# ADIRONDACK MYSTERIES

*Gripping Thrillers, Detective Stories, and*
*Crime Fiction Tales in the Mountains*

## VOLUME 4

## EDITED BY DENNIS WEBSTER

BOOKS
NORTH COUNTRY BOOKS

North Country Books
An imprint of Globe Pequot, the trade division of
The Rowman & Littlefield Publishing Group, Inc.
4501 Forbes Blvd., Ste. 200
Lanham, MD 20706
www.rowman.com

Distributed by NATIONAL BOOK NETWORK

British Library Cataloguing in Publication Information Available

**Library of Congress Cataloging-in-Publication Data**

Names: Webster, Dennis, 1966– editor.
Title: Adirondack mysteries : gripping thrillers, detective stories, and
   crime fiction tales in the mountains / edited by Dennis Webster.
Description: Lanham, MD : North Country, 2024. | Summary: "Venture into the
   unknown in this collection of mysterious short stories set in the
   mountains and lakes of the Adirondack Park. This installment features
   thrillers and mysteries by popular Adirondack authors, award-winning
   crime fiction writers, and locals born and raised in the shadows of the
   high peaks."—Provided by publisher.
Identifiers: LCCN 2023028156 (print) | LCCN 2023028157 (ebook) | ISBN
   9781493080625 (paperback) | ISBN 9781493080632 (epub)
Subjects: LCSH: Detective and mystery stories, American—New York
   (State)—Adirondack Mountains Region. | Suspense fiction, American—New
   York (State)—Adirondack Mountains Region. | Adirondack Park
   (N.Y.)—Fiction. | LCGFT: Detective and mystery fiction. | Thrillers
   (Fiction) | Short stories.
Classification: LCC PS648.D4 A285 2024  (print) | LCC PS648.D4  (ebook) |
   DDC 813/.0872083587475—dc23/eng/20230804
LC record available at https://lccn.loc.gov/2023028156
LC ebook record available at https://lccn.loc.gov/2023028157

♾ The paper used in this publication meets the minimum requirements of American National Standard for Information Sciences—Permanence of Paper for Printed Library Materials, ANSI/NISO Z39.48-1992

*The authors dedicate this collection of stories to all those who embrace and preserve the beauty and grandeur of the Adirondacks. May these stories inspire travelers to seek out Mother Nature's gravitas that nestles between the peaks and pines.*

# Contents

# Dead Man Walking

*Cheryl Ann Costa*

**ADIRONDACK GENERAL HOSPITAL, DOCTORS' LOUNGE, THURSDAY, 27 NOVEMBER 1941, 3:10 P.M.**

"It's your move Ruth," I reminded intern physician Ruth Hall as she quietly studied the chess board.

"Sorry, Dr. Patterson, I'm rather rusty at my chess game; I really didn't have time in med school." She moved a knight. I moved a bishop and took her knight. "Oh, crap, I didn't see that," she groaned. "Do they always have the single people cover the holiday weekends?" she queried as she moved a pawn.

"Yep," I answered. "It's a strange custom for holiday weekends that goes back to the founding of the hospital. The assumption is that single folks are usually new in their careers and generally don't have the same family obligations that married folks have," I explained as I took her bishop.

As she sat pondering her next move, she queried, "But I heard that you're married." She moved her rook.

"Oh yes, I'm married, but since my husband is out of town they consider me locally unattached." I took her other knight.

"Crap!" Ruth moaned as she moved a pawn. "Your husband, what's he do, and why is he out of town?"

I thought for a moment. If I tell her the situation it will probably rattle her, and she'll probably have a zillion questions I really don't want to answer and the chess game will end. "I'm married to a German Luftwaffe wing commander; I haven't had a letter in three months. If he's still alive, he's probably flying a mission over London right now and the Brits are trying to shoot him down and kill him as we speak. Needless to say, I can't do a thing about it." I moved my bishop. "Check and mate!" Ruth had an astonished look on her face. Frankly I wasn't sure if it was about the chess move or my statement about my husband Rudolph.

She sat quietly with her hand over her mouth. "Where did you meet him?" I figured it might be fun to go down this rabbit hole with her.

"I was at a medical symposium in Frankfurt, Germany, in '37 and I met Colonel Kastner at a fancy dinner and dance club in Frankfurt. We courted each other during our flight over on the *Hindenburg*."

Her jaw dropped and her eyes opened wide, "Were you on the airship when it . . ."

I smiled, remarking, "Yep, when the thing blew up. We both barely survived," I explained.

While Ruth was processing what I had said, an orderly came in. He said, "Dr. Patterson, Dr. Clark in the emergency room needs you stat."

I stood up. "Tell him I'm on my way." I looked at Ruth. "Dr. Hall, would you care to shadow me in the ER?"

She perked up. "Sure!" she answered.

In the emergency room, Dr. Walter Clark was writing notes on a clipboard. "Hi, Angela, I've got a strange one." I glanced at a man in his sixties or perhaps seventies lying on the ER table.

"Dead?" I presumed.

Clark nodded in the affirmative. "Mr. Liam Guenther, age forty-three."

I gave Clark a shocked look. "Forty-three? I had him pegged for sixty or seventy something."

Walter shrugged his shoulders. "Me too. He came here in a really bad way. His reported symptoms suggested that he might be in renal failure. I sent the orderly to find you. A few minutes later he let out a moan and just expired."

I just stood staring at the body. My intern spoke up. "On first glance, I suggest that what was ailing him has been a long time in coming. I mean look at him, he's a wreck."

I gave Walter a glance and nodded with Ruth's assessment. Walter gave me a slow nod of concurrence. Then I stated, "Hospital protocol states that all unexplained deaths in the ER must be followed up with an autopsy to determine the cause of death."

Walter simply answered, "You are our pathologist; he's all yours."

I turned and looked at Ruth. "Dr. Hall, care to assist me with an autopsy?"

She looked almost excited. "Absolutely."

"Go find us an orderly to move our patient down to the morgue," I directed. She turned and left the ER with a slight skip in her step. After the intern physician left the ER, Walter just rolled his eyes, and he began filling me in on the admission symptoms.

"The patient initially told me his stomach hurt, that he had been vomiting, and that his joints were very painful. My initial impression was that perhaps he had a case of influenza."

I nodded in concurrence. "That might have been my first notion, too."

Walter continued, "I was getting ready to take his blood pressure. Then I noted that he was acting all fussy; he even had tears rolling down his cheeks. If he'd been a three-year-old, I would have sworn he had colic."

I pondered what my colleague had just told me. After a few moments I asked, "Did you manage to get his BP or get lab samples?"

With a frustrated look, Dr. Clark remarked, "Angela, he was lying on the table less than ten minutes before he expired. I did manage to get his blood pressure—it was 185 over 130."

I winced. "Ouch! Well, hopefully the postmortem will get to the bottom of it. Is there anybody with him?"

Walter nodded. "I believe that his wife is out in the lobby. I'll have to tell her he's dead, but perhaps I can get some more history on him."

I studied the clipboard with the admission information. "Walter, you go talk to her and get some history and deliver that bad news. I'll go down to the morgue and get the autopsy started." I paused for a moment. "Good luck, Walter, I don't envy the task ahead of you." I turned and left the emergency room.

## ADIRONDACK GENERAL HOSPITAL, MORGUE,
## THURSDAY, 27 NOVEMBER 1941, 3:45 P.M.

When I arrived at the morgue, young Dr. Hall and the orderly had already weighed the deceased and moved the body of Mr. Liam Guenther to the autopsy table and covered the man with a sheet. I looked around for my postmortem assistant and morgue diener Shelley. "Crap!" I groused.

"What's wrong?" Dr. Hall queried.

"My diener Shelley Burton who assists me is on holiday. I have been assigned a temporary, and she's not here." I explained while stepping over to the phone and calling the hospital switchboard. As the operator connected, I simply requested, "Please page Lisa Davis for the morgue."

I reached over to a couple of wall hooks and removed a pair of rubber aprons. I handed one to Hall. It was about then that the acting morgue attendant, Lisa Davis, leisurely walked in. "Hi, Doc!" She paused and squinted at the corpse on the autopsy table. "I see we have a customer."

I finished tying my apron. "Miss Davis, please step over here."

She walked over to me saying, "What's up, Doc?" Out of the corner of my eye, I could see Ruth Hall cringe and looking like she wanted to leave the room.

I addressed the acting morgue attendant, "Miss Davis, you are the morgue attendant. Your job is to be here attending to morgue-related duties and ready to process an intake at any time. By morgue procedures, you should have been here to accept the deceased. In addition, the deceased is *not* a customer, a stiff, or a cadaver. The decedent is our patient, and as such we will continue to respect our patients whether they are breathing or not. Is that understood?"

Davis looked at me. "Sure, Doc, anything you say."

I paused for a moment and stared at the ceiling trying hard not to scream for the lack of decorum. "Miss Davis," I began. "In this operating theater you will address physicians and nurses as doctor and nurse or sister, do I make myself perfectly clear?"

Davis's eyes looked like she had seen a ghost. She stammered, "Yes, Dr. Patterson. My apologies, Dr. Patterson."

I nodded politely and simply said, "Attendant, please undress the patient and wash him per procedure."

Davis replied crisply, "Yes, Doctor."

The acting morgue attendant removed the sheet covering the remains. She stepped over to a drawer and removed a pair of heavy-duty scissors and proceeded to start cutting the man's pants off starting with the cuffs of each leg. After all the clothing had been removed, Davis grabbed an overhead spray nozzle and hose. Then she proceeded to carefully apply a light stream of lukewarm water and gently scrubbed the patient with a large sponge. When she was finished, she removed several large towels from a stack on a counter and dried the body. When she was done, she picked up a clipboard. "Doctor, there is a weight already indicated."

I requested her to weigh the clothing and shoes, then subtract the measured weight to compensate for the weight of the patient's clothing and shoes. She did as requested; moments later she reported, "Doctor, the patient was 105 pounds at the time of death."

"Okay, let's measure him," I requested. Dr. Hall held a tape measure at the patient's heel while Miss Davis pulled the tape to the top of the head.

"Seventy inches, Doctor," Davis called off.

I wrote it down on the clipboard form. Dr. Hall remarked, "If memory serves, a man five feet, ten inches would average from about 150 to maybe 180 pounds."

I looked at my young colleague. "Dr. Hall, any initial thoughts about what ailed our patient?"

The intern stood at the foot of the autopsy table and studied the general condition of the body for a few moments. "Given his very low body weight, the decrepit look of his overall body, and the degenerated skin tone, my first guess would be cancer or perhaps some form of long-term poisoning. In any case, he's been a dead man walking for some time now."

Dr. Hall's assessment was spot on, I thought, especially the remark about him being a dead man walking. I directed the team to assist me in turning the patient over. Immediately, Dr. Hall noted a pattern of perhaps thirty-five or forty healed-over blemish-like bumps on his upper buttocks and lower back. I quickly noted two badly scarred, badly stitched old gunshot entry wounds on the buttocks.

Dr. Hall remarked, "My God, he looks like he was in a war."

Using a magnifying glass, I took a closer look, and as I did, I explained, "I was a front-line field surgeon during the Spanish Civil War. These don't look like any combat wounds I've ever seen on the battlefield in Spain or on Great War veterans here in this morgue. But they do look like evidence of gangland wounds."

Dr. Hall raised an eyebrow. "Gangland?"

I gave Dr. Hall and Attendant Davis a knowing look. "Back during Prohibition there was a very active business of illegal liquor running from Canada down here into the States. The competition was fierce, and from time to time gun fights ensued. Some died and many others were wounded, but they weren't treated by a professional, because doctors and hospitals would report the wound to the authorities. In that case, usually someone who was a medic in the war or a veterinarian, or perhaps some midwife would stitch up the wound."

I looked at Miss Davis. "Please ask the duty X-ray folks to bring the portable X-ray machine. I want film of this guy's buttocks and lower back." She nodded her head and stepped out of the room.

I looked at Dr. Hall. "Why don't you get a scalpel, some tweezers, and a petri dish and open up four of five of those blemish bumps and see what's in there."

She wrinkled her nose. "I doubt they're bullets."

"Ever hear of birdshot?" I asked. She shook her head in the negative. "Where did you grow up, hon?" I asked.

Dr. Hall, with a slightly vacant look, answered, "The Bronx in New York City."

Miss Davis returned to the morgue with an X-ray tech and an orderly pushing a portable X-ray machine. I directed the X-ray technician to give me films of each buttock, with films from the lower back in order to get images of the suspected birdshot. As they were setting up for the films, I continued with my chat about birdshot with Dr. Hall.

"Birdshot is designed for shooting game birds. The small pellets form a pattern that gives the hunter a better chance of hitting his prey and does less damage to the bird."

The X-ray tech spoke up. "Yep, at close range a load of birdshot will blow a big hole in you!" He looked at me and remarked, "Dr. Patterson, the rest of you might want to step out while I shoot the films." I nodded and motioned for everyone to step out of the morgue. As we waited in the hall, I quietly remembered treating a few shot-up bootleggers on the sly—usually in the wounded individual's home.

## Autopsy Report

Dr. Angela Patterson, attending pathologist, Adirondack General, and assistant county coroner. Hospital case number 121 on 27 November 1941; patient Liam Guenther. The body is that of an emaciated, 43-year-old Caucasian male, graying-black hair and brown eyes. The body is 70 inches long and weighs 105 pounds. Time of Death: 27 November 1941, 3:21 p.m. EST. The body has been dead approximately 90 minutes and has early non-fixed liquidity and still blanches to the touch. There is no rigor mortis as yet detected.

Upon physical examination of the body, there are two very old, healed, but badly stitched gunshot entry wounds, one on each buttock. There is also evidence of healed-over birdshot wounds on the patient's lower back. A small quantity of birdshot was removed from surface scar tissue. These birdshot wounds appear to be younger than three years.

Internal examination of the liver and kidneys indicate deterioration and damage consistent with long-term lead poisoning from old gunshot wounds where the bullets were never removed. X-rays of the buttocks show only small fragments of lead from the bullets of undetermined caliber in the buttocks. The X-rays also indicate that they mostly have dissolved within the body.

The makeshift stitching of the gunshot wounds clearly indicates the patient was never taken to professional medical personnel for bullet removal. X-ray films suggest that these wounds could have been easily treated and removed by any doctor at the time. It's assumed that the decedent didn't wish to have professional medical care because that would have alerted authorities at the time and questions may have revealed incriminating activity.

The deceased's wife has stated that his health had been slowly deteriorating over the past five years. She also indicated that his mental condition over the past two years had been degrading significantly. This is consistent with the neurological toxicity from the high lead levels in the body. She also confirmed that Mr. Guenther never served in the armed services.

Nevertheless, the two bullets slowly dissolved and leeched into the decedent's system over a period of about 10 to 20 years. The cause of death is diagnosed as acute lead poisoning. Given that murder has no statute of limitation, this slow lead poisoning death of Mr. Guenther is hereby ruled as a homicide.

## PLATTSBURGH CITY POLICE BUREAU, LEAD DETECTIVE'S OFFICE, FRIDAY, 28 NOVEMBER 1941, 9:30 A.M.

"Angela! What you are talking about is nearly a twenty-year-old cold case. We barely have the resources to chase our current case load let alone something that old," Chief Detective Michael Phillips explained politely to me as I sat quietly pondering a cup of Joe he had given me. After a few minutes of my silence, Michael, feeling uncomfortable, spoke up.

"Angela, I understand your passion for solving cases you discover during your postmortems. But you have to understand my position. I have to think about the case from the perspective of evidence, witness testimony, and other things that will hold up in a court of law. Those bullets in the victim's ass are three-quarters dissolved. Even if you removed them, I doubt we could get any ballistics imagery that we can compare to test fired bullets, even if we had a suspect weapon in hand, presently."

Again there was just a hideous silence between the two of us; I still said nothing. "Angela, we have old records on Liam Guenther, granted he certainly wasn't a saint. We know he was running liquor down from Canada and sold it to underworld distributors all through New York State. My best guess is that either a Revenue agent shot him in the butt or perhaps it was one of his competitors." Mike paused for a few moments and as an afterthought remarked, "For all we know it might have been a state trooper giving chase and shooting him as a fleeing felon; in any case, it certainly wasn't in our Plattsburgh jurisdiction. Angela, my dear, give it a rest. It happened a long time ago, and Liam Guenther is dead, God rest his soul!"

I put the coffee cup on the edge of his desk and stood to leave. "Michael, thank you for your valuable time this morning. I won't bother you further regarding this finding."

He pushed himself away from his desk and stood up. "Angela, I hope you know that it's nothing personal. I respect your past investigative work. This finding just isn't actionable in my best judgment."

I reached out, and the two of us shook hands. "Michael, thank you for your frank wisdom and best judgment. If I don't see you before the holidays, I wish you and your family a merry Christmas season."

He broke into a warm smile. "Thank you, Angela, and the same to you."

As I left the Police Bureau Headquarters building, the bitter cold November air hit my face. As I walked down the steps, I simply remarked to myself, "Maybe there is another way to skin this cat!"

## South Side of Plattsburgh, St. John's Catholic Cemetery, Sunday, 30 November 1941, 11:00 a.m.

*The morning sky is clear*, I thought to myself. It sure beats a rainy or snowy day for a funeral. Ever since I was appointed to be the staff pathologist at Adirondack General, I have tried in earnest to attend the funerals of the people whose death I declared a homicide. I suppose it's my way of paying my respects to them given that their deaths were from unnatural causes.

Mr. Liam Guenther's death in my mind was no different. While his death wasn't immediate after a couple of gunshot wounds, the bullets from those wounds certainly were the eventual cause of his untimely death as well as years of related suffering and debilitating deterioration.

My parents taught me that if you aren't family or close friends, it's proper to make room for those people who knew the deceased. At the graveside funeral, I stood at the back of the group of approximately thirty people in attendance. Guenther is a French Canadian name, so I wasn't surprised to witness a clearly Catholic interment ritual.

The family members each followed the widow performing the practice of throwing a handful of dirt on Mr. Guenther's humble pine box.

It's a time-honored custom to indicate an acceptance that the deceased's remains would now be returned to the elements of nature.

As the widow walked away from the graveside, she caught sight of me and gave me a knowing nod. Then she leaned into a male family member, said something, and gestured toward me. The man acknowledged her and began walking the short distance toward me. When he reached me, he introduced himself. "I'm Gilbert Force and one of Mrs. Guenther's brothers." He extended a handshake to me, I reciprocated, and I introduced myself. Then Mr. Force added, "Our family would be grateful if you would attend our wake, Dr. Patterson." It was Sunday, and I had nothing else planned so I graciously accepted the invitation.

The family had arranged for the banquet space at a local Public House. Many family members dropped by my isolated table in the banquet hall and introduced themselves. The odd part was that they all knew who I was. Finally, one family member outright thanked me for declaring Mr. Guenther's death a homicide. "Doctor, perhaps your declaration will bring my cousin a degree of long-overdue justice!" the man said bluntly as he shook my hand before he rejoined the family.

I sat down, sipped my pint of ale, and had a few mouthfuls of poutine. From behind me, a woman's voice said, "Docteur Angèle Patterson, it's nice to see you again." I turned to see an elegantly dressed older woman. She could see that I was straining my memory to recognize her. In an amused tone she remarked, "Docteur, you treated my late husband François several times."

Then it hit me. It was Madeline Riendeaus Baril. "Madame Baril, it is such a pleasure to see you again," I said as I gave her *la bise*, a two-kiss friendly French greeting. I offered her a chair, and she graciously took a seat.

"Docteur Angèle, as you know my late husband François was very successful in his public businesses." She took a moment to look around for prying ears. We were curiously alone in the noisy banquet room.

Madame Baril continued, "As we both know, his more clandestine enterprises were very profitable as well." I gave her a subtle smile and slightly nodded my head in acknowledgment. She opened her purse, removed a small silver bell, rang it briefly, and returned it to her bag. A dignified, well-dressed woman left the gathering of people at the other end of the banquet hall. As she approached, Madame Baril simply said, "*Un peu de xérès, s'il vous plaît.*" Dutifully the younger woman smiled, bowed slightly, and left for the bar area.

Madame Baril directed her attention back to me. "Since François passed away, I have employed a well-traveled and educated lady's companion. We travel and enjoy adventures together." The traveling companion quickly returned and set a small glass of sherry down next to Madame Baril and quietly left. "We have a private code for a private conversation. If I ask for sherry, she will bring me one and keep people from disturbing us," Madame Baril remarked.

I gave her a puzzled look. "Madame, do we need such privacy?"

She simply said, "*Oui.*"

I took a sip of my ale and replied, "You have my confidential ear, Madame."

She began, "As you know, François had many businesses. Monsieur Liam Guenther was in my husband's employ in both the public—and darker—sides of his businesses."

I thought to myself, *Good God, is the dead gangster's wife going to spill the beans on who shot Guenther?*

Madame Baril continued, "It was the 19th of May 1923, two days before Fête de la Reine, or as you might call it Victoria Day. François and his employees were bringing a large shipment of spirits down to the American side near the village of Champlain. A Montreal gangster named Emile Edouard Pelletier and his *voyou*, or hooligans, intercepted François and his people and attempted to steal the shipment of liquor. A gun fight transpired. Men on both sides of the fight were killed or wounded. One of the wounded survivors of my husband's team was Monsieur Guenther. A midwife related to my household staff cleaned his wound and stitched his *croupe* [hind end]." She took a sip of her sherry.

I spoke up. "Madame, we can't go to the authorities and accuse Mr. Pelletier based on what you just told me. It was all illegal activity to begin with, and the law would see it as hearsay evidence. Besides, the bullets in Mr. Guenther have long since dissolved, so there is nothing to match in ballistics tests," I explained.

"Docteur Angèle, you misunderstand me," she remarked. "You privately removed a similar bullet from my husband in 1931. You did so at great risk to your legal standing as a *docteur*. My family and I respect you for that and consider you trusted like family. I told you this story so you will not waste your time trying to find who was responsible. We know who did this. Monsieur Pelletier will be dealt with; we will invoke justice for poor Liam," she explained as she rose from her seat. I rose as well. She stepped over to me and gave me an endearing hug. As she did, she whispered, "The next time you offer me two kisses please consider it *bisous*, a more than friendly kiss; you are now my family." She bowed slightly and left my presence.

I drove home, changed my clothes to something a bit more casual, then walked to my neighborhood bar. There I nursed a pint of brown ale. I considered the last four years of my life as a strange adventure: nearly being killed on the *Hindenburg*, marrying a German Luftwaffe wing commander, and being kidnapped by the Spanish leftists while on our honeymoon in Barcelona—only to be pressed into service as a battlefield surgeon for the POUM (Workers' Party of Marxist Unification) during the Spanish Civil War.

I took a mouthful of my pint of ale. As I swished the marvelous brown ale in my mouth to capture its full flavor, I considered yet another new kink in my tempestuous life. It would appear that I have become the revered personal confidante to the widows of French Canadian gangsters! I could only reconcile the matter by simply indulging myself and getting quietly drunk!

Two weeks later, I was intrigued to read in the newspaper that noted Montreal businessman Monsieur Emile Edouard Pelletier was tragically killed in a freak automobile accident. Madame Baril told me Monsieur Pelletier would be dealt with. Perhaps this is Liam Guenther's justice. May he rest in peace.

# What's in a Name?

## *Marie Hannan-Mandel*

JANE FREELAND, THE WOMAN I WAS TO MEET, SCUTTLED TOWARD ME IN the dark, crab like, looking behind her every other step. Oh yeah, she was one of ours. Just the kind to contact the website wanting her moments of fame.

This part of Manhattan was almost deserted; now it was dark. It wasn't my choice of a meeting spot, but now that I was here, I could see its attractions.

Simon Shawell, my boss at the goofy website I wrote for, had been insistent that I interview her. Jane wanted to meet here in front of the building in Manhattan where she worked. At night. So, I rode the subway across the city from my hotel. Simon won't pay Manhattan prices. Simon wouldn't normally pay what this Queens hotel wanted for this tiny room either, but he had no choice now that all five boroughs of New York City had become a crazy pot of rich bastards and wannabes with the kind of stories the website subscribers love.

"You're Jake Harrison, right?" She turned and walked to the door of the glass-walled tower, expecting me to follow.

"Hi, George," she hollered, moving through the huge lobby like the bailiffs were after us. The lounging doorman, with more years behind him than he'd like—given the fake black hair under his hat—got up and stood behind the desk.

"Mr. Runcorn just left," he said. He nodded toward a huge portrait of a man who thought a great deal of himself. A mane of carefully dyed blond hair swept over a face sculpted by the best plastic surgery his money could buy.

"Thanks, George. I forgot my keys," she bellowed. Then dropping her voice, she hissed at me, "Keep your head down." She added, to George, "This is my brother, visiting from Vermont. I just picked him up at Penn Station. He doesn't have to sign in, does he?"

"Naw, I trust you." George's smile broke open, but I couldn't place the look on his face, paternalistic or yearning.

"Thanks," Jane said. "Works every time," she muttered. Brittle as an old piece of plastic, I knew her type. Wind blasted by life. But she was pretty, I had to give her that. Tall, blonde, athletic, and brown-eyed.

"Who's Runcorn?" I asked.

"The boss. Don't worry, George won't tell him you're here."

I hadn't been worried. Until then. I'd have to look him up and see what danger he might be to her, and to me.

When we were inside her office, the door closed, she sighed long and loud. "They don't have cameras in the private offices."

The room was tiny and filled with fringed lamps and perky sayings. Trying way, way too hard to look like it was all fun and games. I particularly liked the lamp in the shape of a bemused sheep.

"Did you look up the people I told you to?" Jane asked.

"I did." I took out my phone. She'd texted me the names two days before.

"Now search again." She sat on the corner of the desk, her legs planted either side like she was on a mechanical bull and bracing herself against being tossed off.

I entered "Arnold Randolph." The well-known financier. The kind of person who'd swap his mother's false teeth for a nickel.

I waited for the story about his wife's visit to the hospital with a broken nose, and the one about his links to Middle Eastern sheiks. Instead, the first item was about a writer with the same last name who had self-published a crime novel set in his hometown in upstate New York. Way down the page an article about Randolph, the financier, told of his charitable contribution to a cat shelter on Cape Cod. If you have to be abandoned, I'd say Cape Cod was a nice place for it to happen, even before Randolph's donation.

"You see." She nudged me hard enough to leave a bruise. "I can clean up anyone's internet presence. It's marketing the brand."

The brand. Like this guy was a weed whacker, which, now that I thought of it, he kind of was. Clearly, Simon hadn't told me what I was wandering into because he knew I'd have said no. No to Randy the rat, no to Jane, and no to the whole sickening business.

"Why would you want to make this writer famous?" I asked. Before I filmed her, I wanted to be sure I understood what this was all about.

"Not him; Randolph needs people to think he's a good person. It's my job."

"And who's this other guy? The writer? Any relation?"

"I don't think so. I never thought of that." She crinkled up her face. "I just used him to push our client and his stuff down the list."

"What's his book about?"

"I don't know, a true crime story—I mean they have a huge prison up there."

Another feckless person loose in the world, changing perceptions, one keystroke at a time.

"Hmm," I said.

"Tomorrow I'm going to work on getting his archenemy's secrets to the top of the list for his name." She put her arms over her head in a stretch, the dog with the Frisbee.

Archenemy. What the hell was this?

"Why are you telling me? You'll be fired as soon as you turn up on the website."

"I'm a whistleblower. You can't use my name or my face, or anything."

"Wait a second, Simon agreed to this?" My unhappiness with the situation ramped up.

"Well, I assumed he knew that a whistleblower has to be protected." For the first time I saw the twenty-something woman under all that smugness.

"I wouldn't count on it. Simon isn't very well versed in corporate matters. He inherited his money." I stood up and made for the door. "I'll talk to him, and you can call me on your disposable phone in the morning."

I got to the door before she said, "You mean the one I bought at the Duane Reade?"

She and Simon were well matched. Two crazy innocents in a world of scavengers.

♣♣♣

The main thing that's wrong with my job is every single thing about it—my boss, his website, the interviewees with their weird hobbies and nutty pastimes. A modern-day *I've Got a Secret*. What kind of person makes miniature kitchen utensils out of ear wax, or sleeps hanging upside down, or wants to donate a kidney to get his helper monkey off dialysis? "We share 99 percent of our genes with apes, after all." Helper monkey, if you don't mind.

I ran away from my job at the biggest newspaper in the world and took this one, and guess what? Hate it or not, I couldn't tear myself away from the craziness of it all. Kind of like picking at the same scab over and over and enjoying the pain enough not to stop. When I called him, Simon, of course, had forgotten all about Jane. I explained to him what a whistleblower was and that she wouldn't show her face on camera, and he pulled the plug. Before he could obsess about dead air and disappointing the viewers, I suggested following up on Randolph, the writer's success. I'd checked. He'd been selling pity copies until Jane's manipulations had made him a best seller. Simon was delighted—an underdog always did well with our subscribers.

♣♣♣

I was on my way in a rental car to visit the writer when my cell phone rang.

"I'm calling from the throw-away phone," Jane said as soon as I answered.

"That's great. No way they'll figure out what you're up to now." I released my voice dripping with sarcasm.

"I know, right? When are we filming?"

"I'm sorry, Jane, but the piece won't work for us. Simon won't let you be anonymous. The viewers don't like it."

"What? But that means . . ."

I waited while she figured out whatever this meant for her.

"I won't be able to leave my job."

"You can leave your job. Nothing's holding you there."

"But I won't be famous. I won't be offered other jobs. How am I going to build my brand?"

"Listen, building brands is reality TV bullshit. Get out of the city. Get a job you can be proud of and live a good life." Here I was, getting involved and giving advice. What the hell was wrong with me?

"Like you? You don't even work for the *New York Times* anymore." Of course, she would have fastened onto that. Simon made sure it was mentioned as often as possible.

"Yes. I don't and I'm happier about it. Go for happy." I hung up.

🌲🌲🌲

In common with more than a few upstate New York towns, Joseph Randolph's had once been prosperous with large, gorgeously furbelowed houses, executives hosting dinner parties, and a wide and fully stocked main street. All of that was gone now except for the houses, many of which were for sale and had been for years. And the sound—the tiny buzz that all dying towns have. The flies on the carcass. Too far from the glamorous Adirondack resorts, this place had one main employer—the maximum-security prison.

Joseph Randolph, now bestselling author, worked in the bank in the middle of town. An eighties brick building with permanently cloudy windows, discolored trim, and a sagging poster hanging outside near the door. It had been easy to track him down. Self-published authors don't want to remain hidden. I pulled into the parking lot, much too large for the bank's needs. One thing there's plenty of in upstate New York is land for parking lots. And storage facilities—sheds big and small, crouching around the edges of towns and villages ready to gobble up the things that should have been taken to the dump. My feet squelched through the dead leaves scattered in lumps over the newish tarmacadam.

There was one young woman, Chassidhe, according to her name badge, at the faux red maple counter. A dusty bowl of purple and pink potpourri, smelling of old clothes, stood next to the FDIC notice in a chipped plastic display frame. Dressed in a tight red dress that rippled over her ample and various skin folds, she was crying. Not even trying to hide it, she snuffled and blew into a tissue without regard for the customers—well, the one customer, me.

"I'm here to see Joseph Randolph," I said.

She yelped and ran into a back room slamming the door behind her.

Chassidhe quickly returned with an older, suited man. He, too, looked upset.

"I'm afraid our small business manager, Randy, has been killed," he said.

"Randy?"

"Yeah, he was always called Randy, never Joseph." The man shook his head like a bobble-head.

"Killed? How? When?" I said.

"He was knocked down by a car, right outside the bank. This morning. On purpose, not by accident," Chassidhe said between sobs.

"And he wrote that book about—"

The manager cut in. "And he was due for a raise."

I walked out the door and headed to the police station, which I'd seen on the way into town.

🌲🌲🌲

"Who are you again?" the young cop behind the counter, Officer Brennan, asked me.

"I'm Jake Harrison, and I'm a reporter. I'm in town to interview Joseph Randolph, the writer. When I heard he'd been killed, I came here to see what happened."

"Yeah, well, we already know who did this." He stared at me, his hair dancing in the blasting heat from the overhead vent.

"You do? That was quick."

When an inner door opened, he turned and stared at the man who stood there.

"Hey, Sheriff," Brennan said.

"You're from the *New York Times*." The sheriff smiled at me, relaxed and friendly.

"Not anymore." How did he know this?

He frowned. "She said the *New York Times* reporter on the web would be able to save her."

"Who?"

"The suspect."

The reporter from the web. What was I? Spider-Man?

"Jane Freeland? Jane Freeland's your suspect? What's she doing here?"

"Killing Randy," Officer Brennan said.

"Come into my office, would you?" the sheriff said.

"Sure," I said.

The sheriff closed the door. I sat opposite in a wooden chair with some sort of crest on the back.

Once he was seated behind his desk he asked, "So why are you really here?"

"I came to meet Joseph Randolph, Randy, to ask him about the success of his novel. You are the lead officer, right?"

"Yes, and I've got to get to a press conference in a minute. You can be there with the rest."

We got up and left the room, walking down the hall to a door with "Briefing Room" on it. There was only one other guy there, dressed in a suit and tie and looking like he was going for a job interview.

The room was large and white with dozens of fluorescent lights overhead.

The sheriff walked behind the podium and pulled a piece of paper out of his top pocket. "At approximately 8:45 a.m., Mr. Joseph Randolph was struck by a car as he crossed Cook Street. The car hit him, backed over him, and then drove away at speed. A witness at the ATM saw the whole thing."

"Did the witness get the license plate?" the other journalist asked.

"No, Henry, it was from out of state and didn't have a front plate, besides the ATM is way over across the parking lot."

That big parking lot. No way anyone could see a license plate from that distance.

"We have a suspect in custody."

"Come on, Mark, why didn't you start with that?" The man swirled his pencil and erased furiously before beginning to write again.

"Listen, Henry, I've told you before. I give the information the way I do and stop hassling me about it just because you have to have everything in a certain order."

Henry kept his head down, writing.

"Why do you think she did it?" I asked.

"Can't talk about that."

"Anything more you can tell us?" Henry asked.

"When there are further developments, I'll let the press know." He came around from behind the podium.

"So, this woman you got locked up, was she his girlfriend, or something?" Henry asked when the sheriff came near.

"He has a wife."

"What does that matter?" Henry said.

"No. Nothing like that."

"Who are you?" Henry asked me, pointing with the eraser end of his pencil.

"I'm—"

"What does that matter, Henry? The readers of the *Pennysaver* need to know that?"

"Just because I haven't hit the big time yet, doesn't mean I don't know how to do my job." Henry drew himself up and walked out of the room with as much dignity as a man wearing a too-tight suit over construction boots could muster.

I raised my eyebrows at the sheriff who laughed. "Small towns," he said.

We walked out of the room.

"So, what's your connection to my suspect?"

"I only met her the other day. I was going to interview her, but then I decided to interview Randy instead. Can I see her?"

He studied me and shrugged. "I guess so."

At the end of the hallway, he pointed at a cell where I could see Jane through the bars on the top half of a steel door.

"I knew you'd come." Jane rushed at us like a puppy at the pound looking for someone to take her home.

"What are you doing here?" I asked.

Jane made a face in the direction of the sheriff.

"Can I speak to her alone?" I asked.

"Sure, but I can't let you in the cell," the sheriff answered.

I didn't want to be in a cell with Jane, so that suited me fine. The man left, closing the door at the end with a bang.

"My boss, Mr. Runcorn, told me to come and see what you were up to. He wants me to make sure you don't put anything up on the website," Jane said.

"He knows about me."

"Yeah, I had to tell him. He knew you'd been up in my office. Turns out there are cameras in the private offices. Sneaky, don't you think?"

"Very. Who'd have thought. Wait, how did your boss know where I was going?"

"I told him, I mean I had to. He's scary." She shuddered like a toddler sucking on a lemon. "You seemed really interested in the writer, so I thought you'd probably come up here to interview him." She leaned against a bar.

That impressed me. Perhaps she was smarter than I'd given her credit for.

"Why do the cops think you killed the writer?"

She slumped again. "Well, I rented a car and it's red, but someone stole it and they say it's the one that hit him." She shuddered, quivering from head to toe.

"Stole it? How? Cars have electronic keys—wait, you didn't leave the keys in the car or something?"

"I might have. Or maybe they were stolen, too." She was crying. She reached through the bars for my hand. I didn't want to get involved with this, but she was so pitiful, I gave her hand a squeeze.

"It'll be all right. I have to go now, but I'll be back as soon as I can."

"Don't leave." She grabbed at me, but I managed to dodge her grasp.

"It's going to be okay. I'm going to find out who did this."

"Okay. You promise?" She tried a smile that barely succeeded.

"I promise." What was I doing promising her anything? Why was I getting involved when all I'd wanted was a nice human-interest piece about a guy who wrote a book and got lucky?

🌲🌲🌲

"Did you find the car?" I asked the sheriff when I returned to his office.

"Yup, parked outside of the Howard Johnson where she was staying, keys inside. Very little damage, considering." I guess he'd decided I was part of the team and that he could tell me what was going on.

Howard Johnson, only a forgotten town like this would still have a Howard Johnson.

"I'm going to talk to the widow," I said.

"Good luck with that. We already spoke to her, and she doesn't know anything."

"Thanks," I said as I turned and left. I stopped in the parking lot to look up Runcorn and there wasn't a lot about him, but I now knew enough to start looking. He might have nothing to do with this, but he could have.

🌲🌲🌲

"He was such a wonderful man and now he's a famous writer. I suppose he'll be more famous now." Mrs. Emily Randolph had ushered me straight into the room she called "the parlor." The large Victorian house oozed with moldings and old wood.

"I don't want to bother you, but I had an appointment to meet with Joseph this morning. It's such a loss," I lied.

I knew the right words. I'd used them all of my adult life. This was the part of journalism I hated. Pushing people into interviews they didn't want to give, probing people's sorrow and grief and holding it up to view like a child's drawing. That's why I only deal with those seeking that kind of manipulation, unless I get caught up in a murder. Then, I'm just swept along like the rest.

"I know. He was so excited when you called him yesterday. Well, your secretary." She shook her wispy blonde hair around her head like a model in a shampoo commercial. "It's such a shame Joseph isn't here to meet you," she said, as if he was out running errands or getting his teeth cleaned.

I took out my recorder and put it on the wrought-iron-and-glass coffee table. She straightened up and ran a hand through her hair.

"Did Randy have any enemies?" I started.

"No. Of course Joseph didn't have any enemies. He was very prominent in the community. He will be missed by everyone."

"And his book is—"

"A best seller. He's on the best seller list. He's so happy that everyone loves his books. Especially because those publishers wouldn't print it and he did it all by himself. With me, of course."

"You must have been very proud."

"What is his book about?" I asked.

"Oh, it's about an unsolved murder. Well, everyone says it was suicide, but Joseph knew that it was murder. People weren't happy."

Unhappy enough to kill him?

"Do you think this terrible thing will increase the sales even more? I mean, you're a writer."

"Not that kind of a writer. But I suppose it will."

"I mean, when famous artists pass away their pictures sell for a lot more money, don't they?"

Passed away? Being run over by a car was murdered, surely.

I've seen grief in all shapes and sizes, but this woman puzzled me. Was she just odd? Her long skirt and crocheted sweater seemed to indicate so. Or was she involved in her husband's death? Hard to know.

"So, who do you think killed your husband?" I asked.

"Someone who was jealous of his success. A stranger. A stalker."

"But wouldn't someone have noticed a stranger hanging around?" I asked.

"You'll have to ask Millie."

"Who's Millie?"

"She runs that nasty late-night diner. In an old, abandoned railway carriage." Her face puckered up so that her nose almost met her mouth. "She knows everything."

🌲🌲🌲

Millie Bailey's diner was behind the stores on the main street. Even though she only opened at night, I took a chance she might be there. I knocked on the door and watched her through the glass, cleaning down the cracked Formica counter.

"Not open," she shouted without looking up.

"Not even for a reporter from the *New York Times*?" I called. Okay, so Simon isn't the only one who uses that.

Her head jerked up like I'd hit it with a reflex hammer. She let me in.

"I'm Jake Harrison. I'm interested in Joseph Randolph," I said.

"He's dead," Millie said with no sign of emotion.

"I know."

"Why ya here?" she asked.

"Did a strange guy come in here last night?" I was happy with the minimalist approach.

She reared up and laughed. "They're all strange."

"No, I mean someone you didn't know."

"Yeah, there was one guy. He didn't think much of the place I could tell, but I'm the only game in town at one in the morning."

"What did he look like?"

"Tall, clean shaven, and angry looking, and he had awful, fake blond hair and looked like someone had sucked his skin tight. He stiffed me on the tip."

Sounded just like Runcorn. So, he'd come as well. He didn't trust Jane, and I'd have to say that was a wise decision.

"Thanks, Millie."

"Want some coffee?" she asked. No "when am I going to be in the paper?" or no "did I want a photo?" Nothing. Millie was a class act.

🌲🌲🌲

"Just in time," the sheriff said when I walked into the cop shop.

"How's that?" I asked.

"Come to my office." He opened the door and let me through.

When he was seated behind his desk and me in the chair facing him, he said, "I'm releasing her, and she'll need a ride to wherever she's going."

"So, you figured it out?" I asked, disappointed that he'd beaten me to it.

"Nah, just couldn't have been her. We finally tracked down Brianna, the girl who cleans mornings at the HoJo. She saw Miss Freeland in her room at the time Randy was killed."

"You should be looking for Harold Runcorn. He was in town last night and he killed Randy."

"Hmm, how d'you spell that?" He leaned over the pad on his desk and scribbled without looking up.

I spelled it for him.

"Wait, who is he, and how do you know this?" He sat back in his chair and stared at me, suspicious for the first time.

"He's Jane's boss. He's involved in cleaning up messes for the rich and powerful, and Jane was a mess. She told me what they were doing, and Runcorn probably was afraid it would come out. Particularly as Jane told me all about it. He called Randy yesterday and arranged to meet him this morning. The widow thought it was me."

"But why Randy? What did Randy do?"

"Nothing. He did nothing except have the same name as a very bad, very rich man. Runcorn figured he'd get rid of the evidence and the leak in one move. Get Jane convicted for killing Randy and neither of them can tell anyone what happened to make him a best seller and clean up the other Randolph's act." Now that he'd released Jane, the fun was gone out of the investigation.

"So, her rental was stolen. Hmm. How did you know he was in town?" The sheriff straightened up and picked up his pen.

"Millie. She saw him last night."

"Good ol' Millie. I should just put her on the payroll," the sheriff said.

"You should. Nobody would mess with Millie." We both smiled.

"When's your show going to air?" he asked.

"No show. I couldn't prove any of this, and anyway, that's not the kind of thing we do." I was regretful not to have met Randy, the writer, with his goofy story. Though maybe not. I didn't want to have been the one to tell him his "best seller" had nothing to do with his writing.

"A big waste of time, then," the sheriff said.

"No, actually. I enjoyed meeting Millie. And you." I got to my feet and put out my hand. "I'm going to leave now."

"You're going to leave her here?" The sheriff motioned with his head out the door.

"She didn't come with me. I'm not responsible for her." I hadn't saved her single-handedly, so I didn't have to get her out of town single-handedly, either.

The door opened, and Jane flung herself across the room. I put out my hands and managed to stop her before she plastered herself over me like a wet towel.

"I didn't do it," she said.

"I know. Knew it all along."

"You see?" she demanded of the sheriff who didn't react.

"Where are we going?" she asked me.

"I'm going home, and you're going, well, where's home for you?"

"Wherever it is, the bus leaves from in front of Carmen's Café," the sheriff said.

"But what about my rental car? I'm still paying for that, you know." She looked about ready to stomp her foot but didn't.

"It's evidence. We'll contact the rental company."

She looked from the sheriff to me.

"Good luck," I said.

"I could be your assistant," she said, grabbing my arm.

"Nah, you couldn't. Get yourself a bus or another rental and go home."

"Miss Freeland, Miss Freeland," Henry, the journalist, rushed in the door. "Where is she?"

"What are you doing here, Henry?" the sheriff asked.

"My job," he said. He gazed at Jane as if she were a prize razzleberry pie at a county fair.

She looked at him with a scowl on her face.

"Now give me a chance, I know I'm not a famous journalist. But I know I could sell a piece about your ordeal to the *Sun-Bulletin* in Binghamton."

"You could?" Jane gushed. "I'll be famous?"

"Yeah, maybe in the paper in Syracuse, too."

"Okay then," she said, leaving us without a backward glance.

"Bet she doesn't even know where Binghamton and Syracuse are," the sheriff muttered.

"That's not a gamble. That's a sure thing," I said.

# 3

# A Death in the Adirondacks

## G. Miki Hayden

ANNA GARDNER WOKE UP IN THE MIDDLE OF THE NIGHT AND, ON HER way back from the bathroom, looked out the window. She lived in the back of an oddly shaped apartment building and happened to be in a position to peer into the second floor of the house next door. Sometimes she caught a glimpse of old men playing cards or sitting on the red leather couches and smoking cigars.

Now at 3 a.m., the light was on, and she spotted a young man, a man she had once or twice observed at the front of that building, dragging a woman's dead weight into the next room. The woman had curled blonde hair like that of an angel, and her arms resembled sculpted ivory. Anna watched, holding her breath until the two figures were gone, and then she sat down to try to understand exactly what she'd seen. Her heart thudded away like mad, and she felt ill.

She recreated the image in her mind several times, trying to determine if the woman had been dead, or, preferably, simply unconscious. Anna could hardly believe in or trust her own eyes, but the horrible truth was that the building next door was some kind of social club suspected to be an organized crime hangout. Organized crime here, in her own city, Lake George? Anywhere illegal activities could be profitable, it seemed.

In a minute or two, after deciding that she refused to be afraid of doing the right thing, Anna picked up the phone and called the Lake George police, reporting what she thought she'd witnessed.

She made clear she was a Warren County assistant district attorney who prosecuted felonies in the local courts not far from where she lived. She didn't want to be dismissed as a crazy.

The desk sergeant was quite polite and promised to send a squad car as soon as possible. Anna said she'd come by the next day and make a statement.

She then lay down and, after a while, fell into a restless sleep. A couple of times she woke up again, rose, and glanced out the window. The room in the other building was dark. She supposed the police had come and gone—hopefully catching any killer in the act of disposing of his victim.

🌲🌲🌲

The next day, Anna got up early despite her lack of sleep, because she had a case to prosecute in court. She dressed carefully in a very nice suit and did her makeup so that she looked a good decade younger than her fifty-two years—or so she imagined. Then she walked down the double flight of stairs instead of taking the elevator.

Outside, seemingly waiting for her, was the man Anna only a few hours before had accused of murder. Though she tried to ignore him to get on her way, he got in front of her and wouldn't let her pass. At the same time, he tendered her a dazzling smile. He was handsome, as she'd noted previously—not Hollywood, prettily handsome, but masculinely and strikingly so. And he was young, certainly no older than in his thirties. Too young for her, even if he hadn't killed a girl the prior night.

"You called the cops on me," he said, though he didn't seem angry.

"What gives you that idea?" She tried to sound as cool as possible.

"I know who you are. And your apartment is the only one that has a view into our building."

"Well, I didn't call the police about anything," Anna denied. "Were you noisy?"

"Aw, come on. You said that I had killed someone, which is ridiculous. You didn't know what you were looking at—not that you should have been looking into someone else's house—but this girl was dead drunk, and I was helping her out. Honest to God." He was sincere, but then so was she in denying that she'd called the police.

"I don't know what you're talking about," she said, and tried again to maneuver around him.

He put out his hand. "Let me buy you an espresso at Venietta's and I'll call her up. She'll come over and show you that she's very much alive. Come on. I'm not dangerous, I promise, and you probably haven't had your coffee yet." The smile this time was innocence itself, and though she didn't trust that look one bit, the expression cut through her. He radiated charisma and an abundant, entirely wholesome, sexuality.

Anna checked her watch. "All right," she said. "Though I'm not the person you think I am." She must be insane, really, giving way to temptation like this.

She walked with him through a shortcut, through an alley no less—really a driveway—where he might have killed her quickly and silently if he had wanted. What in heaven's name was wrong with her?

She felt relieved when they finally sat in the public restaurant. And while they ordered, the man made his call.

"You're Anna," he said once he'd hung up, though she hadn't told him. "But not Italian?"

"How would you know my name?" she asked instead of answering. Her blood ought to run cold, but she felt flushed.

"We're neighbors, after all," he answered.

She might well have prosecuted some friend of his, one of his fellow "soldiers," as the gangsters called them. She shivered a bit internally, but wasn't really very frightened. The old-style Italian Mob left the prosecutors alone; only the Jamaican and other, more recent, gangs could be ruthlessly vicious in pursing vendettas against criminal justice personnel.

He'd probably gone and looked at the doorbells, Anna reassured herself. Even though only her last name was posted there, he could then have gotten her first name from. . . . Oh, hell, pay $12.95 online and find anyone's name, birthdate—anything at all. She reddened again. She was at least a good fifteen, maybe twenty, years older than he, and here he was smiling at her so winningly from across the table.

His double espresso and her cappuccino arrived, handed off a tray by an efficient, blank-faced waiter, who undoubtedly knew all too well who her companion was. Anna ignored the sugar cubes and sipped.

"I'm Nick," he said. "And here comes Ariadne." A proper gentleman, he stood for the girl.

Anna almost did so, too, the young woman was that glorious.

With hair so blonde you could call it white, and wearing a lacey, pale-pink frock and a pair of sunglasses, perhaps to hide the traces of the past night's binge, the not-really-dead girl took a seat and completed a triangle design of three at the table.

Of course Anna was only here momentarily. She'd get up and leave, and the young, beautiful couple would go back to their twosome.

"Say something, Ariadne, to prove you're alive," Nick told the tall woman.

"Of course, I'm alive," Ariadne replied. She removed her glasses, revealing not the bruised eyes that Anna expected, but cautious ones. "Nicky would never hurt me." She still didn't smile.

"I'm so glad," said Anna. She very much was. She twice had prosecuted murderers. She hated murder. Murder was unthinkable.

She looked at her watch. This morning, she had an embezzler to send up for the duration. She drank her cappuccino quickly and stood.

Surprisingly, Nick got out of his chair, called out something to the waiter, then left a twenty on the table. He gestured Ariadne up. The girl hadn't even had a chance to place her order.

Nick followed Anna onto the street. "Are you satisfied then?" he asked as he stuck with her in the direction of the old courthouse.

"I wasn't the one who called the police," Anna reminded him. "But I'm delighted that a lovely girl like Ariadne is alive."

The two hustled their way across the crowded sidewalks of the business district. "You people have an overactive imagination," he told Anna. She had no idea why he continued to keep up with her, or who he meant by "you people." Prosecutors who unfairly targeted mobsters?

"I'm taking you out to dinner tomorrow night," he added as they emerged from the color of the narrow streets into the gray, "official" portion of the government-office area.

"You needn't do that." Anna stopped her fast-paced walking and turned to him. She herself had been pretty once, had enjoyed her fair portion of male attention. But that time of life seemed to be in the past for her.

"I hope you like Italian food." He began to back away, without saying goodbye or giving her a time or place for them to meet.

Then he spun on his heels and walked off.

She watched as he went, but Nick never turned around again to see if Anna had moved on or not. He must be supremely confident, and for every good reason in the world, except for one. He was manly and attractive, and had the means to leave a twenty on the table for a service of half that. He also knew she felt his pull. But he was a criminal. If he hadn't murdered this girl, he had murdered another poor soul or had done something very, very antisocial, very wrong—and more than once.

What was going on here? she wondered, as she hurried away to take up her case. The image of what she had seen last night came back to her. Had the girl been dead? No. . . . Was someone dead? Had someone drugged and raped this girl perhaps, accounting for what had seemed to be her state?

How would courting a random senior attorney, an older one at that, help him exonerate himself? Maybe he naively imagined that it would. Or he was just toying with Anna as a cat does a mouse—not for any reason aside from simple instinct.

In court, she gave a somber summation to the jury, explaining the terrible effect on society of financial crime.

🌲🌲🌲

At four that afternoon, she left her office and walked to the police headquarters building. There, she sat and waited on the benches near the desk until Detective Szabo came down to take Anna upstairs to the detective unit.

Anna showed him her official identification card. "I'm sorry," she said, and sat. "The call I made last night reporting a dead girl at the Grand Street Social Club. . . . The officers didn't find anything, I suppose?"

Szabo, a man with only a few wisps of graying hair, a man whose awkward form stuck out in an odd array of bulges and folds, gave her a cop-like, noncommittal look. "No dead body," he agreed at last. "Did you expect they would, or they wouldn't, find one?"

"I saw a girl being dragged out of the room. Her eyes were closed. She looked dead to me." Anna felt troubled and knew her face must reflect that emotion. "But I saw her again today, and she was alive."

Ah, she'd surprised him, probably something that not many people could do anymore.

"I have to tell you that when your call came in last night, you caused quite a stir," Szabo said. "We leave the Mob boys strictly alone, or as much as possible. Not that we're unaware, but they're in the hands of an upstate federal-crime task force."

She knew that. In her own office, the Rackets Bureau dealt with criminal enterprises, such as the Mafia, the Chinese tongs, the Russian Mob, the Nigerians ... such as they were in this remote corner of New York state. The cases brought were often made by a joint New York State–FBI task force.

Szabo brought a folder out of his desk and opened it up, not a photo array as the police would ordinarily show a citizen, but candid photos, snapped by a long-range lens—shots of the various men Anna routinely saw around the social club. She pointed at a picture of Nick.

"Nicky the Charmer," said Detective Szabo. He showed her a few more pictures, some of women who obviously came or went from the premises. Anna put a finger on a photo of Ariadne. Even caught unaware in an awkward pose, the girl was breathtakingly beautiful.

"I saw her today," Anna told the policeman. "Ariadne. I don't know her last name." How stupid of her not to have asked.

"Someone undoubtedly has that information," Szabo said.

Anna wanted ... well, she didn't want. ... She wanted Nick ... Nicky the Charmer ... to want to have dinner with her tomorrow night. And she wanted. ... "Could she be a twin?" Anna asked. Her voice cracked slightly.

"I'll find out," Szabo said.

Anna gave Szabo her business card. ... She wanted to be in Nick the Charmer's presence again. But she wanted more.

She might have gone home by another route that evening, yet she went past the social club in question. No one went in or came out. Anna affected a preoccupied look and hurried to her building. Upstairs, she peered down into the gangsters' second floor. One old man was on the sofa either sleeping or dead. Undoubtedly Anna hadn't seen a dead woman, after all. Maybe she did have an overactive imagination.

▲▲▲

The next day at work, Anna received a call from Detective Szabo. Ariadne Sposeto had no sisters, nor any female cousins the task force knew of. She was the niece of a minor underworld figure, and she was sometimes seen in the company of Nick "the Charmer" Perosi. Szabo clicked off in the abrupt style Anna found typical of most of the officers she dealt with.

Anna wondered what she would wear that night if Nick took her out. She had a little black dress. But no. Not to dinner. . . . She had another dress.

She could look attractive, though she would never look young. But maybe he had forgotten about her. More likely than not.

She deliberately walked the short way to her home that afternoon and didn't pass by the gangland club.

And there, sitting on the stoop of her own building was the Charmer, reading the *Lake George Mirror*. Anna nearly fainted, but not from the surprise. Just from the utter, radiant physicality of the man. He was a prize she didn't deserve. That was funny, maybe, that life could be lived on at least two different levels. In the world of pure animal magnetism, he was a top specimen, and she was a female who'd had her day. In the rational world of human morality, of course, she was his superior. But social hierarchy escaped her mind when she saw him there.

He spotted her as well and rose right up. "I couldn't get your cell phone number," he told her with a magnificent smile.

"You're not supposed to be able to," Anna answered. Her heart fluttered. "But I would have given it to you." She muttered the last statement in a low tone, the first spoken acknowledgment of how she felt.

He folded the newspaper and put it under his arm. "I'll drop by at seven," he said. "I do know the apartment number."

"I'll just come down." A wave of heat poured off Anna as she spoke.

Nick saluted her with his newspaper and then left.

Climbing the stairs, Anna stumbled once. Nerves. Stupid nerves. While she bathed and dressed to meet him, her head whirled. She was glad she worked out regularly at the gym. Her body was fit enough to be made love to. But she wasn't fresh minted, as Ariadne was.

🌲🌲🌲

They went to Carbellini's, a restaurant Anna hadn't ever before stepped foot in, but one that he was obviously familiar with. He immediately ordered a bottle of red wine—an Italian brand.

"Maybe you want a nice veal," he suggested. She recoiled a little, and when she did, she saw from his amused response that he'd anticipated her reaction. "Too barbaric?" he asked. Men simply liked to see a woman jump, and she'd entertained him. But rather than being offended, her heart, already open to him, melted further. She smiled as secretly to herself as he had to himself.

They both ordered steaks. Not as cruel as veal for which the rancher caged the calf forbidding movement. Cruel, of course, but relatively less.

"Why do you want to be a prosecutor?" Nick asked. "You could make a lot more money as a defense attorney." He appeared to be instructing her in the art of fording life's more perilous streams.

"I don't like crime."

He laughed a little, outright. "No? But the people you approve of are probably criminals themselves. The politicians. The cops. Even the other district attorneys you work with. Not only can they be bought, but they are bought. Every day."

"And you think that's good?" Almost too tense to eat, she broke a breadstick in two, scattering crumbs on the spotless white tablecloth.

He picked half of the breadstick off her side plate, an affecting gesture.

"So crime is good?" she pursued.

"Crime is natural." He gave her a serious look and brushed a lock of dark hair from his forehead. "Competition is natural. What's unnatural are the laws people make because they're weak. So we have crime—people acting naturally. I'm not talking about the way some street punks behave. I'm not talking about beating up old ladies. I'm talking about

35

natural competition for what we all need to live, to have a nice life." He finally bit into his piece of breadstick.

She couldn't think of a response that might make any sense to him. He had rationalized away the damage that his lifestyle did to others, even to himself. She'd save her arguments for her juries.

When she didn't answer him, he smiled. The wine arrived. He tasted what the waiter poured for him and nodded. The waiter poured them each a glass of the merlot.

"To us," Nick said, saluting Anna with the deep crimson liquid. "To both of us and everything we have in common."

He followed her into her building, into her elevator, and into her apartment. The arrangement they apparently had made, had been made without speech.

"You don't have a cat?" he asked looking around.

"No. Do the women you see usually have cats?"

"I just thought you might be the type." He looked out through the slats of the living room blind, then walked into the bedroom. She trailed after him and watched him pull up the blind in there and look down. "Wow, you really can see into our building," he said. "I mean the angle."

She didn't say anything in response, but perhaps as a witness to whatever he had done, she ought to feel some fear.

He pulled the blind back down. "Don't worry about it," he reassured her. "I can see that you're the nervous type. You thought something had happened."

He took off his jacket and sat on her bed. "Come here," he said.

She entered into his arms, and he enfolded her, the intensity of her emotional response obliterating all reason. Her behavior these last two days had been uncharacteristic, but she understood herself completely. This moment with him was one of life's most precious gifts, like a perfect shell cast up from the sea by a treacherous storm.

In the middle of the night, she opened her eyes. He was dressing and looked over at her, then away. They did have something very much in common. They had an awareness alive in them, something that was dead in most others. So despite their being polar opposites, they were the same.

And that, she thought, was why he had gone after her. No cat and mouse game. Only a kind of sensing of the other, accompanied by curiosity. He had wanted to unify their two existences, their two halves.

His suit on, tie in his pocket, he came over to the bed, where he soothed her forehead in a single, light touch. "Get up and lock the door after I'm gone." With a gesture, he restrained her from accompanying him.

He left. She rose and locked the door. That was all. That was all she might ever expect.

🌲🌲🌲

Still, a couple of times in the week after, she walked on his street past the social club. The old guys playing cards at their table on the sidewalk saw her passage, she noted, then bent back to their game. Nick didn't seem to be around.

She knew she shouldn't be looking for him. She knew that.

Finally, the week after that, however, she didn't just pass the social club, but went up to the table where the men played.

"I wondered if Nick is around," she said.

"Everybody wants to find Nicky boy," answered one of the old men heavily.

"Who else?" she asked, as if she had a right to.

"Pretty nearly everybody, honey. Forget about Nick."

She wasn't going to forget about Nick, but she could act as if she had. She went away, putting work at the forefront of her life again. If she just saw him once in a while, just saw him, that would surely be enough.

🌲🌲🌲

A couple of days later, Detective Szabo called and asked her to come over, so she hurried to the PD headquarters without waiting until the end of the day.

37

Once Anna sat, Szabo placed a picture in front of her.

She gasped. The girl ... dead. Dead!? Unrecognizable as someone who had once been beautiful when alive—yet the girl, indeed. "Yes," Anna said. She had to clear her throat. "But I saw her alive." She was confused.

"No," Szabo disagreed. "This wasn't the woman you saw alive."

"Ariadne?" She looked away from the horrible picture.

Szabo moved the photo to his side of the desk. "Yes, Ariadne. But the woman you saw wasn't Ariadne. Ariadne's remains were found in a remote area of the park a few days ago."

She felt the detective watching her. "You mean ... he did kill her. I did see her dead ..."

"I'll tell you what happened as I envision it," Szabo said.

She declined a coffee or anything else, and he began to tell Anna a story, a story she could almost see acted out.

"Ariadne Sposeto worked as an accountant for her uncle, Paul Terrazzino, a minor figure in the Grabino crime family. Nicky Perosi met her at her uncle's home. He found her attractive. He took her out."

Anna could envision Nick with the woman she'd had met as Ariadne. She could imagine his flirtatious manner, his radiant sexuality beamed directly at the girl. Irresistible, even for someone as young and attractive as Ariadne. The real Ariadne, of course, not the look-alike.

"He took her to dinner and listened to her talk about the job she did for her uncle. They became lovers, and he bought her little tokens. Maybe he began to hint that the two of them could go away, leave the country, if only she'd get her hands on her uncle's money." Szabo was a lumpy man and his eyes were clouded with some condition of age.

But he was also obviously a person of a certain acumen. Anna felt he was right as to how Nick had approached Ariadne—ever so discreetly, as if the thought of the money was really not at the forefront of their relationship.

Szabo shot a look at Anna. "But Ariadne was reluctant. She knew her Uncle Paul would kill her, kill them both, if they stole his money. And maybe, too, she had a little bit of family sense, this girl. She refused and Nick shrugged it off as if he'd only been joking.

"A short while after that, he met another girl, an aspiring actress—aren't they always? Where did he meet her? At a café? In the street? Anyway, he met her. She was about the same height and build as Ariadne, and had some facial similarities. All she had to do was a little of this and a little of that to recast herself. He courted this girl, too, of course, and invited her to join him in a modest criminal engagement. Maybe he explained how little risk there was to the effort, how he was really entitled to the money—maybe the money had been his father's. You see?"

Anna nodded. The world was competitive, and a man like Nick wanted so many things.

Szabo seemed satisfied that she did understand, and he went on. "Nancy Jackson is her name. She's from Ohio. He taught her how to present herself as Ariadne. He had her practice Ariadne's signature. Terrazzino's millions minus enough cash for them to travel on went into a numbered account offshore."

Szabo put another glossy photo in front of Anna—Ariadne, or the Ariadne Anna had met—Nancy Jackson. Pictured here with dark hair, she wandered in a crowd in a public place. Anna could see that the snapshot had been taken at an airport.

Szabo set down one more photograph, this one of Nick. Anna's heart ached to look at his absolute beauty. She wanted to ask Szabo if she could have the picture, but she restrained herself. She ought to act as if she were sane, even if she wasn't entirely.

"The task force tracked them to the point at which they disappeared," Szabo said. "The two could be anywhere by now. With cash, and they had plenty of it, getting a new passport isn't hard. And then, after some time, he'll tire of Nancy from Ohio. And he'll want all the money for himself."

"How did . . . Ariadne die?" Anna asked.

"She was drugged, taken out and shot, then dumped along a trail," Szabo told her. "He couldn't just shoot her anywhere they might be."

"How awful," said Anna. "How very, very dreadful."

"Yes," the detective agreed. "And her uncle must think so, too, now that the investigators have told him what happened. But worse than that, Paul Terrazzino's money is gone." Szabo smiled. "You really don't want to steal the money of a mobster."

Anna stood up. Her legs felt like rubber. She sat back down. She sat there for a very long time, and Szabo went and fetched her some water.

Not that night but the next one, Anna had a dream. The dream was of great emotional intensity—one of those dreams that you remember for a long, long time, a dream that she would probably be able to bring to mind many years from the original experience.

In Anna's dream, she was prosecuting Nick for something or other. She wasn't sure what, and she hoped she found out before making a fool of herself in front of the court. At any rate, she set out her case, cleverly avoiding having to refer to the crime or any of the facts, which she didn't know. She felt she might be able to make her argument convincing enough without all of that anyway.

Just as she was about to rest the case, Nick came to her and gave her a very soulful look. He wanted Anna to agree to a plea bargain before the trial went any further. He said he'd sleep with her again in return for her dropping all of the charges.

Then, she remembered that Nick was on trial for killing a girl.

Anna pondered what she ought to do, debated sending him to prison, where she knew he wouldn't do well, versus having sex with him one more time.

In the middle of her internal debate, she woke up.

"No, Nick," Anna said out loud. "No plea bargain. You go to Dannemora."

She turned on her side to fall back asleep. . . . If only she had something to remember him by, a photo, a token.

In court next week, in her real case, she would say what the prosecutor always said. "Show this man as much mercy as he showed his victim and the victim's family.

"None at all."

Would someone say that to the jury when Nick finally stood trial?

4

# Reward or Revenge

*Marianna Heusler*


Vintage Values, Inc.
To: Sagesullivan13@gmail.com

Hi Sage,
Congratulations! I have some great news for you. For the fourth quarter of last year, you were number one in the district. You crushed the competition!

So, because of your diligence and hard work, you're going to be rewarded.

Vintage Values has planned a wonderful four-day vacation in the Adirondack Mountains. You will join me and four other high-level producers for a long weekend of skiing, snowboarding, hiking, and delicious meals by a roaring fire.

The weekend begins on Thursday, January 13th and will extend to Sunday, January 16th. More details will follow.

Again, congratulations! You've earned this trip. And thank you for everything you have done to make Vintage Values a success.

Kristen


Sage stared at the e-mail for several minutes and then reread it.

"What's up, babe?" The door burst open, and Noah, Sage's boyfriend of four years, entered.

"I won a trip."

"Is it a trip for two?"

"I don't think so. At least it doesn't say that."

Noah leaned over Sage's shoulder to read the e-mail. She could smell his musky, sandalwood scent, and the coffee on his breath. She found the scents comforting, just as she found the small room in her apartment on the Upper East Side of Manhattan a safe place.

"You don't seem too excited," Noah said as he straightened up.

"It sounds far and cold."

"Don't be ridiculous. The Adirondacks are only 250 miles away. And as far as being cold, Manhattan is cold at this time of the year. Would you feel better if it was a trip to one of the islands and you had to take a plane?" Noah paused. "But that's not it, is it?"

"My heart," Sage whispered.

Impatience flashed on Noah's face. "There is nothing wrong with your heart. You had every possible test, and it was determined that those skipped beats were caused by anxiety."

"And that's what I'm going to have, plenty of anxiety."

"Look," Noah couldn't keep the exasperation out of his voice, which made Sage even more anxious, "since COVID you have barely left this room, and thank God, you were able to continue to work remotely. I understood your fear at first, but life has moved on. People are socializing. I have a hard time getting you to go to a restaurant. You won't go to the movies, forget a Broadway show. You wouldn't even go to my company's picnic, and that was outside."

"And just when I was feeling better, that crazy man tried to hit me with a brick." Sage reached inside her shirt and touched the whistle pendant necklace from Tiffany's that Noah had bought to reduce her anxiety.

But Noah didn't understand. He was outgoing and confident, unlike Sage, who never knew what to say. Opposites might attract, but Sage feared that Noah was growing less and less attracted to her.

"I'll go," Sage said.

In the meantime, she would pray that she'd catch some sort of contagious disease, or that a major snowstorm would hit the Northeast.

And she would ignore the e-mail.

Vintage Values, Inc.
To: Sagesullivan13@gmail.com

Hi Sage,

I haven't heard from you. I'm assuming you are just as excited as I am about our upcoming trip. The address of the bed and breakfast is below. You can check in any time after two.

You can use your own car, if you have one, or you can rent one. If you don't drive, you can hop on a train and take a cab from the station. Of course, we will cover all expenses.

I'm looking forward to the trip and finally meeting you.

Thanks for acquiring those colorful poodle skirts!

Kristen

*Wait until Kristen meets me,* Sage thought. Her bio picture had been taken ten years ago, and in the meantime, Sage had gained thirty pounds. The right lighting had disguised her less-than-perfect features.

The other ladies were sure to be chic, pretty, and young, while Sage was over forty.

She ignored the e-mail.

But she couldn't ignore the phone call.

"I'm sorry, I haven't been feeling well," Sage lied.

"You are planning on coming next week?"

"I hope I can."

"I didn't mention this in my e-mail, but this is not just a vacation. We're going to be training you women to become leaders. I'm promoting you. You'll oversee your entire district. There will be some traveling involved, but you'll receive quite a nice bump in salary. This is a wonderful opportunity for you."

"I don't know what to say." Which was the truth.

"I'm trying to put together a menu. Any dietary restrictions? Or something you must have?"

"No." Except maybe arsenic.

"Great. I'll see you next Thursday. And be sure to pack a lot of warm clothing. It can get nippy at night."

Sage hung up and sank into her chair. There was no way out. She had to go. She had a feeling if she didn't, she would lose her job. Kristen wouldn't like the fact that Sage didn't want to advance in the company.

And Sage would probably lose Noah. That relationship was already shaky. He was moving on, while she was just stuck. Well, at least if he left her and she got a raise, she would be able to afford the rent by herself.

Maybe.

As she looked out her window, she glanced below at the bustling streets of Manhattan. She heard the roar of the passing traffic, accompanied by blaring horns. The clouds above were gray, dark, and threatening.

She had a very bad feeling about this trip. She couldn't shake the thought that something was about to go horribly wrong.

Much to Sage's surprise, the train ride was enjoyable. She bought the ticket for business class, and she occupied a single seat. She relished the peace and quiet, which, in no doubt, would be shattered once she reached the inn.

At first sight, Sage was impressed. The inn stood further back on a property that was now blanketed with snow. The brick building looked solid and well kept. Sage made her way up the walk and opened the stained-glass door. She found herself in a small hall. A woman with flaming red hair and bright turquoise eye shadow welcomed Sage in a high-pitched voice.

Sage introduced herself.

"I'm Clara; my husband and I own the Golden Light Inn. These are our mascots." Two Golden Retrievers entered the hallway, almost on cue. "This is Sunset," Clara pointed at the smaller dog, "and this is Sunrise. You can pet them if you like. They love attention."

Sage did not like it, but she managed to tap the tops of their heads.

"You're the first to arrive. It's a good thing you ladies are coming today. They are predicting a northeastern, a real blizzard. I was afraid you might cancel."

Sage felt her heart quicken. *Be careful what you wish for*, she thought. "I didn't hear anything about that."

"Well, we're hoping that it blows out to sea. But no matter, we have a backup generator, although we haven't used it for years. Your room is at the top of the stairs, first on the right. If you need anything, you can just pick up the phone. My husband, Ronald, can bring up your luggage."

"No, I can manage. Thank you."

"Tea is served at four. By then the rest of your party should have arrived. I bet you're anxious meet them."

Yes, that is exactly what Sage was. Anxious.

▲▲▲

But at least the room was a happy space, done in shades of pink and white. The canopy bed was enveloped with crisp, white linen and a fluffy comforter. The carpet below was dense and soft, and hydrangeas danced across the wallpaper and across the oversized chair. A fireplace occupied one wall, and a bouquet of pink roses had been placed by her bedside, filling the space with a sweet scent.

*I could stay here forever*, Sage thought.

She was unpacking her suitcase when she heard a movement in the hall. She drew a deep breath, and then she noticed the knob on her door turning. The door burst open, and Sage screamed.

A large man, with a long, messy, white beard and watery blue eyes, towered over her. "I'm sorry. I think I got the wrong room."

"Who are you?"

"I'm Ronald, one of the owners. Someone complained about a draft."

"Well, it wasn't me."

Sage looked up to spot a woman peeking into the open door. "Hi, I'm Bailey."

Ronald strode out of sight as Sage shook Bailey's hand. Bailey was young, clearly in her twenties, and she didn't look like a diva or a mean girl. Her full face was friendly, and she was wearing tan corduroy pants and an oversized sweater. Clearly, she was no fashionista.

"He gives me the willies," Bailey said as she plopped on the bed. "So, what do you think of the company?"

Sage soon learned that Bailey had just moved from Oklahoma to New Jersey, just getting settled in a new state. And she wasn't thrilled about a leadership position.

"I guess we should go down and meet the rest of the women," Bailey said in a discouraging voice, which cheered Sage.

The ladies, who seemed like a cheery lot, were already assembled in a cozy room steeped in chintz fabric. Tea was served, silver trays full of tiny scones, salmon on crisp melba toast, small bites of crabmeat, brownies drenched in chocolate.

The moment they walked into the room, Sage saw Bailey's face pale. *Why is she as nervous as I am?* Sage thought.

They sat down on plump chairs and introduced themselves. Kristen, the leader, was just as Sage expected, a blonde with high-priced highlights, dressed in a beige pantsuit and wearing bright red lipstick. Lara was a petite redhead, who seemed stoned or slightly inebriated. Olivia babbled on about her love of fashion and relayed her various jobs that led to Vintage Values. Bailey confessed that she didn't like traveling, and this was the furthest northeast she had been. But it was Avery who caught Sage's attention.

Avery was beautiful with her brown hair highlighted in gold. Her eyes were so blue they looked like sapphires. Her skin was bronze, and even in her expensive cashmere sweater and her designer jeans, it was obvious that she didn't have an ounce of fat on her.

And she was smart as well. "I'm a Harvard graduate. I went to private school in the Berkshires, and I spent a semester at Oxford. I live now in Boston with my fiancé, who is a heart surgeon."

Everyone nodded and said that was wonderful.

It was while Sage was reaching for a brownie that Avery sauntered over. "I hear that you're first in the district."

"Not me," Bailey answered, reaching for a scone.

"I wasn't speaking to you," Avery said in a snippy tone. She then looked at Bailey and shook her head when she saw the scone Bailey was about to consume.

Bailey put it down.

"Tell me, Sage, what's your secret? I don't like being second best."

Sage resisted the urge to say that she treated people nicely. Instead, she just muttered, "I work hard."

Avery shook her head, walked away, leaving a trace of gardenia behind.

"I've got to get out of here," Bailey said. "What do you say we go for a walk in the woods before dinner?"

The moment she was outdoors Sage felt jubilant. She loved it all, surrounded by fresh, white snow, icicles hanging from the trees, branches reaching to the sky, shining like diamonds.

"I'm not comfortable here," Bailey said, destroying the mood. "When I returned to my room, I found that guy, Clara's husband, looking through my underwear drawer. He said he wanted to fix the drawer, but I didn't believe him."

Sage agreed that he was weird and suggested they should both stay clear of him.

It started to snow. It came quickly, big, fat flakes, but Sage didn't mind. She didn't even care about the wind. It invigorated her. So did the odor of the pine trees; the air smelled so clean. Sunset and Sunrise joined them, running with glee, their mouths open, leaping, trying to catch the flakes. Bailey dropped her glove, and Sunset ran away with it. She chased the dog right into the open garage. Sage approached the garage as she watched Bailey yank her glove from Sunset.

"I think we can enter the inn from the garage door," Bailey said.

For some reason, Sage didn't want to walk through the garage. Instead, she went to the front door, wishing she could stay out just a little longer.

She wasn't anxious to go back inside and face the others. But she hardly had a choice.

Dinner was lovely, and the food was delicious. A roasted chicken with potato au gratin, assorted vegetables, hot buttered rolls, and an ample supply of wine. They enjoyed warm apple pie topped with cheddar cheese for dessert.

As they ate, Sage was aware of the howling wind and the lights in the dining room, which flickered off and on.

No one else seemed to be concerned except Bailey, who was quiet.

Kristen told the ladies that they were going to play an ice breaker game, which meant that Sage would have to speak, answering silly questions—would you rather vomit or have a headache, win the lottery if it meant giving up ten years of your life . . .

The game ended before Sage could make a fool of herself. Kristen explained that they were all going cross country skiing the next day if the weather permitted. Sage doubted that the weather would permit, which was fine with her. After they finished enjoying the outdoors, they would return to the inn for a power presentation.

"Before you retire for the night," Clara said, "I have made hot toddies. Just give me a minute and I'll bring them out."

"Will this evening ever end?" Bailey whispered. "I'm going to the bathroom."

"Don't you dare disappear on me!" Sage warned.

The chattering of the ladies stopped when they heard some crackling outdoors. "That doesn't sound good," Lara said shakily.

Bailey came in, holding a drink. Ronald passed out the drinks and then disappeared, and Clara entered. Sunrise and Sunset burst into the room, and Bailey apologized for keeping the kitchen door open. "I went to pet them through the gate, and they escaped."

Avery wasn't thrilled. She stepped back. Maybe she was afraid that one of the dogs would ruin her winter white pantsuit.

"Let's toast to the best weekend ever," Kristen said, holding up her glass.

At that moment, Bailey stepped back and bumped into Sunset, which caused Avery to spill her drink. Avery screamed, as though she had been shot and then dropped her glass on the coffee table. "This pantsuit cost three hundred dollars!" she raged. "You clumsy oaf!"

"I am so sorry," Clara said. "Of course, I will pay to have it cleaned."

"And if it can't be cleaned?" Avery asked.

"It's my fault," Bailey admitted. "I let the dogs out. Here, take my drink."

"I could use a drink!" Avery gulped it down.

Clara offered to get Bailey another, but Bailey declined. "I just want to go to bed."

Sage noticed that Bailey seemed to be staring in the distance. It took Sage a moment to realize that Ronald was now standing in the doorway, smiling in a strange way.

"I think I'll go upstairs with you." Sage put down her drink. It was a little too strong for her.

Suddenly a huge crash erupted. Olivia and Lara screamed, Avery cursed, and Bailey jumped into Sage's arms.

"What was that?" Kristen asked as the lights went out and they were thrust into darkness.

Ronald opened the front door, letting in a gust of cold air and wet snowflakes. They stepped back and slammed the door shut.

"I'm afraid that one of the power lines came down," Ronald said. "But no problem, we have a backup generator."

"Oh, this is just great!" Avery said. "We are trapped in here with no electricity while there is a blizzard outside."

"Ronald will check on the generator," Clara said. "In the meantime, I'll give you all flashlights."

"It's freezing cold," Olivia complained.

"We have a wood-burning stove," Clara said, "but it needs electricity to run. Why don't you all go to your rooms?"

"Think of it as an adventure." Kristen twitched a weak smile.

After Clara passed out the flashlights, Avery led the ladies up the stairs. Sage thought that she must be drunk; stumbling, Avery hung on to Kristen. "I don't feel good," Avery moaned.

"You'll feel better after a good night's sleep," Kristen said.

"I doubt it."

It was growing cold in Sage's room. There was no way to light the gas fireplace. She was too cold to undress so she climbed into bed fully clothed. But she didn't go to sleep, not easily, aware of her heart racing.

At 5:15 she turned on the lamp. It didn't work, and the room was freezing.

What happened to the emergency generator?

She walked to the window, but the pane of glass was thick with ice.

Chatter broke out in the hall.

"It seems that the backup generator is clogged from not being used," Olivia said as she tightened her coat around her. "I think we should all go home."

"Yes, like we can get out of here," Lara said. "I'm betting my car is buried under the snow!"

"It can't go on much longer," Kristen said. "Where's Avery? I would think she would be the first to complain."

Kristen approached the only shut door and knocked loudly, calling out to Avery. There was no answer.

"Can you open it?" Kristen asked Clara, who was coming up the stairs.

"I don't know if I should."

"She wasn't feeling well last night," Sage reminded everyone.

Clara reached inside her coat pocket and took out a row of keys. Slowly she inserted the key into the lock.

Everyone gathered around. Sage was thinking that maybe Avery wasn't in her room at all.

She was there, on the floor, still and silent.

"Is she dead?" Olivia asked in a faint voice.

"She seems dead to me." And as though Lara didn't want to look anymore, she retreated into the hall.

Bailey was crying, but all Sage felt was numb.

"I used to be a nurse," Kristen said, as she approached Avery. She bent down and put her thumb on Avery's neck. Then she rose and shook her head.

"What happened?" Olivia asked. "Do you think it was a heart attack or maybe a drug overdose?"

"Look what's on the rug," Lara shouted from the hall.

Everyone turned around and walked cautiously. Sage was afraid to look, expecting to see a blood stain. Instead, she noticed an orange blotch. She watched as Olivia bent down and sniffed the rug.

"What is it?" Clara asked. "I just had the carpets cleaned in the hall."

"Is that what you're worried about?" Kristen lashed out. "There's a dead body in one of your rooms, and you're worried about a stain on the rug?"

"I only meant it wasn't here yesterday," Clara said.

"The stain on the rug is antifreeze," Olivia announced in a grim voice. "My boyfriend is a car mechanic."

"Antifreeze!" Bailey said. "Why would antifreeze be on the floor?"

Sage felt like falling on the floor herself when she thought about how unsteady Avery had been climbing the stairs.

"I don't like this at all," Bailey said as she stepped away and looked at Clara. "We have to call the police."

"Of course, we have to call the police," Clara said. "But we can't do that right now. All the lines are down."

"Well, we can't just leave a dead body in the room," Lara answered, looking as though she might be sick.

"That is exactly what we're going to do," Kristen said. "In fact, no one should go into the room or touch anything until the police arrive." She closed the door of the room for which Sage was grateful. And then Kristen turned toward Clara. "Do you think that something was in that hot toddy?"

"Absolutely not!" It was obvious that Clara was horrified by the thought. "I poured those drinks myself. The woman was probably on drugs."

"Did you wash out the glasses?" Kristen asked.

"Well, no," Clara said sheepishly. "It was dark, so I decided to leave the cleaning to the morning."

"Olivia," Kristen turned toward her, "would you be able to tell if antifreeze was in one of the cups?"

"I think I would."

Sage and Bailey held hands walking down the stairs, and Sage was grateful for that. All eyes were on Olivia as she lifted the cups, one by one, to her nose. She put the third one down. "It's in here," she said.

Everyone stepped back as though she had discovered a bomb.

"I don't understand," Clara began to wring her hands. "This can't be happening."

"Why would anyone want to kill Avery?" Olivia asked. "No one even knew her."

"You knew her, Kristen," Olivia said. "You worked with her."

"Me! I never met her! Besides she was one of my top billers. I wouldn't kill her; I needed her."

Suddenly Sage felt her heart beating fast and furiously. Because she remembered. "Bailey, it was you," she said breathlessly. "That glass was meant for you."

"You're right!" Bailey cried out. "My God! I bumped into Avery, spilling her drink. And I felt so bad for staining her beautiful outfit, so I gave her mine! Oh my God!" She sank to the floor.

"This has to be a horrible mistake," Clara said.

"I don't see how putting antifreeze in someone's drink can be a mistake," Sage muttered.

"Maybe the killer wasn't targeting anyone in particular," Kristen said. "Maybe they just wanted to destroy your inn's reputation, Clara, one of your competitors."

Clara looked baffled by this theory.

The front door slammed, letting in a gust of freezing air. The room erupted in a series of screams as a face suddenly loomed. It took Sage a few seconds to recognize Ronald. His hulking figure was covered in snow, his beard wet and wild. He stomped his feet on the rug, and bits of ice flew into the air. "There are fallen trees all over, impossible to get to the road. Even if we could, it's not plowed. We're stuck here for a while." He paused. "Why are you all looking at me this way?"

"Someone murdered Avery, Ronald," Clara said. "One of the drinks we handed out contained antifreeze."

"Who's Avery?" Ronald asked as he unbuttoned his thick black coat.

"Except it wasn't Avery," Bailey said. "That drink was meant for me. Let's be honest. I caught you in my room, Ronald, going through my underwear drawer. I threatened to tell Clara."

"What?!" Clara thundered.

"I—I," Ronald stuttered. "I got a text about a drawer being stuck in room 12. So, I went upstairs—"

"I didn't send you any text," Bailey interrupted.

"Could we see that text?" Sage asked.

"Yeah, maybe, if my phone was charged, but it's not."

"I saw you," Olivia said, "in the kitchen, helping Clara with the drinks. You were the one who handed them out."

"This is crazy!" Ronald threw his coat on the floor. "Do you really think I'd murder someone over that?"

"All I know is that we're trapped here with a murderer!" Bailey cried.

"But it's not me!" Ronald shook his head violently.

"How long do you think it will be before the roads are cleared?" Kristen turned toward Ronald.

"I don't know," Ronald said. "First it has to stop snowing."

"I'm not eating anything that I haven't prepared myself," Olivia insisted.

"I took a cooking course one summer," Lara said. "I could do the cooking."

Everyone stared at her, mute.

"The question is," Kristen said, "who had access to those drinks?"

"The person who prepared them," Olivia said. Everyone looked at Clara.

Clara's face went bright red. "Why would I do something like that?" she cried.

"It was in my drink," Bailey said. "I need to get some air."

"I wouldn't go out there," Ronald warned. "The snow is four feet deep. If you should get caught in a drift, it could be dangerous."

"Somehow I think it's more dangerous in here." Bailey headed up the stairs.

"I'll go with you," Sage offered.

They couldn't go far. Not with the icy wind blowing snow in their faces and their boots crunching into the drifts.

But in a very strange way, Sage felt at peace. *I should be afraid*, she thought, but she wasn't. Instead, she felt as though the entire world had paused and been wiped clean.

Even in the middle of a murder.

Bailey suddenly stopped. "I feel terrible. After all, I gave Avery that drink."

"But if you hadn't, you would have been the one dead."

Bailey didn't deny it as they walked on, and then she said, "It must be him. Ronald, I mean. No one else had a motive to kill me." Sage didn't deny that. "If this was about our sales records, I'm only number three. The murderer would have gone after you, you're number one."

"Not comforting," Sage mumbled.

"Sorry. I've never seen a blizzard like this. Even in the Berkshires. I think it's only going to get worse. We should head back."

Sage thought that was a good suggestion because suddenly she realized how vulnerable they were in such a desolate place.

They walked in silence as they approached the garage. Sage was wishing they could go through there instead of walking the extra steps to the inn. But the garage door was closed.

Not like yesterday.

The garage where the antifreeze was kept.

And just like that, Sage knew.

"You did it," she said. "You killed Avery."

Bailey stopped dead in her tracks. "Are you crazy? Why would I kill Avery? I mean she wasn't a nice person, but I hardly knew her."

"You spiked your own drink. I saw you carry it in from the kitchen after you said you had to go to the bathroom. Then you purposely bumped into the dog, spilled Avery's drink, and offered her yours. I'm not sure but I'm guessing you knew her before. You said you moved from Oklahoma to New Jersey, you had never been this far northeast before. But you just mentioned the Berkshires, and that's where Avery went to high school."

For a moment Bailey didn't say anything, and then, "She didn't remember me. She bullied me relentlessly in high school—she and her mean girlfriends. And now, it's as though I didn't even exist. You won't say anything, right? You know she deserved what she got. Besides, it will put me in second place in sales."

Sage knew what she should do. She should play along instead of standing there, paralyzed, but before she could utter a word, she felt a tremendous jolt in the center of her abdomen, and she fell into the snow.

She wanted to cry out, but suddenly there was snow in her mouth, and more was coming. Bailey must have caused some kind of avalanche right on top of her. Now, buried in the snowdrift, she was fighting for every breath.

How did Bailey think she could get away with this? Well, maybe she wasn't thinking at all. Even if she was caught, Sage would still be dead.

*Don't move*, Sage thought. *Let her think you're dying and then when she leaves . . .*

Sage closed her eyes and started to pray. She heard footsteps above her moving away. She waited and then she tried to push the snow off her. But she couldn't. The snow was too heavy and getting heavier.

She was going to die here, buried in this winter wonderland. They would find her frozen to death when the snow melted.

She started to cry, and the tears turned to ice.

She was on her second Hail Mary, praying for a miracle, when a miracle occurred. She remembered what Noah had given her to keep her safe, buried underneath her clothes. With her teeth, she removed her glove and unzipped her jacket. It took her several seconds, but she found it. Her silver whistle.

Except it didn't work. It was too wet. She fished around in her pocket and found a tissue and wiped it. She blew on the whistle.

Too low to be heard.

She wiped it some more.

It was a bit louder.

And then again.

And again.

And again.

She heard voices.

"It's over here," someone said from a distance.

With her heart pounding, Sage kept blowing.

She heard digging above her, and then Ronald's face was the first thing she saw, a kind, concerned expression. He helped her up.

"Bailey," said Sage, spitting out the snow.

"You guys didn't come back," Kristen cried, putting her arm around Sage. "We were worried."

"Let's get her inside," Ronald said. "Then she can tell us what happened."

🌲🌲🌲

After a cup of tea with a splash of brandy and a cheese Danish, wrapped in a blanket, Sage was relieved to tell the story. Everyone was so nice and understanding, and she was grateful to be safe.

Ronald went out to check and said in a gleeful voice. "It stopped snowing!"

Everyone cheered.

"What now?" Kristen asked.

"We wait," Ronald said.

🌲🌲🌲

And wait they did as the hours dragged by. It was early evening when Ronald went out and came back with the news that he had seen a snowplow. They were going to send the police.

The next few hours were chaotic. The police found Bailey wandering in the snow, and they placed her under arrest. They removed Avery's body and gave Sage access to their phone so she could call Noah.

"There is a chance you might have to return for the trial," Ronald told her. "Hopefully, that will be in the spring."

"I'd like to be here in the spring," Sage said. "I bet it's beautiful."

"It's beautiful in the Adirondacks all the time," Clara said, "despite what happened here."

"I'll be back," Sage said, "because in a strange way, this beautiful place has changed me for the better."

5

# I'm Sorry

*Margaret Mendel*

DELIA WAS A PATIENT WOMAN, BUT THE RAIN, WIND, AND AN UNSEASON-ably late snowfall within the Blue Line of the Adirondacks had seriously messed with her plans to forage the early crop of wild mushrooms.

It wasn't as if Delia didn't have anything else to do. Quite the contrary, she was hopping all over the mountains, writing freelance articles for several local newspapers.

Finally, however, the weather broke, and the sky was as blue as it could ever get. Delia gathered up her mushroom-collecting gear and headed for her secret early spring gathering spot. Hopefully a yummy dish of sautéed morels would be on the dinner table tonight.

The time might have been too early in the season for the average person to take a motorcycle ride, but for Delia, the day was perfect. Though a deep chill was still in the air, Delia knew her Harley was up to the challenge. So, layering on the clothes, Delia headed out the door. The bike started up with a huge roar that never failed to bring a smile to her lips.

The ground was, nonetheless, miserably wet. In several areas, the boggy earth sucked at Delia's boots, making the going extra rough. She liked the way the land forced her to struggle. Your reaction was all a matter of how you looked at it. Mother Earth, that quirky old lady, controlled the weather, the land, the storms, and even the mushrooms; and for Delia this was part of the big picture. The outcome all made sense to her.

As Delia climbed around a tricky jagged outcrop of boulders, she saw someone asleep in the bushes. At just that moment, a sudden biting wind blew in from the north. A small bank of clouds slowly drifted overhead, casting a shadow on the area. A lock of the reclining person's dark hair frantically flapped in the breeze.

"Hello," Delia called out.

She received no response. She approached. Kneeling, Delia brushed aside the flapping hair. The person was a young man. He was cold as ice, and she felt not the slightest throbbing of life in his carotid artery.

She recognized the young man. He was Ronald, Will Everett's stepson. A trickle of blood trailed from the corner of his mouth. This was not good. Why did she, of all people, have to find him? Uncomfortable thoughts came to her mind, and she whispered, "Don't go there."

Delia knew better than to mess with the scene before a forest ranger or coroner arrived. But something wasn't right. This guy was not dressed for the weather. And she could see a large, dark stain on the front of his sweater. No doubt about it. Blood.

Delia needed to contact the authorities. She had to go back out to the main trail, find a signal, and call the ranger station. Ranger Robin answered. Delia related what she'd found and where the body was located. Then with trepidation, Delia said, "I'll meet you there."

Delia took out a notebook. Obviously, this was going to be her next article. This was certainly not how she expected the day to turn out.

As Delia headed back to where Ronald lay, she looked for clues. But the weather had been so brutal this winter and spring that deciphering which twisted and broken branch might have been man-made or the result of a storm was impossible.

She knew that the scene needed to be preserved. But Delia couldn't help looking for something out of the ordinary. Maybe she'd find a shell casing from the gun. Or maybe someone had dropped a cigarette butt. But she detected nothing.

Then, as luck would have it, she found a small patch of yellow morels buried under a bundle of winter debris. Carefully, she took up the fungi and placed them in her basket. She didn't consider taking the morels to be disturbing the crime scene.

Ranger Robin and the coroner took more than three hours to arrive.

The coroner who Robin brought was Angelina Beatelman, an elected coroner and the owner of a small funeral parlor in the area.

By the time Angelina had finished examining Ronald, the weather had turned quite cold. "Don't know if the bullet killed him," Angelina said, "but he does have a bullet wound in his chest. We're going to hear a lot of tongue wagging about this one. And, Delia, looks like you'll have first dibs on the story."

"Yeah, well, I'd rather have first dibs on other things, for sure," Delia said. "You going to call this a case of murder?"

"Don't know what else to call it. But it's not official until my report is turned in."

In the morning, after a restless night, Delia called Angelina. "Anything new?" she asked.

"Well, some interesting issues need looking into," Angelina said. "It's questionable whether the shooting took place where the body was found. Do you know about livor mortis?"

"I think I've heard the term," Delia said.

"That's the pooling of blood at the lowest part of the body after death," Angelina said. "Gravity pulls the blood down. This happens because the blood no longer flows. The body looks bruised and red in that area. And this begins to show up within an hour of death. In Ronald's case, several locations of his body showed spots of livor mortis. He had them on his left side, on his back, and on his belly. So, that means he was moved at least three times for this to happen, and all within several hours of his death. Crazy, right?"

When Delia hung up the phone, she opened her computer. It was time to write the article. But where to begin? She had so much to write about. Sadly, this was not the first tragedy for the Everett family, either. Delia hesitated to delve into the past, but after all, this was reporting. So, she began: "That tragedy should befall a family twice doesn't seem fair. And even the wealthy are visited by the ugliness of death. Almost twenty years ago, a toddler, the second born of Will Everett, tragically fell from a cliff to his death. This week, Will's stepson was found dead on one of our beloved trails, with the suspicion of foul play." Delia gave a brief family history and mentioned that Dylan, the baby's older brother, a child of ten years old, had been present when the toddler fell to his death.

Delia gave only the barest of information about Ronald's case and did not mention livor mortis. When the article was finished, she sent it to Sammy Winters, the publisher of a small newspaper that was scheduled to come out within the next day or two. Delia typed, all in caps in the subject line of the e-mail, "AM I TOO LATE?"

Sammy responded with, "YEOWZA! With an article like that I'd stop the presses anytime! It's going out today. Keep me in the loop!"

The next afternoon, someone came barreling up Delia's driveway. Delia wasn't surprised to see Will Everett stepping out of his SUV.

"Figured I'd see you some time soon," Delia said as Will neared the house. "I am sorry about your stepson."

"You didn't waste any time digging up the past," Will said.

Detecting Will was pissed didn't take much effort. Delia didn't flinch at his words. "News is news," she said. She looked this one-time friend straight in the eyes as honest with him as she'd ever been. She suspected Ronald's death had awakened thoughts of the painful death of the toddler, an ugly tragedy that years ago had tangled them both in heartache.

Will stood by the porch.

"You look tired, Will," Delia went on.

"Yeah, suppose I am," Will said.

Delia didn't think either of them knew how their first meeting would go after all these years. But then she supposed that neither of them thought they'd ever talk to one another again.

"It's been a while since we had our chats," Will said. The bluster that he had first come at her with was no longer present.

"Yes, a lot has happened along the way," Delia said.

The angry look on Will's face had turned to sadness, and now he looked as though he was about to cry as he stepped up on the porch.

"Come inside," she offered softly. "I'll make you a cup of tea."

Delia had never been a big talker. Her strength was writing, gathering mushrooms and wild edibles for her special teas, and diagnosing a person's ills. Sometimes solving a problem was simply a matter of the heart, and sometimes she had to deal with bad living catching up with a drinker. Once in a while, she dealt with someone who was very sick, and in that case, she could neither say nor do anything to help the person. But Delia prided herself in knowing when to keep her mouth shut and when to give comfort and advice.

"The place hasn't changed much," Will said as he stepped into the little house.

Delia put the kettle on the stove. "Made a few changes, here and there," she replied.

They sat quietly for a while. The small window over the kitchen sink let in precious little light, but there was a warm glow from an afternoon sun.

"Why'd you come here?" Delia asked.

"Dylan thought you took too much liberty in the article about our family," Will said. "He's hopping mad you brought up the past. I've bent over backward trying to comfort him about what happened to his little brother. And now you've brought it all back. It's hard enough that we're dealing with Ronald's death here. Now we're having to relive the past."

"The situation is a sad one," Delia said, knowing that no one could give Will comfort at this point. "But why did you come here?"

Will fidgeted with the sugar spoon, turning it over and over. He didn't drink his tea. Then he said, "I've missed you."

She did not respond.

"You were always so kind to me, even when I was a jerk," Will added.

"You were a mess when that little boy of yours fell off the cliff," Delia said. "I just helped you through that time. You and I were over years ago."

The expression on his face startled her. He looked confused and frightened.

"I cannot stand remembering what a beautiful child he was." Will clenched his fists. He no longer looked frightened. "Help me find who did this to Ronald."

Delia was taken off guard. "I write the news. I don't investigate. How could I help?"

"We'll find a way," Will said. "Tell me you'll think about it. We had our problems, but I need your help and I trust you."

Delia took a sip of tea. She put down the cup. Will's request for help touched her, and she recalled the caring times they had spent together. She had once been important to him, and he had responded in kindness.

Will needed her again, and Delia understood his request for her help, and wondered how she could not agree to his request for assistance.

"Does Dylan know that you're asking for my help?" Delia inquired.

"No, this was my idea."

"He's not going to like it," Delia said.

"I'll handle that. So you'll help?"

"I'll think about it and let you know in the morning."

Delia watched the SUV leave the driveway.

Though that first death had occurred many years before, Delia also remembered, as though it was yesterday, the lovely little elf-like boy from Will's second marriage. His first marriage had been a mistake from the beginning and ended in a nasty divorce. Will was then committed to huge alimony payments while Dylan was shuffled back and forth in the joint custody arrangements. But when the second wife came along, a school-teacher newly relocated to the Adirondack school system, life began running smoothly again.

Only after the child from his second marriage fell from a cliff did Delia and Will become close. The second Mrs. Everett, totally distraught by the death of their son, had a nervous breakdown. Then on a doctor's recommendation she left the area for a rest, and she never returned.

A local merchant recommended Delia to Will because he constantly complained about being unable to sleep. An herbal potion to stop the night images was what he requested of Delia. Will said he couldn't sleep because the child kept coming to him in the night. A simple act of kindness was how their relationship began. Delia was a single mother raising a daughter at the time, and she needed the extra money her little herbal business brought in.

The warm glow coming through the kitchen window had disappeared. The room had become dark with shadows that crept across the walls. Delia remembered how Will trembled when he first talked about the child's visits after dark. Her herbs helped him sleep some nights, and then other nights the teas were of no help at all. But he kept coming to visit Delia. It might have turned into a physical relationship, but for her, he was too desperate, too eager to become lost in another person. Now he was asking for her help again.

Delia went out onto the porch. A slight breeze rustled the upper boughs of the trees. The season was beginning to turn. She smelled the early green in the air. But something else was in the air as well, an unnerving sense of meanness. Delia shivered in the fading afternoon light, and she decided to help Will find Ronald's killer.

Ranger Robin called Delia later that night. "Things are going to be busy around here for the next couple days," Robin said. "Ronald's body is being transported by helicopter to New York tomorrow. Will Everett got a special permit from the county. They couldn't land on his property because of the dense trees. So, they'll do the pickup on the local grocery store parking lot. Then the next day, the New York State Police are coming by. They want us to round up a few folks to ask them questions. They'll want to talk to you, since you were the person who found Ronald."

"Sounds like the circus has come to town," Delia said. "Are Will and Dylan going to be there when the state folks show up?"

"They sure are," Robin said. "And from what I've heard, the head investigator is pretty interested to know why Dylan has now changed his story about what Ronald told him."

That following morning the hearse carrying Ronald pulled into the grocery store's parking lot and waited for the helicopter to arrive. A few of the locals stood around as the hearse eased into a parking spot. It wasn't something the folks around here saw every day, nor was the sound of the whirring helicopter blades a common occurrence. Delia stood on the sidelines and watched. Seeing the coffin taken out of the hearse and loaded into the helicopter was quite a spectacle. Ronald's mother, a woman Delia had never met, got out of the SUV and, with Will at her side, walked toward the helicopter.

Will held his wife's hand. She was crying. Dylan got out of the back seat of the SUV and climbed into the passenger side of the vehicle.

Delia watched Will kiss his wife and then let go of her hand. She said something to him, but he did not respond. His wife looked at Dylan sitting in the SUV and then turned and went into the helicopter. Delia didn't know if by unfortunate scheduling or a deliberate act of Ronald's mother, but a major meeting regarding the investigation of her son's murder was to be held the following day, and she wouldn't be in attendance.

Then when the helicopter lifted off the pavement, whipping up great gusts of wind as it headed for New York, Will spotted Delia in the small crowd of bystanders as they were leaving the area.

"So what did you decide?" he asked.

"Yes, I'll help in any way that I can," Delia said and glanced over at the SUV. Dylan was watching them, and she could see from his furrowed brow that he was not happy. "Have you talked to Dylan?"

"Not yet. But he wants to find out who did this as much as I do. He'll come around."

"I heard about the investigators coming tomorrow. I'll be there. Got a special invitation from the forest rangers."

"Good," Will said. He looked at the SUV. "Dylan's having a meltdown today. So much is going on that it's driving him a bit crazy. He's not handling any of this very well. He still holds a grudge against you."

"Figures," Delia said. "Look if it's too much for you, I don't have to involve myself."

"No, no, I want your help. I need your help. Dylan will just have to accept this. You looking into this will be to his benefit, too."

"Okay," Delia said. "See you at the ranger station tomorrow."

Delia watched Will walk to the SUV. Dylan watched, too. Delia had only seen Dylan a couple of times since she and Will parted ways. She and Dylan never exchanged a word, and on those few times they did meet up accidentally at a store, or in the street, he would give her a scowling look as they passed each other. The little boy had grown into manhood, and even as a little boy she remembered his eyes, watching, always watching, yet never meeting a person's gaze. When he was still quite young and she spoke to him, he looked at the floor, the ceiling, across the room, but never looked her directly in the eyes. Delia knew that if the investigating attempt with Will didn't work, the failure would be the result of Dylan's disgruntled attitude about her.

The next morning when Delia arrived at the forest ranger station, the parking lot had a few extra cars but plenty of room remained for her Harley. Will's SUV was parked near the front door and Delia knew that meant he'd arrived plenty early.

The meeting was just about to get under way when Delia walked in. The New York State Police investigator was addressing Dylan. "We're having trouble with the time line you presented us," he said. "It contradicts what you first told the rangers about your stepbrother going missing."

"Why are you questioning me?" Dylan shouted. "Isn't it your job to find the killers and not harass the family?"

"We're just trying to organize our investigation because you were the last one to see or talk to your stepbrother," the officer said. "No one saw him but you."

Delia watched Dylan. He had red blotches on his cheeks and down his neck.

"Are you accusing me?" Dylan shouted.

"Calm down, sir. We know this is difficult for you and your family. No one's accusing you of anything."

The officer directed his attention to Will. "Mr. Everett, when was the last time you saw your stepson?"

"More than a week ago. I was out of town on a business trip in Japan when I heard Ronald was missing."

Until now only the rangers had asked the questions, and they were sympathetic with the family, so they took a gentle approach with Dylan. This investigator from the New York State Police was not a soft-spoken, easygoing guy. Delia could tell he meant business and hadn't come all the way out here to pass the time of day. He was looking for answers.

Still directing his questions at Will, the officer asked, "Do you have guns in the Everett household? Handguns?"

"Yes," Will said.

"When we're finished here, would you mind if we come by your place and take a look at them?"

"Fine. No problem."

The angry look Dylan gave his father told Delia that working with Will's son was not going to be easy, and she wondered how long her arrangement with Will would last.

The state investigating officer pitched a few more questions. But Dylan either couldn't or wouldn't answer, and then complained that the investigators were spending too much time talking to the wrong people. Will looked distraught, and clearly, he couldn't calm Dylan, no matter what he said. At one point when Dylan was asked if he and his step-brother ever got into fights, Dylan stood up, shouted, "This is bullshit," and left the room.

The investigator raised an eyebrow in exasperation, looked at one of his deputies, then said, "Who's next?"

Delia had her turn with the investigator. She could add nothing new to the case. Her evidence was the discovery of the body. And no talk of wild mushrooms. When the investigator was finished with Delia, she left the building and went home to start on another article.

Later that evening, Delia received a call from Will. "A couple guns are missing—a rifle and a handgun."

"What do you mean, missing?"

"I'm a big believer in gun safety. I keep them in a locked box in the basement rec-room, and they're not there."

"Did your wife or Dylan take them out and not return them?"

"They both know better than to do that. I'm a real bug about locking up guns. Dylan is beside himself worried that someone broke into our house and took the guns. Now he wants cameras and alarms on the grounds and in the house."

"What do you think happened to them?"

"Haven't a clue. It could have been a robbery. Really, we can't rule that out. I can't remember the last time I opened the case. But the key was where I usually keep it."

"What did the investigator say?" Delia asked.

"Wasn't happy, I can tell you that much."

"Maybe talk with Dylan. Could he have used the guns, put them someplace and forgot?"

"The investigator asked him that, and boy, that did not go well."

"Talk to Dylan. Ask for his help in solving this."

"He has become so unreasonable in the last couple of years; I'm losing my patience. And the way he spoke to the investigator was very upsetting."

"Don't think I can help you with Dylan," Delia said.

"Why don't you come by for lunch tomorrow?" Will asked. "We'll try to have a conversation about how we can all work together to find Ronald's killer."

Delia agreed to come for lunch, but she didn't have much confidence that her being there would help the situation. She hung up the phone and went back to writing a rough draft of the next article.

The following day, Delia arrived at the Everett estate. It was a big place. Will worked years getting it to be exactly how he envisioned, now he boasted that he lived in a log cabin mansion. Delia thought maybe a couple dozen little houses the size of her place could fit into the Everett mansion.

Lunch was to take place in a gazebo in the back garden. The setting was lovely, but Delia thought Will's mood was a bit testy when he said, "Can't depend on the weather or my cook. Seems she's got a toothache and needs the afternoon off."

"That's fine," Delia said. "Looks as if she did a great job of getting food on the table."

"Yeah, she's good usually," he said. "Maybe she needed a break from Dylan and me. He's been ranting about contacting a security company to set up a new system. He won't let it go, and he goes on and on about it."

Delia sat at the table. Will poured her a cup of coffee and sat beside her. A few birds flew into the garden. A breeze ruffled the cloth napkins on the table. A faint fragrance of lilac was in the air, and Delia was sure she'd find a bush of those beauties somewhere nearby.

Delia heard something stir behind her; she turned and saw Dylan standing in the doorway.

Will turned and saw him, too. "How long have you been there?" Will asked.

"Not long," he replied.

"Hungry?" Will asked.

"Not really," Dylan said. He looked in the direction of Delia. "Is this why you wanted me to have lunch with you? Because you invited her?"

"Yeah, well, we have to work together to help the authorities find Ronald's killer."

Delia could see that Will was approaching this situation quite diplomatically. She knew as a businessman he had plenty experience with negotiating.

"Tell me again," Will said, "so that we can get a good time line, what time of day did you last see Ronald?"

"I don't remember. Maybe late morning." Dylan stepped out of the doorway.

"What did he say?" Will cautiously pursued the questioning.

"Maybe he was going climbing or maybe hang out with friends."

"Want some coffee?" Will asked.

"No."

"Were his college friends in town?"

"Didn't ask."

Dylan moved closer to the table. "She going to eat anything?"

"Suppose we both are, even if you aren't," Will said. Then taking up a small sandwich, Will asked, "So, when do you think our guns went missing?"

"I told you yesterday that I didn't have a clue what happened to the guns. Don't you ever listen to what I say?"

"Yes, I listen very closely."

"The hell you do," Dylan said. "You listen to everybody but me."

"Now, son, you know that's not true."

"I'll bet you listen to her more than me."

Delia could see that this conversation was going nowhere. "Maybe I should leave," she said.

"No," Will shouted.

Dylan turned to face his father. "I don't want her here."

"Be reasonable, Dylan. We thought you'd like to be part of a team that was looking for answers to who killed Ronald."

"You're always asking questions—Where's the gun? When did you last see Ronald? What did he say to you? Where did you last talk to him?" Dylan's face and neck had turned blotchy with red spots.

Dylan glared in the direction of the wildflower garden and said, "Nobody ever believes me."

These last four words that Dylan had just spoken, as pathetic as they sounded, triggered a memory, something Delia had tried hard to forget. The air had been sweet with the scent of lilac that day, too. Delia was undressing her young daughter to give her a bath and discovered bruises scattered all over the child's legs, arms, and shoulders.

"What happened?" Delia asked.

"Nothing," her five-year-old daughter said.

"Something happened. Tell me."

"I can't."

"What do you mean you can't?"

"If I tell, he'll hurt you, too."

In the end, Delia got it out of her daughter that Dylan had tied her to a tree and then threw rocks at her. Will asked his son about what Delia had discovered. Dylan denied doing any such thing. It was quite a scene. Delia's child, frightened that more harm would come to her and to her mother, begged her mother to believe Dylan. But there was no other logical answer. The only time her daughter was out of her sight was when the child was outside playing with Dylan, and Delia was making tea for Will to help him through his grief of losing a son and a wife who would not return home to him.

Dylan cried that day, also and repeatedly said, "Nobody ever believes me."

His father believed him. Now Delia sat in this family's lush garden, delightful food on the table and a nasty memory glaring her in the face. She looked at Will. He appeared helpless and pathetic as he tried to make nice with his overindulged, spoiled son.

She got up from the table. "Nobody ever believes you," Delia said. "Why should they? You're a little lying brat."

"I should kill you for that," Dylan said, and he pulled a pistol from the back pocket of his jeans.

"Maybe you should try," Delia said. "Look me in the eye, you twerp." She paid no attention to the gun.

"Stop it," Will shouted.

"Make her stop," Dylan said. Delia heard a childish whine.

Will looked at the gun. He knew then what his son had done. "What did you do?" he softly asked his son. "What did you do?"

"It was an accident. It was an accident. I didn't mean to do it. Please, I didn't mean to do it."

Will took the gun from his son's hand. This was the missing handgun, the gun that was supposed to be locked away. He looked at Delia, "What do I do?" he asked.

She sighed heavily. She had no comforting words.

"I'm sorry, Daddy, I didn't mean to do it. Daddy, please, I'm sorry."

Will stood in the gazebo, pistol in hand. He said nothing as Dylan repeatedly said, "I'm sorry."

Will looked at Delia. They had both heard this same plea years ago when the toddler had fallen from the cliff. "I'm sorry, Daddy. I didn't mean to do it."

# 6

# The Other Side of the Line

*Jenny Milchman*

**CUTE COTTAGE REDO ON OTTER LAKE**

Lily Michaelson was tired, and they hadn't even set out yet.

The children had been racing around, yelling and bashing things, from the second they woke up at their usual insane hour, a time that had only gotten harder to beat as the little kid years receded into the past. Second and third graders now, impossibly enough. She, the mother of elementary school children? How had that happened? With a nanny harder and harder to justify, the kids being out of the house all day, Lily's morning routine had gotten so compressed she scarcely had time for her flow and was down to one hastily guzzled cold-pressed juice instead of a lovingly composed smoothie: fistfuls of green fed into her Macerator followed by a satiny pour of milked nuts and trickle of honey. No wonder she was exhausted.

"Babe!" she called to her husband, ignoring the din. "We about up?"

"Five seconds," he called back over a fierce gush of water.

Or maybe five minutes? She couldn't really hear him. They'd recently redone the bathroom, and Lily still wasn't used to the echo of the subway tile. Ben was notoriously flabby about time anyway. If he'd been the one responsible for getting the kids off to school, he'd have been physically flabby, too. Instead, he got to put in two hours at his favorite gym, thirty blocks uptown, before strolling into his crypto startup. Chump Change, it was called, as if all of them—VCs, dev, marketing—were laughing at those who thought the mighty dollar would ever fail while at the same time getting rich off them. Lily wasn't exactly one to talk, though. Her does-anybody-really-need-this food styling business kept her dashing all over the city—sometimes even one of the outer boroughs, horrors—and plastered to Instagram after the kids finally conked out for the night.

The kids.

"Reuben! Daydra! We're leaving! Now!"

Somewhere in the morass of motherhood, her voice had taken on the unappealing quality of attaching an exclamation point to every utterance.

Ben ambled out, rubbing his hair with one of the new, plush towels that went with their new, plush bathroom. It was as if his pace had been factory-set to amble. The man wouldn't hurry if he were being chased at knifepoint.

"Check-in is three o'clock," she reminded him. No exclamation point, but her voice wielded an even less pleasant tone now, chiding and prim. Librarian-like. "If we don't leave soon, we'll be losing money on the res."

"And time," he replied agreeably. "Which is even worse. We've only got two days."

Some former part of Lily flickered, a piece of her past that included soaking the cereal dust from an empty box in milk and calling it breakfast, sleeping on the sofa in her mother's rental before walking two miles alongside railroad tracks to school. What would her mother, long dead, have thought about weekend getaways and renovated bathrooms?

The kids came flying out of their rooms, dragging two-hundred-dollar backpacks stuffed to bursting with items they wouldn't look at over the next two days, much less need. Lily mentally ticked off the contents of her wheelie. Tooth stuff, each one's favorite snugglie, outer gear. Up north there might still be snow on the ground.

🌲🌲🌲

Reuben took the stoop steps to their brownstone as one, per his usual. They located their Range Rover on Greene Street, then drove off to join the clogged river of traffic entering the city only to exit it uptown in an endless, unforced migration, its only urgency the pursuit of pleasure.

"I love this part," Lily murmured a few hours later, lulled by the rhythm of the drive. "Where our everyday lives, the city—then what lies beyond it—give way to nothingness." She gestured out the car window. Trees and open space.

"Our everyday lives are great," Ben said, giving her a look.

He was right. They were. They had everything. So why did nothing appeal so deeply?

"K, kids," Ben said. "Time's up."

He never had to clip on an exclamation point to his sentences; both children's hands rose obediently to the sides of their heads. She and Ben permitted the kids to keep earbuds in, or have Kindles out, for half the trip; after that they needed to participate in whatever conversation the grownups were having or look at the scenery. Since both unfailingly selected the first part of the drive for devices—no marshmallow test winners in her duo, which she supposed was okay—they ran out of distraction in conjunction.

Lily decided to revisit this policy with Ben before making the trip home. In what seemed like a mathematical impossibility, two unoccupied children added up to more than one doubled.

"When're we gonna get there, Mom?" asked Reuben, once the squabbling had gone on for so long that even he and his sister seemed bored by it.

Lily glanced out the window. The landscape had grown even more spread out, less cluttered. Enormous trees overhung the road, their branches so heavy with snow they swept the ground. Deeper in the woods that snow was completely untracked, as if nothing and no one had walked there for a very long time.

She shivered despite the blast of warm air from the vents. Nothing no longer appeared quite so peaceful and soothing.

Ben turned the heat up, and she thanked him with a look.

"You all right?" he mouthed.

She nodded.

"Soon," Daydra told her brother optimistically.

Reuben whipped around on the backseat. "You don't know it's soon!"

"Yes, I do!" Daydra shouted back.

Lily stayed silent. Her gaze felt pinned, as if by spikes, to the hummocks of white beneath the trees. Elsewhere the snow had started to melt for the season, but those draping branches shaded the ground, kept it from warming. There'd probably be snow in there till May. She shivered again, a full-body shudder.

"Kids," Ben said brightly, giving the steering wheel a spin. He checked his phone. "I actually do think we're close now. Unless this thing is confused, it's about a mile up ahead."

He made a turn onto a narrow dirt road roofed by spindlier trees so that the snow, that awful blankness, gave way to bare patches of ground, although banks of white still rose up on both sides.

"See," Daydra said. "Told you."

"This isn't soon," Reuben replied nonsensically.

Lily fought to shake off whatever mood had overtaken her. They were on a mini-vacay, something they did a dozen or more times a year, but this felt different for some reason. "Hey, guys, remember that weird place last time?" she said, conjuring up the image. They booked so many stays, the differences tended to get smeared away.

"Which one was that?" Ben asked.

"Oh yeah, I remember," Reuben said, looking uncertain.

The tires fishtailed as the road began to twist, and Ben steered expertly out of the skid. City boy, but her husband could be pretty capable. Lily laid a hand on his thigh, and he looked away from the road to give her a lascivious eyebrow waggle.

"There was all that weird art stuff on the walls," Daydra piped up. "It looked like—"

"Blood!" Reuben said, catching on.

"And guts!" crowed Daydra, not to be outdone.

"How about that other place where they brought us the really huge zucchini?" Ben said. "From their garden—"

Just then a mossy triangle of roof poked its peak from a cleft in the ground, the road crooked, and the rest of the cottage appeared.

"Oh yeah, and Mommy cooked it and you made us eat it, Daddy!"

"Ewww! That was gross!"

"Shh!" Lily hissed, so sharply that Ben jerked his head in her direction.

"What's going on with you?" he asked, sotto voce.

She subsided, sinking back in her seat. "Sorry."

"Seriously," he went on. "What's wrong?"

She stared out the window as the car rolled to a stop. "Where'd you find this place? Airbnb or Vrbo?" She pronounced it the new way—*verbo*—despite a mental scoff. Always one to fall for a marketing campaign, that was her.

Ben threw open the door, letting in a rush of cold air. "I don't remember. Why?"

The kids scrambled out, backpacks left behind on the muddy rubber floormats, so that Lily busied herself clearing out the car without offering a reply. It didn't matter anyway. They were all the same.

🌲🌲🌲

By avoiding the path, scrambling up over an ice-encrusted slope, then slip-sliding the rest of the way, Reuben managed to reach the house first. At the door, he stood with one stubby finger poised over the number pad on the lockbox. Ben read the code off his phone, and Daydra leapt to extricate the key. They were all old hands at this.

Lily pushed the door open. It creaked. Of course it did.

Inside everything was on the dingy side, the light dim. A smallish main room with worn wooden floorboards was mostly taken up by twin couches, their cushions lumpy, and a battered table. A picture window—the cottage's best feature—was concealed behind a waxy shade. Lily drew up the shade, letting in afternoon light, scant, but sufficient to bring into view a circa 1980s kitchen and two narrow doors, probably leading to bedrooms, down a short lick of hall.

"Cute cottage redo?" Lily said. "I dispute both. The cute and the redone."

She went around turning on lamps, all of which fluttered before the bulbs finally consented to give off a grudging yellowish light.

"It's creepy cute," Ben said, trailing her. "Like shabby chic. Next big thing in décor."

He headed over to the kitchen to see what the host had left, always his favorite part. After a brief hunt, he displayed a shallow wicker basket filled with granola bars—and not non-allergenic, vegan ones either—herbal teabags, and chocolates whose wrappers looked wrinkled.

"Six," said Lily, forcing optimism, because, although she couldn't figure out why, this weekend was turning into a disaster and it had barely started.

"No way. Four at best. The last place left wine and cheese and those seeded crackers."

"At least there's no nuclear winter vegetables."

"Fruit," Ben said. "Zucchini is a fruit."

"Really, Ben?" Lily replied.

He shrugged. "I just helped Rube with his botany project."

"You mean did it for him?"

The kids came tearing down the tiny scrap of hall.

"We don't have to share a room, do we?" they both cried, with as much terror as if one had learned the other needed a kidney.

Ben finished gobbling a bar. "Hey, kids, you know what? We're going outside."

🌲🌲🌲

"There's the lake!" Reuben shouted as they all exited the house, jackets zipped, hats and gloves on, boots laced. "Otter Lake!"

"Otters are so adorable," Daydra said, hugging herself through her bulky coat.

Ben topped the crest of land that stood between them and the lake, and Reuben set off in pursuit of his father. Lily sped up, signaling her daughter to follow.

Normally she was in favor of giving the kids room to explore—no helicopter parent, she; Reuben and Daydra had been taking the subway alone since they were old enough to top off their Metro Cards—but this terrain was more rugged than any of them were used to, almost violently so. They shouldn't have come all the way up here, she noted with a pang of something like dread. You had to venture farther and farther these days to really get away, the outlying areas scarcely different from home. Beacon Beats Brooklyn. A slogan she'd seen on a T-shirt once.

But as she emerged through a grove of lacy trees to a thin thread of sun pinkening the lake, a sense of peace descended. She exhaled a puff of white that floated in the air. "Pretty, huh, kids?"

"It's frozen," Reuben said. "There's ice all the way across."

"Not frozen enough to go on," Lily said, alarm returning. She reached for her daughter's gloved hand while shooting Ben a look. *It'd better not be only me watching them this weekend.*

"Mom's right," Ben said, catching her eye. "Up here you know how they test if the ice is solid?"

"Do they jump up and down really hard on it?" Reuben asked.

"That's dumb," Daydra told him. "They'd slip. Ice is really slippery."

"This kind isn't like at the rink," Reuben argued. "It has all dirt and gunk frozen in it. Anyway, some people know how to jump on ice. What about in the Olympics?"

"They drive a truck out on it," Ben interrupted.

Both kids, who might very well have never heard the word *truck* unless it was preceded by *delivery*, were impressed enough to fall silent. They all stared at the lake.

Curved branches pierced the sky like hooks. *What would breaking through sound like?* Lily wondered. A sharp crack, similar to the lash of a whip. She shut her eyes, which brought the darkness closer, depthless reaches of water with ice like a sealed lid.

What were they doing, four cosseted souls from Brooklyn, in land that hadn't been stripped and gutted yet, all its savage scoured out? It was a privileged perception—her past retained enough of a hold to tell her that—since the city could be dreadfully savage to some. But still. Here they might get hurt for real—reality so lacking in their daily lives—or even killed.

Reuben was the first to break the silence. "Hey, what's over there?"

He tore off, in the opposite direction from the lake at least, and his sister ran after him, while Ben started walking, a little zombie-like, toward the scrim of ice on the shore.

"Babe?" she said. "Let's stick together, okay? I'm going after the kids."

"Sure," he called back. "Just one sec. Be right there."

Ben mentally ambled too, possessing a vacant, far-off quality he claimed came with being a coder. Lily was fighting the completely unjustifiable impulse to insist he ignore whatever had captured his attention and come with her now when a shriek sliced the silence. Not a shout or a yell, the bickering voices of her forever arguing children, but a ragged, terrified scream.

She broke into a run, no longer cursing their choice of destination but herself instead, whatever inside had led to this ridiculous life, with its eight-dollar lattes before work, and fifteen-dollar pours up here because people like them had infiltrated the area and liked mixology. Liked, and Likes, digitally bestowed upon filtered pics of food-looking drinks; the world had never seen so many pointless expressions of approbation, meaningless all, all of it gone in an Insta[nt].

Her pricey, seldom-worn boots mashed leaves into the snow-sloppy ground—she was going to get a workout in today after all, first one in weeks—as she fought for breath.

"Reuben! Daydra!" Back to exclamation points. "What happened? What's wrong?"

She stumbled over a slant in the earth, rounded a massive tree trunk, and came upon the two from behind. Yet another dispute was erupting.

"No, uh-uh," Daydra said. "Seriously. That's real."

"Is not! It's fake. I saw a TikTok."

Daydra edged past her slightly taller brother, neck craned to get a better look, and the motion enabled Lily to have a line of sight as well. Something lay still beneath a surf-curl of snow. Suddenly the little girl swerved, changing course so fast she nearly fell over. She caught herself, small mittened hands against a tree.

"It's real," Daydra said, then added, "Come away from there, Rube," in a voice of such maturity, both steely and kind, that it got Lily's legs pumping again, moving quickly enough that she slipped, skidded, arms thrust forward, gloved hands splayed to break her fall, face-first in a scarlet gash beside the body on the ground.

## PALATIAL NEW BUILD ON QUIET DEAD END ROAD

Tim Lurcquer, chief of police in Wedeskyull for more than a decade, was fast on his way to appointing Mandy Bishop deputy. The summer before she'd played a hero's role in a standoff with one of the most frightening characters Lurcquer had ever encountered on the job, and she was intuitive in addition to brave. Sometimes overly so on the intuition part, but still, it was an essential trait in a cop.

"The body was lying beneath an overhang of snow," he reminded her. "Not exactly what you'd call hidden."

"Bad guys be stupid," Bishop replied. "First thing they teach us in police school."

He permitted his lips a brief upward tilt. "That level of stupid is pushing it. And we don't have police school here."

She appeared to take his cue and got serious. "You think the victim was meant to be found."

"Unless our guy's not in the habit of checking the weather. Big thaw coming."

"Which they don't feel in their bones," she noted. "Maybe somebody young?"

He hesitated. "That's a bit of a leap. I'm gonna stick with the premise that they just didn't care if the body was discovered. Maybe even wanted it discovered."

"By that family?" she asked.

He held up a cautioning hand. "We don't know that. The Michaelsons apparently made their—do they call it a reservation?"

"Sure," she said.

"At the last minute," he went on. "And it was the children who spotted the body. Apparently the boy thought it was a prop—he follows this f/x guy on Tik-Snap-O-Gram or whatever."

"Okay, Boomer," said Bishop.

Lurcquer gave a genial wag of his finger. "Eight years shy actually." A pause. "While little sis knew what was what, sounded the alarm."

"You know, when you said prop—" Bishop began.

Lurcquer nodded her on.

"It made me think how something about the scene did look staged. Or positioned. You know? That perfect lip of snow with the body laid out beneath it."

"Possible," Lurcquer acknowledged. "Anyhow, there're plenty of people out by Otter Lake this time of year. Ice is still good. Fishing.

Snowmobiling. Whoever did it probably had no idea the person stumbling upon his kill would be a—guest?"

She gave a nod.

He rubbed a spot between his eyes. "Running that dilapidated old shack as if it's a hotel. Charging people for it."

"Kids these days," said Bishop.

No upward tilt of his lips this time. "So who owns it since the Potters sold? You track down that information?"

"Well, it can be a little hard to tell. Sometimes the owner isn't the owner."

"How's that?" he asked.

"It might be a parent corporation, say, some conglomerate that actually holds the title," she explained. "They in turn lease it—sort of—to individual owners who then run the place as a short-term rental. Never living in it themselves."

"Christ," he said.

Bishop glanced at her phone. "The name I have is Meghan Waters. She lives three hundred miles away from here. Downstate."

"Doesn't mean she was three hundred miles away during the time frame Bursar gave." The medical examiner. "She'd've had a good six hours to get home, maybe more, depending."

Bishop nodded. "I was all set to ask permission to leave town. Go question her on her home turf. But she just left a message saying she's headed up here. Which isn't the most likely move for a murderer, to return voluntarily to the scene."

Lurcquer sensed the faint vee that preceded a real bruiser imprinting itself on his forehead. Lately headaches had been giving him hell. "Unless that's exactly what she knows we'll conclude." He paused. "Bad guys don't always be stupid."

"10-35—" came the voice of Dorothy Weathers, den mother, dispatcher, general overseer of police business—everybody's business actually—in Wedeskyull.

Lurcquer and Bishop stood up at the same time.

"—1 Gibbons Creek Road. Repeat, 10-35 1 Gibbons Creek Road."

They zipped coats, donned fur-lined hats in lockstep as they strode out of the war room.

Bishop paused. "There's no residence on Gibbons Creek."

"There is now," Lurcquer said, outpacing her to the exit, a flip of the hand to say so long to Dorothy. "I watched it go up." His breath vaporized as he stepped outside. "No one's living in it yet, though; I just asked at Harrow Realty. Wanna know what a place like that will go for."

"Stalk Zillow." Then, "Holy shit, Chief—"

Already at his vehicle, Lurcquer half-turned.

"I bet it's another Airbnb."

Croesus Hunt went by Creece. Everyone except his mother called him that. He was short but strong, good at anything that could be done with his hands, from wood to engines to beatings. Only a good slug could talk reason into some people, the bitch in front of him now being one.

"You're telling me this isn't broken?" she demanded.

"No, ma'am," Creece said. "Installed it myself."

She ignored that. "Because I'm already composing my review. You don't charge somebody $600 a night for this."

He had to agree with her there.

But then she spat out more words. "You think I get to do this every day? Not even every week. This is supposed to be my me time! And I get a soaking tub that doesn't fill!"

The image of her nude, not-young-but-fighting-to-stay-fit body sinking into this tub had gotten him through the encounter so far. But the effect began to wane as he witnessed her sloppy and completely unearned display of grievance. A sentence his mother used to say when she gave Creece—Croesus to her—a beating filled his mind like a haze of smoke.

I'll give you something to complain about.

He blocked out the thought of his mother, turning back to the woman at hand. Reddened face, spittle flying. Outrage brought out her wrinkles. Forty-five if she was a day.

"Look," he said, setting down his toolbox, which he wouldn't need. "Faucet is kind of tricky—a lot of these fancy ones are—but you just need to lift the lever, kind of switch over to this valve here. Otherwise all you get is a trickle. See?"

Steam began to billow as the water flowed. They both watched the level in the tub rise.

His mood settled as he pictured one of those womanly admissions of wrongheadedness—a "silly me, I can't thank you enough" kind of thing. Maybe even an invitation of some kind; she'd been giving him looks this whole time, hadn't she?

Well, since the bath seems to work, why don't we . . .

Instead she rounded on him, clutching both sides of her robe as if she knew what he'd been X-ray visioning beneath. "If you think this means I'm changing my review again—"

Creece had a strange and sudden realization. She thought she was holding a .44, whereas he saw a BB gun. "Lady, that doesn't mean anything to me."

She scoffed. "I'm talking one star."

Telltale blotches of red appeared before his eyes. His vision was about to cloud over, and something unstoppable always happened then.

She was still at it. "You think a bottle of cheap champagne in the fridge is going to—"

And Creece, whose hands were good at everything, used them.

🌲🌲🌲

"There's a mess out at Gibbons Creek," Creece said as his wife set a plate before him. "I'm going to need you to take care of it. Tonight."

Becky settled heavily into the chair beside him. "I never do cleans at night. You know that. My eyes." She lifted her fork. "And the Gibbons Creek property? It's all the way at the end of the road. I'd drive right into the water. I suppose if you brought me. Okay." She nodded even though he hadn't said a thing. "I'll do the clean while you see to odd jobs. Knowing that woman, there's plenty piled up already."

She had a way of having the whole conversation herself. Most nights he could polish off dinner without having to contribute anything. "I can't take you. Maybe Elsie can."

Becky set her fork down with its bite uneaten. "Why can't you go?"

"The meeting at the town hall. Remember?"

"Well, I have to be there, too," Becky said. "If Firmament comes in, it'll have a bigger effect on me than you since they use their own house-keeping crew but hire out handiwork—"

He was surprised, not by the ongoing drone of her chatter—which he was used to, soundtrack of his life—but by her resistance. Good ole Beck, docile and yielding as a cart mare usually. Again he saw a red-stained world.

"—and I care about this town as much as you; my kin goes back even farther than your Ole Pop-Pop—"

He slammed a hand—open, his palm not his fist—onto the table. The wooden surface jumped, upending his plate. "Do the goddamn clean. No questions asked. I'll go to the meeting and protest enough for the both of us."

"Okay," she told him, and it was the only word she said.

Becky Hunt's husband was in trouble. It wasn't how he'd hit the table—Lord knew he'd hit worse things, softer surfaces, her own, enough times over the years—but the way he looked when he did it. Imploring-like. Creece believed that he was owed a life and a living, every damn thing she did for him, and a whole lot else besides. He would never beg, not even with his eyes.

That was why she decided not to ask for a ride from Elsie.

Becky looked out the small window over the kitchen sink, the sky gone a late-winter rust. She had thirty minutes till the sun disappeared completely, and with it her ability to see.

At first the drive felt safe; just the usual, blurred-around-the-edges quality everything had taken on when her eyes began to go, like her mother's had, and her grandmother's before that. Becky had known what was coming. The condition lying in wait her whole life, anticipating the moment when it would finally pounce, stealing her vision and so much else along with it.

A lot like that thieving company, Firmament. The campground Creece had gone to take a stand against. Glampground. Robbing townspeople of their money and the land of its resources. Tents were taxed at a lower rate—even if they were really structures that never came down—and the septic and water couldn't support an influx of people willing to pay $500 per night to sleep outside without really being outside, on the ground without being anywhere near the ground.

Becky was able to tolerate her belligerent father and husband with their entitled ways and flares of violence. She cleaned up after a revolving succession of guests in houses they didn't give a fig about. She had found gum stuck to the edges of sinks that cost more than she made in a month, dishes thrown in the trash instead of rinsed, and toilets that looked as if they'd been used for target practice, splashes and gales of yellow on the tank and even the wall behind it. None of it made her as angry as the prospect of Firmament coming to town.

She swiveled the wheel so abruptly that the car swerved. Braking, at a standstill right there in the middle of the road, she twisted to peer over her shoulder. It looked as if someone were standing on the soft shoulder where the blacktop met the forest. Flagging her down. She was about to get out to see who it was, but as she squinted into the descending dark, she was able to make out a tree, one branch thrust forward like an arm. Easing up on the brake, she drove on.

Gibbons Creek came up fast; she could make out only indistinct shapes in a pall of darkness now. She crept forward, clenching the steering wheel so that her hands lost feeling, bloodless and whitened. Allowing the wheel to rotate so much as an inch would send her headlong into the water, whose roar could be heard over the engine.

She must be near the spot where the creek became a falls. Straining to see, she leaned close enough to the windshield that her nose touched cold glass. She got out, letting the door fall shut with a thud, its sound swallowed by the rush of water. So long as she walked in the opposite direction, she should spot the glistening black driveway—the owner had installed some kind of expensive under-asphalt heating system that made plowing unnecessary—which would then lead to the house. To the mess she was meant to clean up.

She stopped short. Hadn't found the driveway yet, but there in the woods, she heard a rustle. Not a bobcat or coyote kind of sound; this was human. Methodical, with pauses between, as if someone were trying to be quiet.

All the trees looked like bodies to her wavery vision. Slim trunks for legs, branches were arms, and the twigs reaching fingers. But she'd been wrong about someone being in the road before. Or maybe the noises, which had quieted for now, had been made by an animal after all.

A ways off from where she stood, the world burst into a carnival of color. Blurred red and blue, a whirling spatter against the night. Somehow she'd gotten badly turned around, for there was the high, sloping roof of the house, illuminated by the lights. If she'd kept going any longer, she might've slipped into the creek, been yanked away by the sucking water.

Her heart gave a hard, painful toll in her chest.

She wasn't safe out on her own at night anymore. Soon her life would get whittled away, like her mother and granny's had, all of them left dependent on men unable or unwilling to care for anyone more than they did themselves.

More sight stolen now, by tears and regret and fear of what her future held.

Police cars. That was the source of the red and blue.

She was too late. Whatever Creece had done, he'd been caught.

Somebody stepped out of the woods.

"Oh, hello," Becky said as the person began to approach. "Ms. Waters, is that you? I'm here to do the clean. Thought I'd get a jump start on the morning; you've been booking up so fast, and this way it'll be done before anyone can—"

The person drew nearer, crackle-crackle through the leaves.

Becky had never met Meghan Waters, the property owner, in person. All their dealings had been over the phone. Still, Becky was getting the distinct sense that this wasn't Meghan.

"Are you a guest? I can get your clean done fast. I'm lickety-split; clients always say so. I'll have this place sparkling before you know it." How she hoped that was true, that whatever Creece had done could still be taken care of, despite the police activity. Foolish to wonder if the cops were here for some other reason? A mass solidified in her throat; she fought to swallow past it. What if that reason had to do with whoever was walking toward her now?

Man or woman, it was hard to tell. A sleek roll of hair, glossy beneath the shine of the rising moon, was visible atop the head that, these days, could've gone either direction, gender-wise. Coat and shoes totally unsuited to the weather. Someone from away.

The person's pace didn't flag.

Becky took a few steps backward, stumbling a bit. "Do you want something? Can I help in some way? You'd be surprised at how friendly we are up here—"

The person's pace quickened, and Becky clamped her mouth shut.

She fought to identify the way back to her car, but the world fuzzed out and she thrust both arms forward, feeling for obstacles as she broke into a blind, shambling run.

Faulty vision or not, she couldn't have mistaken the glint of moonlight on steel.

Or the bite of the blade as it sank into her throat.

Lurcquer and Bishop split up. In a town the size of Wedeskyull, they often had to, with the rest of the force, Landry and Barber and Samuelson—all off-shift for the night—now on their way to provide backup for Bishop out at Gibbons Creek.

He himself was following up on what he thought of as the policing version of a Christmas present. A solid lead just handed over. Which might mean it was too good to be true. Socks when you ripped open the wrapping paper.

He'd managed to raise the homeowner—or title holder or whatever the hell she was—on her way up the Northway. Got her on her cell, which was as good an alibi as any that she wasn't outside, having just dropped a second victim. Cell vacuum in a sixty-mile radius around Gibbons Creek. He wondered how all those guests handled it when the Wi-Fi cut out and they couldn't Google something or make a phone call.

It wasn't yet clear who had called in the body, which meant it could've been Meghan Waters once she got within range. That would depend on the time of death the ME came up with. But for now the information Meghan had offered pointed in another direction.

She'd sent her handyman out to deal with irate guests last night and today, one at each property. Christmas present. Assuming the guests proved to be the corpses, which wasn't too much of a reach, then he could see the handyman getting ticked off, coming to blows. Lurcquer was familiar with the bouts of temper that had put Creece Hunt in lock-up, hauled in on a domestic, although his wife never pressed charges.

Sometimes cases were solved as easy as that, and Lurcquer had to guard against hoping this one would be. You went into a case with a need as strong as he had; you tended to see things through a lens, to turn away—without even knowing you were doing it—from differing lines of thinking or other crucial findings. But he did need this over with fast, and not just because two dead visitors to the region would bring a slew of friends and family members demanding answers, and be lousy for business besides. His head had been hurting pretty badly lately. He didn't know how long he could stand an investigation chewing into his brain.

*Hunt,* he thought. *Did you finally get around to killing someone? Two someones?*

*Got to be,* a new, dawning headache told him. Helluva coincidence otherwise.

*Too easy,* said the cop beneath the impending throb.

Hunt wasn't at home, either his own or his father's, with whom he spent most of his time since his mother's passing. The elder Hunt's neighbor came outside.

"They're at that protest, Chief," she called. "Along with half the town. I'da gone myself except for my rheumatism. Doesn't do well come mud season. Everything so damp."

"Stay inside, Mrs. Moll," Lurcquer said, raising one hand to acknowledge the tip. "And you might want to get some of those quercetin tablets. They say they help with joints."

She lifted a crooked, gnarled hand in return, mirroring his gesture.

Lurcquer drove to the town hall annex / animal shelter, arriving amid a cacophony of barking dogs and shouting people that could be heard inside the car. A vise clamped down on his head. The radio squawked and it tightened.

Homemade signboards and posters tilted in a dizzying array outside; stakes thrust into the thawing ground, leaning against the brick walls of the building and the metal railing on the steps.

Clamp down on Glampgrounds. Get Out of Our Beds. Don't Bulldoze Paradise.

"Chief?" came a voice. "Are you there? Chief, you copy?"

He seized the radio from the console and depressed its button. Something about Bishop's voice was wrong, alarmed, ravaged, even allowing for the fact that she was on-site with a likely murder. "I copy, Bishop. Come at me."

"Chief." She sounded as if she were trying mightily to compose herself. "We found another body. She was lying by a car, and Landry located a purse inside. Chief, we think this is—oh God, it's Becky Hunt. Bus is here, but the medic's—it's Brian on tonight—got nothing. She bled out already. Knife wound to the jugular."

The pounding in Lurcquer's head lifted, replaced by a focused image of blueprints, drawings, the specs of this structure with its myriad of exits. He drew a mental path to the bulkhead doors at the side where he'd be able to enter unnoticed. Two to cover front and back.

Given the number required to clear the woods around Gibbons Creek and seal off the scene, they'd have to dip into part-time replacements. Dorothy, off-duty, would need to act fast. He called her cell, hoping she'd have signal. No twenty-four-hour dispatch in Wedeskyull; it'd never been necessary. Now they had three potential homicides on their hands, in such short succession the ME hadn't formally made that determination on body number 1 yet.

With any luck, Hunt would be here as his father's neighbor had reported, save the work of a search. The protest sounded as if it were just gearing up, though Lurcquer kept a sharp eye out for any early departers. Hunt might exit on his own, no idea what he was in for. About to be brought in for questioning before learning that his wife was dead. Tough night.

Unless he already knew his wife was dead.

A theory composed itself, achingly, tantalizingly simple. Hunt's wife had come upon him while he was tangling with the guest. Hunt had had to make it two for one.

Because despite how easy it was to poke fun and point fingers at the out-of-towners—with their habits and ways as exotic as any safari animal's—Lurcquer knew full well. Anybody could be a murderer. No matter what their walk of life or where they came from.

He reached up to kill the lightbar, letting the night camouflage him while he waited for backup. Praying this wouldn't be socks.

## TINY TREETOP LIVING

"This is definitely the coolest place we've ever been," Marty said, watching her boyfriend throw a log into the real working fireplace. Nothing like that in their city studio. "Wait—don't you need to start with something smaller first? Newspaper or, like, sticks?" She thought back to her camp days. YMCA, not one of those fancy ones with real actors to direct the end-of-summer show and water slides in the lake. She'd learned a few things about nature.

"They left a stack of logs," Shea replied, sending her a glance that made it look as if he were gazing down from a great height, even though they were about equal in stature. "Think it was meant for something besides a fire?"

The tiny flame from the match he'd struck sputtered out.

Marty swallowed her smile. She went over to him, positioning herself so that he didn't have to see the curled and charred matchstick that signaled his failed attempt, and touched her lips to his. At first he kissed her back, slowly enough to light a different fire. But then he pushed her away, restless or wounded or just in one of his moods.

He wandered out onto the 360-degree deck that wrapped around the trunk of the tree twenty feet in the air. Literally and figuratively a long way from their uptown—way, way uptown—digs in Manhattan. Marty was glad they had splurged on this getaway. They both needed it. Their relationship needed it.

Shea yanked down the zipper on his jeans with a rasp and started peeing over the railing.

"Shea!" Marty burst out from inside, looking toward a bank of windows.

Nothing to see besides woods, faded in the dying light. They might've gone on forever. Somehow it was a chilling thought instead of a comforting one.

He echoed the place her mind had gone. "Nobody's here. I can piss wherever I want."

She hugged herself with both arms. Treehouses were cold in March this far north. They really needed that fire. She went out and joined him on the deck. Reignited their kiss for a while.

Then she drew away. "I'm going to take this very cool rope ladder down, gather some kindling," she told him. "And do you think you could unpack the food? Just keep the vegetarian stuff separate, please." She had to remind him every time. "And maybe slice the baguette?"

"I'm going to sprinkle some of my beef in your quinoa. You know that, right?"

"Hilarious," she replied, hand on the first rung.

On the ground, she kept to a circumference of the tree so as not to stray too far while feeling around for twigs and branches, making sure the ones she selected weren't sodden with snow. It was dark with only the distant light of the moon. Why hadn't she brought the flashlight, thoughtfully provided by their host? She had no right to call out Shea on his lack of experience in nature when she herself made an error like that—

She straightened from her bent over position, alerted by a mound to her left.

The wood she'd collected dropped with a hollow clatter. Good, dry wood from the sound; it would've lit beautifully. But she was suddenly sure there'd be no firelight sex—or picnic—or anything else they had planned for this evening.

"Mart?" Shea's voice echoed through the woods, the sound bouncing off the trees. "What was that noise?" When she didn't answer: "Fine, I'll do the bread. Where is there a knife, do you think? Marty! Where'd you go?"

"Shh!" She stood, staring down, heart clobbering her chest. "Be quiet!"

"Mart?" he shouted back, maybe not hearing her, but more likely ignoring her entreaty.

She'd told him she hated being called that. Sometimes he saw fit to tell her what it rhymed with, letting one rip just to drive the point home. He really was a boor, like her mother said, with a way of putting her down whenever he felt lousy about himself. Their relationship didn't need a reboot; it needed to end. She could cut her own damn bread.

The mound lay motionless. With her eyes fully adjusted, and fear offering a cold shot of clarity as well, she was certain of that, of its inhuman, or no-longer-human, stillness. Still, she forced herself to crouch down, feeling the neck to make sure.

She stood up, assessing the woods as best she could given the lack of light while darting back toward the tree. Across ground she'd already covered so as not to create additional disturbance. Crime shows her jam, though Shea always made them watch ESPN. Well, as soon as she found a place—outside the city for sure, no way to afford Manhattan or even Brooklyn on her own—she could watch whatever she wanted.

"Shea!" She managed to tamp the call down from a shriek, but just barely. "Get down here! We have to call 911."

They'd lost signal at the gas station where they had fueled up. Maybe fifty miles back.

"Climb down!" she shouted again. "Now!"

For once he listened without arguing or dismissing her; something in her voice maybe sounding an alarm. He came scurrying down the ladder like a beetle to join her in their rental car. They didn't exchange a word until the bedecked, bedazzled tree intended for their living quarters that weekend had blended into a million of the same behind them.

🌲🌲🌲

"Both of them were found outside," Mandy told Gil Landry, using her flashlight to indicate the two areas she'd cordoned off. One body lay upon a sculptural swirl of snow; the other was sprawled on her back in a mash of leaves. Mandy was aware of a press of tears at the back of her throat upon pointing to the second. Mrs. Hunt, who used to babysit her. Mandy had always been afraid of Mrs. Hunt's husband. She'd told the chief that the woman's throat had been cut, but the beam from the Mag revealed something far worse. Mrs. Hunt had no throat at all anymore—just an open maw of tissue surrounding a pale ivory glisten of windpipe.

"That snow looks kinda funny," Gil remarked.

Mandy nodded. "I thought so, too. Like a piece of marble."

"You think somebody did that to it? Somehow shaped or carved it?"

Mandy was pretty sure of it, but the chief had been cautioning her against supposition so all she said was, "It was the same at the other house. Anyway, come take a look inside."

"Holy shit," Gil said when they reached the bathroom.

The proclamation sounded unbidden, spontaneous. "You're reacting to the fact that it's bigger than my first-floor apartment? Not including that tub and shower part—I think they call it a wet room." She signaled Landry forward. "But look at this."

He let out a whistle this time. "What a mess."

Mandy nodded. "I can't figure it out. If either of the victims was killed here, then taken outside, this place would look like an abattoir. So was there a fight and this stuff got knocked over?" She gestured to the floor, which sparkled like a fairy garden beneath glints of broken glass. "But then how would it have stayed contained?" She dug the toe of her boot into a gritty heap of bath salts, the smell of sage and lavender making her nauseous. "We would've ground it to bits when we walked in. And I didn't hear a single crunch."

Landry interrupted his march across the palatial bathroom, lifting a slim vase that had been placed just so on a marble vanity. "Maybe this'll help clear things up."

He tilted the single sprig of hortense flower so that it caught the light. Concealed within the pistil was a tiny black bead. A hidden camera.

Hunt took a chair at a table in front of the one-way; Lurcquer sat across from him to deliver the news. First, the guest at the property Hunt saw to.

"The bitch got offed? Good. Bet it was some dude she was making miserable."

Socks for Christmas after all? Few guilty people would've been willing to act as Hunt was, practically scrubbing his hands in front of a cop upon hearing news of his victim's demise. But it was his next response that really placed an unsettled pebble of doubt in Lurcquer's gut.

"What're you talking about?" Small, like a child. "I sent her out there to tidy things up. Crap I spilled in the bathroom. Okay, threw. But Beck's not dead. No way. She can't be."

So his wife hadn't been one of the intended victims; she'd been there by accident.

The ragged stitching that held Hunt's face together, lines and fissures in the skin, tore open, and he began to weep. Lurcquer wondered if he were mourning his wife or his punching bag. He asked Hunt to provide alibis for both time frames—a construction crew the first day, half the town who had watched him make a furious fool of himself at the protest tonight. Then, alibis notwithstanding, Lurcquer ordered the man to stay put in town before releasing him so he could go plan his wife's funeral.

🌲🌲🌲

The camera's feed revealed Mr. Hunt; the sight of him even just on film provoking a childish tremor in Mandy. He laid waste to a row of glass canisters, bath salts falling through the air like snow. A berobed woman—the fact that it was the other victim clear despite the blurry image—opened her mouth in a scream that looked more enraged than frightened as she scooted out behind Mr. Hunt. Very much alive, although it was unlikely the ME would be able to pin down the time of death exactly enough for this video to exonerate Hunt on its own.

The chief sat with a fist to his forehead. "You mean to tell me hosts are allowed to spy on their guests?"

Despite having gotten some of the lingo down, the chief still seemed like he was trying to bridge a great divide with his feet. "No way," Mandy said. "Having hidden cameras breaks Airbnb policies and procedures—Vrbo's, too. Especially in a bathroom." She suppressed a shudder.

"It's a break for us that Meghan Waters is a rule breaker then. I have Dorothy downloading feeds from the other properties as we speak."

"Dot's more techy than my little sister who's never known life without a smartphone."

The chief gave a nod. He looked tired. "You ever stayed in one of these places, Bishop?"

"My rent's so high now, it's lucky I can afford one bed to sleep in, let alone two."

"If I paid you what you deserve, I hope you wouldn't hand it over to people like this."

Dorothy entered the war room. "I just took a call. Two tourists found a body."

"Please tell me it was on a mountain in a whiteout," said Mandy. "Or fell off the ski jump in Lake Placid. Coyote attack? Have elk made it this far east? I hear rut season is a bitch."

Dorothy answered with the thin set of her lips.

The chief rose. "The hell with rut season. This place is turning into a human hunting ground."

🌲🌲🌲

The bodies were piling up like snow in January.

By the following morning, four more had been called in by sources as yet unidentified, stumbled across by winter recreationalists, or guests who'd arrived at their short-term rental and surely started composing one-star reviews on the spot. Thank God the dead were from away—except for poor Becky Hunt—because the local undertaker wouldn't have been able to keep up, especially this time of year, with the ground still frozen.

Every property where a body had been found—next to, on, or under a sculpted berm of snow as Bishop had pointed out—belonged to Meghan Waters, who'd finally arrived upstate.

"Mee-gan," she said, exasperation detectible in her tone. "It's pronounced with a long e."

"Ms. Waters," Lurcquer said deliberately.

They sat on opposite sides of the table in the interview room, and before he could continue, she leaned down and picked up a bag off the floor. Ribbon dangled from its handle.

"Here you go, Officer," she said. "Local chocolates. For all the hard work you do."

He let the "officer" go. "Thank you. But we can't accept bribes."

"This isn't a bribe!" she exclaimed. "I leave them at all my properties. Tailored to the space, you know. Like at the little cottage, I assemble a basket that's kind of rustic and retro."

She trailed off, perhaps thinking of the rustic, retro murder that had occurred there.

"Ms. Waters, how do you explain—" he began. He'd been about to ask for her explanation for the deaths, but a different question popped out: "How do you explain owning so many properties in the region?"

Several firefighters and EMTs—hastily deputized—now sat on stakeout at each of the residences in question, including the ones where bodies had not yet been found.

"Last I checked, a person could own as many houses as they want," she replied.

"Not when corpses keep turning up at them," he said, knowing his response lacked logic.

"Do I seem like a murderer to you?" She gestured to her upswept hair, made-up face, and clothing even he could tell cost a lot. "You should question my handyman. He's one of those guys that make their wives cook and clean for them. On *Making of a Murderer*, it'd definitely be him." She gave a shudder that managed to look authentic. Maybe it was.

"In my experience, Ms. Waters, murderers come in all guises."

She snorted, a rather indelicate sound for somebody who looked like her.

"I was ten million miles away at the time. Times. You can check my phone records. Texts, Instagram, calls. They'll clear me since this place exists in some kind of time warp."

"How are you so certain you were on your phone for each of the murders?"

She gave him a patronizing glance, bordering on bored. "I'm never not on my phone."

Her expression made the blood tingle in Lurcquer's temples.

"Now, if I may leave," she continued, "you can go call in some other agency who will do your job for you and find the real criminal."

He glanced at the one-way, signaling with a finger to his jaw.

A knock on the door and Bishop entered. Meghan Waters gave her an appraising look.

"Each of the victims has been a guest found outside one of your residences, Meghan," Bishop said, pronouncing the name correctly.

The information didn't stop the woman from scoffing again. "Nothing new there."

"I wasn't finished," Bishop said. "And each of them left you a one-star review."

Meghan no longer looked quite so bored. She shifted on her seat, and Lurcquer had the feeling it wasn't because the chair was less comfortable than the ones she was used to.

"How would that work exactly? They're dead."

Bishop took a step closer. "Two we found in drafts on their phones. We surmise they'd called with a complaint, alerting you that their review wouldn't be favorable." A pause. "And the other four left bad reviews from a previous visit. You invited them back, offering them a steep discount according to the sums we found on their credit card bills. We conjecture that you were bribing them to write a better review, amending the first or stating you'd fixed all the problems."

Meghan's face had gone winter-white beneath her makeup.

Bishop turned to Lurcquer. "Maybe we won't need the Feds after all, Chief." She looked back at Meghan. "Upkeep must be awfully hard on that many properties. All sorts of issues creep in. It's no wonder your guests were getting crabby."

"I want a lawyer," Meghan whispered. Then ire seemed to overtake her. "You think what I do is easy? What I have is easy? Covering expenses? A month of my meals probably costs more than your rent! And that's not even including drinks! Of course I had to do something to lure those guests back! A bad review is more deadly than any stupid knife wound!"

Lurcquer passed a landline across the table. "Call a lawyer. You're going to need one."

She glared at him, picking up the receiver as if it were either a rare relic or a piece of bad meat. "This is some *Orange Is the New Black* shit. And no one's watched that show in years."

🌲🌲🌲

All was quiet on the western fronts of the remaining properties, although this level of bloodshed was going to take a long time to wash out of Wedeskyull, despite only one of the victims being from here. So far— Lurcquer tapped some mental wood. While waiting for the out-of-town lawyer to arrive, he spoke with his now officially appointed second in command. Helluva investigator she was turning out to be, although he still feared she took too many leaps.

"One piece of good news," he said, topping off a cup of coffee that was helping to quiet the drone in his head.

"Thank God," Bishop replied.

"Firmament got blocked. That parcel they were after turns out to be a wetlands."

"Thank God," she said again, with even more feeling this time.

"Now let's get back to everything else. So your theory is that Waters killed her victims for leaving bad reviews? Isn't that a little extreme?"

Bishop raised an eyebrow. "Spoken like someone who didn't grow up with star ratings determining their self-worth. Didn't you watch that *Black Mirror* episode?"

"What's *Black Mirror*?"

"Point proven," Bishop said. But then she hesitated. "You think I'm on the wrong track."

Her intuition was correct this time. "It was something in her response. To your admittedly excellent and extraordinarily fast investigating."

She shrugged. "Helps to be a digital detective. Less shoe leather."

"The part she homed in on was getting those guests back for a second stay. Even went so far as to admit she'd 'lured' them. As if their deaths didn't even figure into her thinking."

Bishop looked down at the floor, hands squared at her sides. "We gonna let her go?"

"She can cool her fancy heels a bit. Wait for the suit from downstate to get here. You never know, new information might shake out. But I want to be clear on something."

"What's that?"

"Meghan-with-a-long-*e* Waters is an easy person to blame. To laugh at even." He laced his fingers behind his back. "But the day we start seeing things that simply is the day we stop solving cases. Because nothing is ever simple. Not anybody's life, even ones like theirs."

Bishop lifted her head. "Got it. Now I want to go take a look at something."

🌲🌲🌲

She and the chief headed back to a room that ran the length of the barracks. Boxes, filing cabinets, and evidence lockers contained the detritus of centuries of policing. There were probably actual antiques in there, although what Mandy wanted wasn't quite that old.

She pulled out a drawer containing paper maps, and flipped through them until she found the one covering Otter Lake, Gibbons Creek, plus a trail leading to Mt. Casco with its famous summit pool. Some of the nicest land was in Wedeskyull; adventurers came from all over to take advantage of it. Tracing a line around the area, she wound up with an amoeba-shaped squiggle. She drew an *x* at each property where a body had been found, as well as by an outlying cabin.

"Meghan Waters doesn't own that house below Casco. The rest of hers are in town."

"I know. But look at how these are positioned. Almost like neighbors."

"Where's that mind of yours going, Bishop?"

"If you're right—and Meghan isn't the murderer—then this place here," she said as she tapped the cabin, "looks like a likely spot for the next killing."

He looked at her, rubbing a spot on his brow. "I can't move anybody; it'd be too risky. The Meghan Waters link is still the strongest we've got. And I'm so maxed out on person power right now, I'd have to deputize the fry cook at the diner to put another stakeout in place."

She loved him for the person he was. And she wondered: when had that line burrowed so deep into his forehead, become so pronounced? "I guess that leaves us, Chief."

## LITTLE CABIN IN THE WOODS

Delilah's muscles felt loose and wobbly; her whole body relaxed. She lifted a finger to wipe a droplet of sweat off Britt's nose. It looked like a crystal; so pure it practically refracted.

"I love you," Delilah said. "I love this cabin. I wish we could live in a place like this."

"Maybe we can," Britt replied dreamily. "These days you just have to be able to afford the down payment. Then you make your mortgage renting it out."

"Oh, I wouldn't want to do that," Delilah said, clarity starting to return. "Too much hardship around here. Everywhere really. Housing shortages and the like."

"Yeah," Britt said. "You're right. Guess we'll just have to get rich enough to—"

But her plan, whatever it was, got interrupted by a room-rattling shake. Something had struck the stout log wall of the cabin hard enough to rock it.

"What the hell?" said Britt.

Delilah was already tugging on clothes and exiting the cabin.

Lurcquer and Bishop approached the cabin concealed beneath the boughs of still-snow-laden trees. They halted at the same time when two women burst through the door and ran down the porch steps, shirts askew, no coats on, boot laces whipping across the ground like snakes.

From behind a glacial erratic, a giant, scaly rock, stepped a man who must've been crouched there, now rising to his full height. He was clad in a long camel-colored coat with a scarf wound around his neck and sleek leather gloves on both hands. Only his hiking boots, fanged with mini-spikes, seemed suited to the climate. In one hand he held a truncated log, which he let fall. In the other, he gripped a knife, steely and serrated.

Silently and as one, chief and deputy unholstered their weapons. They swiveled, both pistols trained on the man, but before either had a clear shot, the man grabbed one of the women.

He put the blade to her throat, and the second woman let out a wordless roar of rage.

"Del!" A scream from the first woman, so rich with love it pulsed. "Run!"

But the woman called Del didn't move.

The man settled his hand around the knife in a way that seemed to apply pressure; a thin line of red appeared on his victim's throat. She didn't say a word, just narrowed her eyes, thinned her lips. But her girlfriend let out a howl, raising both hands with fingers clenched into claws.

Lurcquer and Bishop stepped out from the trees. They parted in synchrony to buttress the man, and for a moment, all motion made by anybody else ceased.

"Drop your weapon," said Lurcquer.

"Let her go," commanded Bishop.

The man paused minutely. "Shoot me and this blade does its job."

"Drop it and we don't shoot," Lurcquer said.

The man's lip curled. "What do you care about some people who are just driving your cost of living through the roof anyway? You think one more makes a difference? You think she matters?" He began backing away toward the woods, pulling his victim in tandem.

"You better fucking believe she does!" the other woman snarled.

The man continued his steady plod backward, maintaining a hold on the woman. A little to his left, a tree had fallen at the border to the woods, and Lurcquer and Bishop moved in unison to make him shift the path he was cutting. They exchanged looks, tilted heads, matching nods.

Then a pain clamped Lurcquer's scalp, and his ready stance faltered.

The man hadn't sidled over enough. He was going to miss the tree.

Bishop stepped out on her own, unguarded, and the man veered away. His heel nicked the log, and as he started to go over, arms pinwheeling, the woman let her body sag. She dropped to the ground and rolled, once, twice, three times before she came to a stop and lay there, heaving.

Letting out a guttural sob, her girlfriend ran to her.

Bishop leaped over the log, using the man's backward momentum to drive him down. The knife went flying, and then she was upright and Lurcquer copacetic again. He came to flip the man face down in the snow and leaves, yanking his wrists behind him while Bishop cuffed them.

"What'd I tell you?" she said, panting. "Bad guys be dumb. Tripped over his own feet."

"I'll keep an eye on him here." He aimed his chin toward the women, now standing in a huddled embrace. "Call the bus; she's got a wound on her neck." He leaned over and extricated the man's leather-tooled wallet.

"Bishop!"

She turned.

"What's this?" he asked.

She walked back and examined the thin slice of plastic. "That's one of those digital business cards, I think. It won't load here, though. Needs Wi-Fi."

"Never mind," he said, thumbing through the man's wallet. "Here's a regular old paper one."

He and Bishop looked.

No name for the man, just Firmament, and below in an elegant low-ercase font:

*site preparation · community engagement · build development*

After a beat, Bishop said, "I guess this counts as site prep."

"He knew they were gonna get blocked," Lurcquer replied. "Had a backup plan."

"These property owners are so underwater, if their places were to become unrentable even for a few weeks—tied up as crime scenes—no one could make their payments," she noted. "Bank would probably kiss Firmament's feet for coming in, buying up mortgages."

"Raze a few houses," Lurcquer said, looking down, "and you have paradise right here."

On the ground, the man let out a muffled "Fuck." Lifting his head as high as he could before Lurcquer kneed it back down, he said, "Do you have any idea what our sunk-in costs add up to already on this hellhole? My job is on the fucking line if we don't get go-ahead for this region."

"On your feet," Lurcquer told him. "I'll read you your rights and then a holding cell's gonna be your Airbnb tonight."

🌲🌲🌲

Bishop wound a scroll of yellow tape around a tree as Lurcquer fed it out.

"Chief?"

He paused in unrolling.

"You know you need to go see a doctor. Right?"

Well, he had chosen her for her intuition. "Yeah," he said. "I do."

She hesitated. "These companies—all those faceless corporate entities—they're like slime. Another one is just going to ooze in to take over the space. This magnificent space. We can't stop them."

Lurcquer faced her. "I prefer to think of it more like Medusa. And today we cut off one head. There'll be more, sure. So we'll keep lopping. But it's a good day when we know who the monster is. It's a very good day. A lot of cops don't, even if we don't like to say so."

Bishop gave a taut snap of the tape. "Hey, what about all those snow formations where the bodies were found? How they looked almost sculpted. Drips and swirls and waves. I was sure that would turn out to mean something."

"Snow melts," Lurcquer said, leading the way out of the woods. "Even in Wedeskyull."

## 7

# Sunrise on Pleasant Lake

*W. K. Pomeroy*

COUGHING OUTBURSTS FROM DISTANT ZASTAVA M72S HELD BY FACE-less young men in a shoot-or-be-shot killing frenzy evolved into pounding explosions much closer to him, dangerously close.

Damir's eyes snapped open. The dark space around him felt wrong. His feet extended off a soft bed too short for his legs. Not in Bosnia, not in a war zone, yet not in his comfortable Utica apartment; it took him a few moments to establish his true whereabouts and what that muffled pounding sound had to be.

"Come on D'man, you've only got twenty minutes until sun-up. You're the one who said you wanted to get some good shots of the sunrise reflecting on the lake." State police inspector Brian Murphy's muted voice came from the other side of the bedroom door.

"I am on my way." Damir kept his voice just loud enough for Brian to hear it through the antique wooden door.

Damir rolled out of bed. He pulled on the blue flannel shirt and heavy jeans he'd laid out for himself the previous night.

On a nightstand, his phone began to sing the annoying wake-up tune he'd programmed into it to wake him at ten minutes until dawn. Damir grabbed the phone and his highest resolution digital camera, shoved his lanky arms into a fleece-lined denim jacket, and headed out the bedroom door, leaving behind the painful dream memories.

Brian had plopped into a classic wooden chair with a laced wicker seat matching three others around the kitchen table. The deceptively athletic man appeared to be contemplating a cup of weak American coffee.

His off-white T-shirt and camouflage pants gave a false impression of someone ready for one of Damir's favorite pastimes, a hike through the Adirondack forest.

"Is Aleksandra up yet?" Damir whispered.

Brian shook his head slowly as if it hurt to twist his neck. "I believe Leksa is still sleeping off some of last night's vodka."

Damir nodded, remembering how late he'd heard them stay up talking and drinking, while he tried to sleep. "I'll sneak out quietly."

Outside their rented camp, an early spring sky had just enough predawn gray-light in it that Damir did not need his flashlight to make his way across the backyard down to a sandy shoreline.

He screwed his high-end digital camera with its 120X zoom onto the tripod he'd set up the previous evening. He systematically rechecked every setting knowing he'd have to take the low light settings off a few minutes after sunrise; then Damir did what he did best, he waited.

🌲🌲🌲

Caleb's watch alarm got him up before dawn, in time to check Old Bessie. The ancient beast had been cantankerous during the last couple batches of shine. The heat dissipation hadn't been working quite right, and he didn't want to take any chances with losing a batch.

He sat up. Morning cold flowed in through the window he'd cracked open last night, bringing his senses fully awake.

He reached for the opening and pulled the replacement glass down, hearing the seal catch.

He probed around under his army surplus cot with his bare feet until he felt the canvas of his size-eight store-brand sneakers brush against his toes. Soles of his feet protected, he stood and listened for Zedediah's stuttering snore from beyond one of the three thin dividing walls they'd built to section off the abandoned trailer. Muffled nasal grunts from the other side of his beaded curtain door assured him Zed had slept through his beeping watch.

Trying not to make any sound, he exited and began moseying down the well-worn trail toward his still.

Almost no trace of moonlight lit the path. Dim predawn light filtered between budding tree branches overhead, not enough for his baggy eyes to make out the trail. Lucky for him his old body knew the way even better than his eyes.

A warm glow began heating his gray whiskers well before his tired eyes saw the source. Old Bessie created her own climate in the area he and his father had cleared out for her, back while Dad still lived.

He pulled cheap plastic reading glasses out of his pocket so he could check the thermometer. Annoyed surprise ran through him seeing the mash and water only up to 160°F, still 10°F from his goal. One of his family secrets was to bring it up to temperature really slowly to a temp hotter than most others used.

*Last night's cool breeze musta been blowing harder than I expected up here. Kept her from getting up to temp. This'll delay things some.*

He looked up to the sky, noting just a hint of actual sunlight coming from the east. He heard a big blackfly buzz somewhere nearby, though it sounded off, not quite natural. A faint whistle grew louder and louder almost deafening Caleb, before the explosion threw him into inky black unconsciousness.

🌲🌲🌲

Damir clicked his camera's button a third time. He appreciated the way the display framed this shot. Several beams of light pierced the early morning fog reflecting golden shimmers in Pleasant Lake's glassy surface: a good shot, though without some cropping not quite good enough for him to enter in Munson's annual Sidewalk Art Show.

He tapped fingers on the tiny screen adjusting settings to account for the increase in light.

A distant sound, almost a buzz, grabbed his attention. Damir tried to focus on it. A whistle overwhelmed the whirr.

He reacted without thinking to the high-pitched whistle by throwing his body on the ground where a little mound would give him some cover.

He felt as much as heard the explosion.

It had been close, but not nearly close enough he'd needed to dive for cover. He understood on a mental level those reflexes were not needed in peacetime, in the United States, and knew just as well he would always react that way.

♠♠♠

If not for his Army Ranger training, Brian might have believed the slight rattling of the walls to be an earth tremor. He knew how rarely quakes happened in this part of the world. Something this minor might be possible. It felt different, more like a distant mortar round or a grenade.

Instead of ignoring the event like most civilians would, he grabbed his gun belt and bolted out the door.

He scanned the area looking for immediate threats. No craters, no exploded vehicles in the niche just off the driveway. Even his restored Jeep showed no damage. At first glimpse nothing seemed amiss.

On the horizon, a bloom of black smoke appeared in the sky above the trees northwest of where he stood. He estimated the smoke at no more than two miles away, not an immediate danger, still much too close not to be investigated.

Out of the corner of his eye movement caught his attention.

Down by the water's edge, Damir picked his lanky body up off the ground and began to move toward him.

Brian resisted a strong impulse to check on his friend. Instead, he hustled into his mud-spattered Jeep, slid his keys into the ignition, and got on his old reliable radio.

"Hey dispatch. Murphy here. I have some kind of explosion up here near Pleasant Lake. Requesting Fire and backup."

"Aren't you supposed to be on vacation, Brian?" Katlyn Shaw's always calm and collected voice responded.

"Yup."

"Casualties?"

"Don't know, Katie. I'm not directly on scene yet. The blowup was back in the woods, inland from Pleasant Lake." Brian felt the car's shocks move as Damir opened the Jeep's passenger door and slipped into the seat. In a glance he confirmed his initial assessment, his friend's body showed no serious injuries. "I'll be enroute in less than sixty seconds."

"I'll radio back soon as I have an ETA on Fire and EMS."

"Thanks, Katie. We'd all be lost without you."

"Yeah, yeah, skip the flowers and send money."

Brian laughed despite the situation, or maybe in part because of it. He looked at the passenger seat. "You good?"

Damir nodded and pointed through the trees. "It came from over there."

Brian revved the engine, backed out of the niche, shifted his car into drive, and depressed the accelerator enough to start moving forward when an angry dark-haired woman stepped in front of the Jeep. His foot jammed down on the brake stopping the car just barely fast enough to prevent slamming into the woman.

🌲🌲🌲

Sitting up, Caleb spit some of last year's decaying leaves from his mouth. Some bits of leaf and spittle caught in his beard. He clasped his hands to the side of his head trying to clear an annoying buzzing hum from his ears. Pressure from his fingers on his throbbing temples helped enough so he got to his feet without falling.

The smell of burning plastic assaulted his nose.

Bessie???

He peered at her through his broken reading glasses. No, his precious still appeared unharmed.

He threw the useless glasses down on leaf-covered ground and gave her a closer inspection finding no damage.

Only once he assured himself Bessie hadn't been harmed did he turn to look back down the trail. Dark smoke billowed up into the air behind him.

"Oh my God." The expletive sounded faint to his damaged ears. "Zedediah."

He began to jog as fast as his wobbly body would let him, back toward their trailer.

🌲🌲🌲

Aleksandra stepped to the Jeep's driver-side door.

Brian rolled down the window, using the old classic crank.

"And you boys ver going vere, at this ridiculous hour of morning?"

Damir heard how tired she must have been in how thick her accent came out even though she tried so hard never to let it slip out, particularly because she'd been advised she might lose the next Herkimer County Coroner election due to people's reaction to it in her last news conference.

He spoke to her across the driver's seat, while Brian tried to find an appropriate answer. "Dobroye utro, Aleksandra."

"Vy you always use your horrible Russian when morning is not in any vay good?"

Damir held both hands palm up in supplication. "When else would I use it?"

"Perhaps when—"

Brian cut her off. "Leksa, something blew up over there." He dipped his chin in the direction he'd seen smoke. "Are you coming with us or . . . ?"

To her credit, Aleksandra didn't pause to scold Brian for his rudeness the way she would in most other circumstances. "Let me grab my medical bag."

Both men nodded.

Barely two minutes later she emerged from their rented cabin with her coat, Brian's coat, and a large duffel bag with the word *CORONER* stenciled on it.

Without complaining, she slid into the tiny back area behind Damir's seat.

Brian gunned the engine, and the Jeep tore out of the driveway.

Caleb stumbled as he got closer to the site of the explosion. Smoke and fire appeared to be all that remained of their trailer. A few shrubs and small trees burned too, adding more black smoke to the air. He tried to move closer to the destruction. Crippling heat forced him back. He drew in a deep breath of smoke preparing to scream Zedediah's name.

Before he could expel his shout, he saw him lying on his back twenty feet from the fire.

He got out.

Relief flooded through Caleb even as a coughing fit seized his lungs making him collapse to his knees.

Relief evolved into something else as he realized Zedediah wasn't moving.

Caleb tried to leap from his crouch and run to him, only to find a fast crawl the best pace his aching lungs could handle.

He put a hand to his old friend's thick neck, feeling for a pulse like they always did on TV. The bigger man's skin felt hot, slick with ash-covered sweat. Nothing throbbed the way Caleb thought it should have.

Zedediah just lay there not moving a muscle.

"You son of a bitch. I warned you they'd come after you, Zed. Dammit, I told you they'd come."

🌲🌲🌲

Brian's Jeep hurtled down West Shore Road toward Route 29A. He fully expected to come to the site of the explosion well before hitting the crossroad.

From under the dashboard his radio squawked, "Brian, you out there?"

"You got me, Katie. What's the word?"

"Fire and EMTs should be a couple minutes out from Lake Pleasant; do you have an address yet?"

"I'm not on s—" Brian started to answer, then what she said fully registered. "Did you say Lake Pleasant?"

"Yes."

"I'm at Pleasant Lake. Down by Stratford, completely different county, an hour south of Lake Pleasant."

The dispatcher cursed under her breath, breaking her professionally helpful tone for a split second. Brian appreciated the control it took for her not to play the blame game and stay on point. He thought he'd said Pleasant Lake. He supposed in the moment he could have said it wrong.

"I'll get correct units rolling toward you, soon as I can. Do you have an actual address yet?"

Brian looked at the little floating compass built into his dashboard. "Explosion happened somewhere northwest of Pleasant Lake, off West Shore Road. Can't you just locate me via satellite?"

"Not with that ancient radio in your car." For the first time, something in her tone hinted at real annoyance.

"Thank you, Katie. Sorry for the mix-up."

Damir tapped him on the shoulder.

"WHAT?" Brian put all his frustration into one word.

Damir pointed back behind them using a hooked thumb. "You've gone by it."

"I have n—?" Brian realized he couldn't see any smoke in the sky through the barely sprouting trees ahead of them, swallowed his response, and looked for a place to turn around.

🌲🌲🌲

Caleb took a deep gasp of air and blew it down Zedediah's throat, before going back to pounding on the thick man's chest.

Ribs broke under his hands. He paused for a second, before deciding he couldn't be doing any worse damage than the explosion had.

Thirty thrusts and two breaths, thirty more elbow-aching pushes against his chest, and two more breaths.

Heat and effort made Caleb's head spin. He tasted chemicals in his mouth almost like medicine.

The world swayed again, and for the second time blackness overwhelmed him.

🌲🌲🌲

"A dirt road over there on the left, goes about the right direction." Damir used his awkward thumb point again.

"Yeah, I see it." Brian's clenched teeth made him hard to understand.

"Not much of a road, more an ATV path." Aleksandra's voice sounded more awake than earlier, still not quite her normal self-control.

"The Jeep can take it." Brian said a small prayer in his head as he turned off the paved road in a spray of mud. Don't make a liar out of me baby.

Puddles of spring rain and snow runoff made the Jeep slide and bounce. From the look of the smoke they probably only had a half mile to go. Brian noticed the smoke had turned gray making it almost raincloud colored. He didn't want to slow down. Curves, bumps, stumps, and holes in the road forced him to go a little slower.

At one point, a fallen tree over the road made him creep through, scraping the top of his old restored Jeep. A little straightaway afterward allowed him to speed back up.

A pea-green Volkswagen camper, probably from the late 1960s, perched on a rise to their left. Brian noted the camper's entire suspension had fallen and part of its roof had collapsed. They did not stop to investigate it.

Up on a short hill to their left, the source of the smoke became obvious well before he stopped the car where the path forked up what had been someone's camp driveway many years ago.

As Damir and Aleksandra got out of the Jeep, Brian got back on his radio. "I'm on site, Katie. Way up a dirt road. Not sure a standard fire truck or ambulance will make it back here. Looks like a trailer fire. Get them up here ASAP so the fire doesn't spread."

"Got it, Brian. I'll let them know. Be careful."

"I always am."

He checked his cell phone. "I've got no signal here, so it may be a while if they can't get to us."

"Understood. I'll do what I can to get them to hurry."

"Appreciate it, signing off."

Caleb's mouth tasted more like chemicals than wood smoke. His body hurt now. Hazy images made their way through his eyes, like seeing through old plastic wrap. Something acrid in the air burned his lungs. He felt displaced, as if he wasn't really inside his own body.

He had something important to do; something about brotherhood. No, that wasn't quite right; not his real brother, his blood brother.

Caleb tried to make his eyes focus. Zed's limp body lay face up, close enough to him he could reach out and touch him. His blood brother had protected him so many times. He needed to step up, to be the one to protect him. Everything seemed so foggy.

Images evolved out of the haze. He felt hands on him as if they came from a thousand miles away.

Voices penetrated his consciousness.

"Hey, are you all right?"

"Can you walk?"

"Ve have to get you avay from dis fire."

The last voice sounded foreign. He hated accents. They made it hard for him to understand. Words he should know made no sense. He tried to swing a fist at the source of the voice, and found himself being dragged by his flailing arm: away from flames, away from his home, away from Zedediah's motionless body.

▲▲▲

Aleksandra began running toward two bodies lying on the forest floor near a trailer engulfed in flames before she said anything.

"Two down. Over here," she yelled.

Ten steps later, she heard Damir and Brian sprinting through wispy yellowed grass to catch up with her.

Though Damir's body made him look more like a runner, Brian passed her first. "Hey, are you all right?" He didn't even sound winded as he shouted up toward the bodies.

Damir drew even with her and paced her the last twelve steps. He knelt on the ground next to the smaller of the two male bodies farther from the fire. "Can you walk?" Damir's voice didn't have Brian's steadiness after the sprint. She did note his Bosnian accent didn't come out.

The gray-bearded man's body curled almost into a fetal position. An unintelligible croaking sound burbled up out of his throat.

She leaned in toward the man. "Ve have to get you avay from dis fire."

His hairy knuckled fist swung at her in slow motion. It came straight at her mouth. She pulled her hands up to deflect the blow and began to duck her head away.

Damir caught the man's arm by his elbow before the punch could get close to landing, flipped him on his side, and dragged him away from the burning trailer.

"This one's alive, too." Brian had the back of his hand under the bull-like nose of a man with the physique of a heavyweight boxer who needed more repetitions in the weight room to get in actual fighting shape. "I'm not sure I should move him, though. He's barely breathing, and his chest looks funky."

Aleksandra glanced at Damir. The semiconscious victim who had tried to punch her had stopped flailing and appeared well under his control.

She moved next to Brian and began to check the enormous man.

He had a pulse, breathing shallowly, but fairly regular. She started to use scissors from her medical bag to cut off his dark blue sweatshirt and stopped when the wind shifted some smoke in her direction. "Ve need to get him avay from da heat."

Brian took a quick breath. "I think smoke is the bigger issue."

"You know how to do shoulder drag?"

Brian gave her a look even a blind man would interpret as, are you kidding me?

She ignored his annoyance and gave direction. "Gentle as possible. He may have some internal bleeding."

"Got it."

Brian grabbed the left shoulder of the man's shirt while Aleksandra took his right.

His weight forced them to go slow. As they slid him along the ground toward where Damir had taken the other victim, Aleksandra noticed his bare feet showed some blistering from the fire.

Once they had him far enough away heat no longer warmed her back, she nodded to Brian. "Dis is far enough."

She checked his vital signs again, checked his feet, went back for her bag, then completed cutting off his sweatshirt.

Maroon-red pre-bruise marks would be painful later—if the man survived.

"Ve keep him stable and vait for ambulance."

Brian grimaced. "If they can make it up the road."

"You've got to save him." The man on the ground next to Damir sat up glaring at them like this whole thing was their fault.

Caleb's shoulder throbbed in the joint above his arm where a man almost as tall as Zedediah, though much less flabby, had tugged at when dragging him across the ground. New pain allowed him to break through the tingling fuzziness filling his head and focus a little more.

"You are safer here, away from the heat."

Cooler air further from their trailer did taste better in his mouth. The aching burn in his lungs lessened. He took some time to think about everything. Sounds, pain, fire, running, it all had to add up to something.

Without sitting up he tried to examine his rescuers. The tall one who'd dragged him stood tall with a soldier's posture. The woman with such a severe face had spoken with a foreign accent. He didn't trust her. She appeared to be directing Zedediah's medical care. The last guy might be one of them: an ex-athlete, a little extra flab in the middle, maybe a little too close to his Irish ancestry; probably his family's been around America long enough to know the score. One thing about the man bothered him, he wore a holstered gun around his waist.

The tall one asked him a question. "What happened here?"

"Uhhh . . ." Caleb started to answer. He stopped as the other two started dragging Zedediah toward him.

"Ve keep him stable and vait for ambulance."

Brian grimaced. "If they can make it up the road."

Caleb heard the doubt in the man's tone. He sat up, his head still spinning a little from smoke and everything else. "You've got to save him!"

♣♣♣

Damir repeated his question. "What happened here?"

The man pointed his gray beard toward Brian and ignored Damir's question a second time. "Zed's dead, ain't he?" Despair in the man's voice came across as palpable as the smoke.

Aleksandra answered him. "If dis is Zed. He is breathing, for now."

"Sir," Brian shifted into police mode, "can you tell us Zed's last name?"

"Jones . . . Zedediah Jones." His hesitation told Damir the answer was a lie.

"And your name would be?" Brian's voice maintained his typical professional calm.

"Caleb Forrester. Zed and I grew up together round these parts. He's good people, if you know what I means."

For a third time, Damir repeated his question. "And what exactly happened here to cause such a big explosion?"

"The Vee Boyz happened. They blewed up our damned home, tried to kill us both. If I hadn't been out, I'd be deader than Zed."

At the old man's mention of the Vee Boyz, Damir locked eyes with Brian.

Brian gave him a nod of acknowledgment and went back to questioning Caleb with a little bit harsher edge to his voice. "And why exactly would a Utica gang blow up your trailer?"

Could his old friend Nhat Huu Quan have anything to do with this?

Caleb's face scrunched up. "Uhmm, well, they kinda threatened Zed. Said they'd get him. I don't knows why. Zed rubbed them wrong somehow."

Damir took everything the man said as a lie. Nothing tracked. He tried to make his question come out in a smooth rather than accusing tone. "Please tell us how would these Vee Boyz get a bomb in your trailer?"

Caleb didn't look at Damir; instead he maintained his focus on Brian. His eyes kept flashing down to the gun secured in its holster.

"I think I figured that all out. See, there was this noise before a whistle. I didn't recognize it at the time, but I think it was one of them drones. You know, like what they use to video stuff now."

Damir remembered the odd buzzing sound the man described.

"A drone?" Brian sounded skeptical.

"Yeah, them Asians love those things, an' I'm betting they used it to launch some kinda missile at us."

Damir tried not to show how much disgust he felt at the man's racist stereotyping.

"And that rocket musta been what made the whistle."

"While you just happened to be out for a morning walk?" Brian's disbelief almost radiated off each word.

"Exactly." The old man either didn't hear Brian's tone or didn't care.

Aleksandra chimed in from where she knelt next to the unconscious behemoth. "And how did Mr. Jones get out of trailer before explosion?"

"I don't know. I wasn't in there." He glanced in Aleksandra's direction. "You gotta get Zed some help."

Brian nodded. "Help's on the way. While we are waiting, maybe you can help me understand why anyone would go to the kind of trouble you've described just to blow up a trailer out in the middle of the woods?"

Caleb closed his eyes as if an answer would appear on the inside of his eyelids. When he opened them, he seemed a little clearer. "They were . . . mad at him. They threatened him, said they'd kill him if they caught . . ."

Something in the fire popped loud enough to startle them all, temporarily interrupting the conversation. Whatever exploded sent a new plume of black smoke up into the sky.

A deep cough as if from underground sputtered up out of the chest of the large man Caleb had called Zed.

"Who are you?" He let out a long groan as he tried to move. "Something's broken in my chest. What . . . what happened?"

He closed his eyes again and tried to answer his own question.

Zedediah peeled open his eyes earlier in the morning than he usually would. Something wasn't right. Hot sweat soaked his sweatshirt and cargo shorts. A vague warning bell rang in his head. Hot in the trailer was bad. Why?

"Oh shit." Zedediah leaped off his cot. His bare feet got tangled in the sheet for a second. He kicked it away with his left foot and stumbled toward the back wall. He leaned an open hand against the plastic cover on the partition he and Caleb had built. It didn't feel any warmer than the air. That was good.

Panic reduced a bit, he took time to flick on the battery-powered camp-light he'd hung from the ceiling to brighten his section of the trailer.

"Hayseed, you up?"

Caleb didn't answer his call. Old man probably went out to take a piss. At least noise from the big fan wouldn't wake him up. Zedediah hated the incredible volume the industrial fan produced. Damn thing broadcast their location to anyone in a couple miles. A necessary evil from the salvage yard, it always cooled down the cooking room fast enough to avoid serious problems.

He pushed his hand through the zip strip in the plastic and pushed the button to turn on the fan. The thing's engine warmed up fast, making its loud buzzing noise almost deafening in the trailer.

Then, a second sound started to compete with it, a whistle, so loud it drowned out any whirring fan blades.

He saw plastic in front of him start to bulge out like an inflating balloon.

He started to run. He went through the beaded entrance to Caleb's section and shot out the trailer door, barely glancing at his blood brother's cot to be sure he really wasn't there.

He got a few steps away from their home when the whole thing exploded in a fireball.

He turned back to look. A wall of heat hit him knocking him farther back.

He took one quick breath that tasted of ammonia, and someone reduced the dim morning light into a tiny pinhole collapsing into itself.

Is this what it's like to die?

🌲🌲🌲

Aleksandra shined her penlight into Zedediah's right eye.

His pupil constricted appropriately, which made her feel better about his chances of getting through this without severe brain damage. "We heard the explosion, came up to investigate, and found you two here."

His deep voice rumbled, "Is Caleb okay?"

The old man replied for himself. "I skinned my knees pretty good. My noggin's seriously frizzed. My shoulder's throbbing something awful. Otherwise, nothing more serious than our trailer being blowed up. You all right?"

"Hurts to breathe. Feels like that time Bull Falkner tackled me back in high school."

Aleksandra placed a gentle hand on his bruised chest. "I think you have a couple broken ribs."

"You some kinda nurse?" The deep accusing tone of the man sounded more hostile than she expected.

"I am doctor." She didn't see any need to tell him she was a coroner. "I think you fine to move when EMTs get here."

"Why don't you run back to our car and see if you can get an update?" Brian looked at her hard, like he wanted her to understand something. "Let them know we need transport for two injured people."

A hot flush of anger burned her cheeks. Why would Brian of all people be trying to send away the best medically trained person? Her aggravation probably kept her from getting whatever message he'd been thinking at her.

She looked at Damir for support, only to see a "please go" expression on his face.

"Fine."

Brian tossed her his keys to the Jeep. She caught them and started jogging down the grown-over driveway toward the radio.

Damir examined the shriveled face of the bearded man who called himself Caleb Forrester. "How long have you been working for the Vee Boyz?"

"I ain't never worked with them."

The older man's answer came so quick Damir wanted to believe it. "You have been distributing your moonshine through them, have you not?"

"Not. I mean no. Never through them."

"They wanted you to, and you refused, so they blew up your still in the trailer?"

"They ain't never touched my still."

"Shut up, Hayseed," Zedediah boomed. The giant man seemed to be about to say something else, a spasm of wet coughs stopped him.

Damir allowed Caleb to see a thin smile. "You will do better telling us than the police when they get here."

Damir hoped Caleb didn't see how his friend Brian stiffened at that statement.

"We only came here to help you. I'm not working for the Vee Boyz or the police." Damir did not elaborate by explaining sometimes he did consultant work for the police.

Without warning him, he grabbed the cuff of the older man's sleeve.

The old man tightened up but didn't resist.

Damir rolled the cloth up so he could see Caleb's bare skin. No tattoos of any kind had been inked on his arm.

He shook his head so Brian could see.

Brian tipped his head in recognition before turning toward the bruised man with his shirt cut off. "May I examine your right arm?"

"You some kinda doctor, too?" Even with what Aleksandra had diagnosed as broken ribs, the man projected his voice like a weapon.

"Never had the patience for medical school. I just wanted to look at that air force tat you've got." While talking, Brian flashed his Army Ranger tattoo.

"You served?"

Brian nodded, without adding any more explanation.

"Look all you want." With a wince, he held up his arm a little. The USAF design had the *U* colored red, the *S* white, and *AF* in blue above an abstract bird design intended to resemble an eagle. No other tats.

Damir felt satisfied. "I believe you. Neither of you are working for the Vee Boyz."

The big man's voice resonated with the power and fading weakness of a bellows. "Like he told you . . . we got attacked . . . by them."

"Bullshit."

Damir's head throbbed just a little. Brian almost never used any kind of vulgar language, especially right before saying, "You are both under arrest. You have the right . . ."

🌲🌲🌲

After securing his flexicuffs on the larger man's enormous wrists, Brian snapped his metal handcuffs on the smaller man's wrists, tight enough he would have a little bruise the next day, and it would pull on his injured shoulder. "I've always hated drug dealers, but I've learned to hate the idiots that cook the stuff even more."

Damir's mouth dropped open. "Cook?"

"D'man, I always admire the way you puzzle stuff together. You got this one all wrong, but you kept them talking long enough for me to get what I needed from them."

Sirens started sounding closer to them. Brian could see Aleksandra moving back up the hill toward them. He knew he'd need to make it up to her, for sending her away.

"Let's start with this mythical whistling missile. I know you had enough military training to know these days most smaller rockets, like one that would have done this," he pointed at what remained of the trailer, "don't whistle."

Damir nodded slowly.

Caleb gave a tug on his handcuffs. "What about the drone? I know I heard one."

Damir scratched some morning grime from his face. "I did hear a whirring sound, sounded deeper than a drone."

Brian shrugged his shoulders. "I doubt there was one. If there was, it was probably some kid from one of the camps playing."

"At that time of morning?" The old man couldn't keep derision out of his tone.

Brian shrugged again. "I don't know what you heard. I'm betting the whistle came from gas building up in your motorhome trying to find a way out before your propane tanks went up from the extreme heat of a meth fire."

Both handcuffed men went silent.

Aleksandra trotted up to them. "Backup officers will be on scene in two minutes. EMS will be here in three minutes. They say pumper truck can't get up past the tree fall; there vill be volunteers in smaller vehicles in less than ten. Oh, and Katie says you owe her big time. Something about interrupting her breakfast?"

Brian flinched. "Thank you, Leksa."

"What is with ze handcuffs?" She tipped her head at the two men on the ground.

"As I started explaining to Damir, I've unfortunately been on scene for several meth lab fires over the past few years."

"Folks who came to help us hadda be with a cop. My luck couldn't run any worse."

Brian didn't let Zedediah's moaning interrupt his explanation. "Meth house fires have a particular smell to them. The chemicals burn hot once ignited and create some pretty toxic fumes. I should have known earlier, except I focused on getting these guys safely away from the fire. Once we got a moment to think, I started to put it all together."

"You were crystal meth chemists?" Damir looked doubtfully at the bearded man.

"I wasn't. Not me. Not never."

The mountain-sized man shook his head. "Hayseed, you've talked too much since I was a kid."

Brian nodded at Aleksandra. "The arson squad will have to confirm. I have no doubt they'll find all sorts of methamphetamine residue in there."

"I ain't going down for no drug pushing. That was all Zed."

"Shut up, Hayseed."

"I told you it was a bad plan. We coulda done fine just selling batches of Bessie's juice, but damn it, you weren't satisfied."

Brian surveyed the area. "Who's Bessie? Should we be looking for . . ."

The old man let out a dry cackle of a laugh. It sounded completely inappropriate for the situation. "Bessie ain't no person. She's my still. If you let me turn her off so she don't explode, too, I'll show you where she is."

Brian, Damir, and Aleksandra all looked at the old man skeptically.

"I promise. Bessie's been part of my family since before Zed was born. I tends to her, while he makes the other stuff. I swears."

Brian looked down on Caleb, and couldn't help thinking a good slug of moonshine wouldn't taste bad about now. "Once my backup gets here, you'll show us your still. We don't need anything else blowing up this morning."

🌲🌲🌲

Back at their rental cabin, Damir looked out across Pleasant Lake as the sun began to set.

Brian and Aleksandra were sharing the shower, using the pretense of saving water as they rinsed the stink of smoke off them.

It had been a long crazy day of explaining and reexplaining how they came to be there, what they had witnessed, what they had been told, and what Brian had figured out.

Caleb and Zedediah had been arrested. From what the lead investigator said it seemed likely they'd get minor charges if Zed rolled on his real distributors, apparently not the Vee Boyz.

Damir put on his jacket and went out to the lakeshore to pick up his camera. Sunset didn't light the lake the way the dawn did. Maybe he should reset the tripod for the following morning's next sunrise on Pleasant Lake.

8

# When the Bears Come

*Cheyenne Shaffer*

WE FINALLY REACHED THE CAMPGROUND AT A QUARTER TO THREE. THE main lodge loomed in front of us, a log building with an overhang shading its front. I pulled into the parking lot.

"Welcome to your first ever camping experience," I said, cutting off the engine. "Are you excited?"

Mark studied the lodge before pointing to a sign in the window. "Looks like they have a café."

"That's not a 'no,' so I'll take it," I said, trying to stay positive. This trip was the latest in a line of arguments—all small on their own, though they added up. In med school, I was always 'too busy' or 'too emotionally unavailable.' Then I wanted to find myself again, and he was thrilled—until I mentioned my love of camping. I couldn't win.

I popped open my door, and the hot air slammed into me, threaded with sweetness from the baskets of flowers suspended from the overhang. I stood, and my phone clattered to the ground. I swore.

"What's wrong?" Mark asked, coming around the front of the Subaru.

I knelt, turning the phone over in my hands. No cracks, thank God. "Just these stupid shorts." These 'pockets' were ridiculous. I really needed to start buying men's pants.

Stuffing my phone into my butt pocket this time, I twined my fingers through Mark's and led him inside. The interior of the lodge was 80 percent gift shop, at least, filled with everything from mugs and T-shirts to miniature bear sculptures and as-seen-on-TV trinkets. Along the wall to the left was a tall registration desk, and I steered Mark up to it.

"Welcome to Old Forge," a stern-faced woman behind a computer said, taking our names. "Let me find you in our system."

Mark pointed at a yellow Bear Crossing sign hanging on the wall nearby, smiling thinly. "Are there really bears around here?"

"Of course. This is the woods, boy." A final keystroke accentuated her words. She retrieved a pile of papers from a filing system behind her and slapped them down on the desk. "Here's a map. You're at site 629." She circled the spot with a pencil, then flipped through the stack, reviewing the rules and logistics listed on each page. The last sheet was bright orange. "Here are our bear safety rules. Clean up all food products and wrappers after eating. They will attract bears. Do not bring food into your tent. When not eating, keep all food and packaging in your car, and keep your car locked. Bears can open car doors." She jabbed at the paper with one finger. "Up top is the number for the ranger's office. This is who you call when the bears come. Any questions?"

"No, I don't think so," I said.

Mark shook his head, his tan face paling.

"Excellent," the woman said. "In that case, we'll process your payment, and you can be on your way."

Mark didn't speak as we climbed back into the car and I eased it onto the dusty road leading into the campground.

"Navigate me to 629," I said, jerking my chin toward the papers in his hands.

"Did she say, 'when the bears come'?" Mark asked.

"Sorry, what?"

"That ranger. When she gave us the phone number, did she say to call 'if' the bears come or 'when'?"

I replayed the conversation in my mind. "I think she said 'when.'"

He slumped in his seat. "You've got to be kidding me."

"I'm sure it's fine. I've camped out in the middle of nowhere several times, and I never saw a bear. It's probably just a liability thing." I reached over, smacking the papers to draw him out of himself. "Now, where am I going?"

Sighing, he examined the map. "It looks like we're right here, which means . . . we just passed it."

"Great."

"No, it's fine. Turn left here. It loops back around."

I turned. The road wound deeper into the woods, with a mixture of tents and cabins nestled among the swaying trees. "At least we get a chance to take in the scenery."

"How scenic." Mark gestured out the window toward an old man reclining on a folding chair, a stained baseball cap pulled down over his face.

"We chose this for you, remember?" I tried to keep the irritation out of my voice. He'd agreed to try camping on the condition that we chose a busy campground where he could feel close to other people. That meant, sometimes, Old Man Jenkins would be sleeping in the middle of the scenery, and he'd just have to deal with that. "Can you try to enjoy yourself? Please?"

"Fine. I'm sorry."

We took another left turn, and the road widened into a parking lot in front of another large building—the bathroom. Behind it stood a denser patch of forest that ran uninterrupted for who knew how far.

"There's some scenery for you," I said.

To his credit, Mark stared out at the deep woods in appreciation as we drove past. Before long, we'd looped back around, and he guided me toward a small clearing designated 629.

"Whoa, I didn't notice that our first time around," he said.

"What?" I asked, backing into the campsite.

"It looks like a beach."

"There's supposed to be one on the lake here somewhere."

"Let's go." Mark hopped out of the car.

I followed, my phone mercifully staying in my pocket. "You don't want to set up the tent first?" I hiked a thumb toward our empty campsite.

"I'm finally excited about something on this trip, and you want to stop and make me do work?" He winked.

I rolled my eyes dramatically for his benefit. "Sorry I asked. Carry on."

We linked hands and started down the road, and the little beach unfolded before us: a wide patch of sand ending in the lake. A string of blue-and-white buoys cut out a small slice of rippling water for swimmers.

As we approached, an older woman got out of the lake and wrapped herself in a towel. Despite her graying hair, her arms and legs were toned with muscle.

"Hi, there," she said, padding toward the cabin directly across the road. "Haven't seen you two around before."

Mark and I exchanged glances. We weren't usually the chatting-with-strangers type.

"It's our first time camping out this way," I said. "I'm guessing you come here a lot?"

"Every year since I first got married." Toweling off, she dropped into a folding chair on the cabin's lawn. "Of course, it's just me now."

"I'm sorry," I said lamely.

"Don't be."

"You've got the best view in the campground," Mark said with a nod to the beach.

"I know. I request this cabin every year." She looked to the side, where a small flowerbed bloomed. Among the blossoms lay a trowel and a hand rake. Sunlight glistened off the pin-sharp tines. "They let me start a garden last year. The other campers who rented after me were pretty good about taking care of it."

"That's really cool," I said. Despite myself, I pictured what it would be like to vacation while single, not having to constantly appease another person. Then, I shook my head. Mark was doing this for me. It wasn't in his nature, and it scared him, but he was trying. I needed to give him a chance.

"Can I ask you a question?" Mark said, glancing at the trees. "All the bear stuff when you check in . . . is it actually a problem?"

"The bears?" She chuckled. "They're no strangers. That's for sure."

"So you've seen them?" His grip on my hand tightened.

"Heard them, mostly. Don't worry, though. You mind your own business, and they'll mind theirs."

"See?" I gave him a reassuring squeeze. "We'll be fine."

Mark didn't look convinced.

I woke up in the middle of the night to the specific pain of a tree root digging into my full bladder—the downside of sleeping on your stomach in a tent. I crept out of the bed we'd made with our unzipped sleeping bags and used my phone's flashlight to find my shorts. Mark kept snoring. All that bear anxiety must have really tired him out.

Dressed, I stepped outside, where the porch lights of the cabins and cottages formed an ambient glow. I turned off my light, pocketed my phone, and set off.

One man—I'd thought of him as Old Man Jenkins earlier—was also awake. As I passed his campsite, he slipped into the trees, lost in his own adventure. Once he was gone, everything was still, and it gave the campground a magical quality.

I took a deep breath, soaking in the feeling that I'd stepped into some alternate universe. I imagined living here, spending my days in the forest and forming a community with the campers who slept all around me. Here, I wouldn't have to balance an all-consuming job and other people's expectations. I'd owe the world nothing but to wake up every morning and live my life. I'd be free.

I rounded a corner, and a floodlight nearly blinded me—the bathroom. The two entrances sat on opposite sides of the building, giving the women the benefit of the floodlight and the parking lot while men had to creep around to the more dimly lit side facing the forest. On the surface, it felt sexist, but I supposed it made sense. There was a reason most men didn't think twice about walking alone at night.

I was still thinking about this as I stepped into the bathroom stall. At least, that's my excuse for forgetting to be careful about how I pulled my shorts down. The soft plunk of my phone diving into toilet water from my tiny, girly pocket reminded me. Swearing and gritting my teeth, I pulled it from the water bare-handed and yanked on the toilet paper. Spinning out a fistful of single-ply, I dabbed at the phone, then gave the screen a couple test taps. No response. Pressing buttons on the side lit up my lock screen, at least, and I quickly powered the phone down. I'd dry it off, and maybe it would work in the morning. If not, I guess upgrade time had come early.

I finished what I'd come to do then wrapped my phone in flimsy, brown paper towels and walked back toward the tent. People always said to stick your phone in rice after this happened, didn't they? But where to get rice at this time of night? Reflexively, I glanced down at my phone to Google it, then felt incredibly dumb.

Something rustled in the woods nearby, and my head shot up. I was almost past Old Man Jenkins's campsite. At first, I assumed he was making the trek back from wherever he had gone, but the movement didn't sound as straightforward as footsteps. The underbrush whispered in a long susurration, like something was slipping smoothly through the bushes. I stepped closer, squinting into the darkness, but the dancing flames of the old man's campfire blinded me to anything more than a few feet beyond it. A twig snapped. Goosebumps crept up my neck, and I hurried away.

I slipped back into our tent, trying not to worry about whatever I'd heard. It was probably just a racoon or something. It wouldn't bother us in here. I knelt by my bag and focused on finding some cloth to wrap around my phone in lieu of rice. Settling on a pair of cotton underwear, I tossed the bundled-up phone into my bag, peeled off my shorts, and crawled back into bed.

Mark stirred when I moved the upper sleeping bag and reached for me. I scooted closer, wrapping my arms around him. Buried in the warmth of his touch, it was easy to believe we were safe.

"Where'd you disappear to?" he asked in a sleep-roughed voice.

"Bathroom."

I considered mentioning the phone incident and maybe even the noise in the woods, but then he kissed me, and it suddenly seemed like the kind of thing that could wait until morning. I was threading my fingers through his hair when something rumbled outside the tent like a giant, corrugated tube scraping against metal. We both froze.

"Was that a bear?" Mark asked.

I hesitated. I'd been trying so hard to keep him from worrying about the bears that I almost said no without thinking, but after what I'd heard moving in the woods, I couldn't dismiss the idea. "I don't know."

The sound came again, this time more erratically, and I jumped. I'd never heard a bear in person before, but it did sound like a roar.

"That was definitely a bear." Mark sat up. "I've got to get out of here. Get dressed."

I reached for my shorts and stood to put them on, our sleeping bags and the tent tarp under them rustling. Mark shushed me.

"Do you want me to get dressed or to be quiet?" I whispered.

"I'm listening." He stood completely still. "I don't hear it moving."

"Good, then maybe it's not that close. You want to make a break for it in your underwear?"

Even in the darkness, I knew the glare he was giving me. He pulled on his pants, and I paused again at the tent's entrance to listen. Still nothing. My hand shook as I reached for the zipper.

I pulled.

Outside was empty darkness. For a moment, all was still. Then, Mark leaned forward to get a better view.

"Anything?" he whispered.

I took a breath and plunged my head outside. Enough light filtered through the trees from other campsites that I would have seen at least the silhouette of a bear. "Nothing."

We were alone, at least for now.

We slipped on our shoes and scampered to the car, locking ourselves in. I partially lowered the windows to listen. Voices rumbled in the once-silent air. The campground was coming awake.

"I can't believe this," Mark said. "You told me this never happens."

"I said it's never happened to me."

"Can't say that anymore. Roll the windows up so we don't get eaten."

I shook my head. "I want to hear. Do you have that bear number?"

"You mean the one we're supposed to call when the bears come?" He reached for the backseat, where he'd tossed the pile of papers earlier.

"Actually, never mind." I pointed toward a pair of hulking vehicles creeping along the campground road, their blinding headlights cutting through the trees. "Looks like someone already called."

The crackle of a radio scanner pierced the night. I focused on it but couldn't make out the staticky voices.

"This sucks," Mark said. "We should go home."

"We're safe in here. Let's see what happens." It felt morbid, but I was enjoying the excitement. Black bears—the type depicted on all the merch in the lodge—could be dangerous but didn't usually hurt people, so even though my heart was pumping, I didn't really believe anything bad would happen.

We'd been sitting in silence for a while when a man materialized from the shadows and approached my window. His hat and button-down shirt gave him away as a ranger. He held up a hand in greeting.

"Sorry for the disruption to your evening," he said. "Is everyone okay?"

"We're fine," I said. "What's happening?"

Mark leaned over. "Did you find the bear?"

The ranger's eyes flicked between our car and the darkness around him as he spoke. "No, we haven't found it yet. That's why I'm speaking with you. This is very rare, but we suspect the bear may have attacked a camper."

Mark slipped his hand into mine. "Are they okay?"

"I'm not at liberty to say," the ranger said, which was an answer in itself.

"Do you need help?" I asked. "I'm a doctor."

"Thanks, but the situation's handled for now. However, this does mean we're closing the campground. I'm sorry for the inconvenience, but it's for everyone's safety. You can contact us Monday about the refund."

Once the ranger was satisfied that we'd gather our things and leave, he melted back into the darkness. I turned to Mark, trying to focus on logistics; I'd have the whole drive home to feel guilty about getting my thrills while someone else was hurt or dying nearby.

"We need to get the rest of our stuff," I said. "Ready?"

Mark's eyes widened. Had he just planned on leaving it all? "I guess. Let's just hurry. I don't even want to fold the tent. We'll deal with it at home."

I nodded in agreement before plunging into the night air and racing around the car. In less than ten minutes, everything we'd brought was piled haphazardly in the back, and we were climbing back into our seats.

"Ready to go?" I said, reaching to shift into drive.

He hesitated. "Yeah, I just—never mind. Yeah."

"What?"

He spoke in a small voice. "When I get scared, I kind of . . . have to go to the bathroom. That's all. But let's get out of here. We'll stop somewhere else."

"We're in the mountains in the middle of the night. How many places do you think are open?"

"Probably at least one. Maybe."

"We're stopping at the bathrooms on the way out."

He drummed his fingers against his knee, staring at the blackness outside his window, and sighed. "Fine."

I pulled out of our campsite, and as I turned toward the bathrooms, my headlights raked over the cabin by the beach where that older lady was staying. A ranger stood behind the cabin, spooling out bright yellow caution tape.

"I guess we know who got hurt," I said weakly, trying not to picture the details.

"It was so close." Mark squeezed my wrist. "You were out here right before we heard the bear. It could have been you."

I flashed back to the sounds I'd heard in the woods near Old Man Jenkins's abandoned campfire. Had that been the bear or Old Man Jenkins? Or both? Old Man Jenkins was heading in the direction of that cabin when he'd entered the woods. He could have stumbled right into the bear's path.

I couldn't help but slow the car to a crawl as I passed his campsite. I leaned into Mark, craning my neck for a view. Had Old Man Jenkins ever come back?

At first, all I saw was the campfire, now burned down to embers. The chair behind it was still empty, and his tent and truck looked untouched.

"What? Do you see the bear?" Mark asked.

I was about to sit upright and answer when I saw it—the silhouette of a person standing at the edge of the forest a ways past the campsite, their arms crossed. I couldn't make out details, but it had to be him. My neck prickled. His face was lost in shadow, but somehow, I knew he was watching me.

It only lasted a moment before we'd passed the campsite, and I sat up straight, giving Mark a half-hearted explanation that I'd seen the man from that campsite go into the woods and I'd been concerned.

"Looks like he's okay," Mark said dismissively. So he'd seen the silhouette, too.

Something was off, though. I thought about it, even as I pulled into the bathroom parking lot, angling my car so my headlights lit the narrow walking path that led around the building to the men's entrance.

"Why couldn't both bathrooms be on the same side," Mark muttered.

"We're the only car here," I said. "Use the women's. No one will ever know."

He shook his head. "It's fine. I'll be right back."

He ducked out, and I locked the car behind him, watching him trudge down the path and around the corner. Beyond the edge of the building, my headlights illuminated the first few layers of trees. The rest dissolved into blackness. I waited for dark fur to emerge from the shadows like a shark fin from water.

Or, if not fur, a man.

Old Man Jenkins's posture as he watched me from the darkness had been menacing. And why wasn't he packing? Even if the rangers hadn't told him about the bear yet, he'd surely heard it. He should have been taking shelter or breaking camp to leave, but he just stood there, as if there wasn't really a threat.

Or as if he was the threat.

We suspect the bear may have attacked a camper. That's what the ranger had said: suspect. No one had actually seen the attack. They'd found a victim and heard some bear noises and put two and two together. What if they were wrong?

I shifted in my seat, scanning the parking lot for movement. Mark needed to hurry up.

What if Old Man Jenkins had been sneaking over to the cabin when I saw him? He could've taken the woods to avoid being seen, hurt that woman—who he knew would be here since she always is—and faked the bear attack as cover. A forest ranger in the dark might not know the difference, especially since bear attacks were rare—the ranger had said so himself.

If that were true, I could have been the only one with enough information to figure it out. And he saw me looking; I was sure of that. I was a witness. Bad things happened to witnesses, and here I was, my car lit up as if by a spotlight in this empty parking lot. I could practically feel the bead of a rifle's scope training on the back of my head. What was taking Mark so long?

Unable to wait any longer, I burst from the car, dancing away from it as if a hand would snake out from underneath and grab my ankle. I slammed the door behind me and locked it before anything or anyone could climb inside. Then, I charged down the path to the men's room, now much darker with my headlights off. I made it almost to the corner and froze, listening. Maybe I'd been on display in the parking lot, but out here, anyone could be anywhere. Still, I heard only quiet—no human footsteps or bear claws, no whispered words or snuffles or growls. Taking a breath, I stepped around the corner—nothing. No bears. No Old Man Jenkins. No Mark.

A bare outdoor lightbulb hung above the door, burned out—of course—though a strip of light glowed from the gap underneath. I swung the door open and stepped in.

"Hurry up or I'm leaving without you," I called, turning to face the stalls.

The door swung shut behind me, and my head exploded in pain. It all went dark.

🌲🌲🌲

The first thing I became aware of was the worst headache of my life. Behind that, I felt myself slide over rough terrain, scraping against it where the back of my shirt rode up. Something—no, someone—held my ankles and was pulling.

I opened my eyes and saw nothing. Was I blind? I'd been hit in the head. Where was I? Where was Mark? Was he okay? Who was doing this to us? But I knew who—Old Man Jenkins. I'd been too curious, and he was disposing of his witness.

I wanted to kick free of his grip and escape, but I couldn't see. I'd be defenseless. For now, he was just moving me. Maybe he thought I was dead, and if I waited long enough, he'd put me somewhere and leave. It was worth a shot.

I kept trying to open my eyes in narrow slits, and after a while, the blackness took on some depth. I wasn't blind; it was just dark. Judging by the litter rubbing against my bare back and arms—leaves, sticks, and stones, from the feel of it—I was in the forest. Was Mark nearby? I tried not to consider what might have happened to him. He'd only gone camping because of me. If he was hurt, it was my fault. But no, he'd be okay, and I'd see him again. I had to.

Finally, Old Man Jenkins dropped my feet. I let them fall limply to the ground, hoping his footsteps would disappear into the night. Instead, he shuffled alongside me and stopped. Fabric rustled above me. What was he doing? My skin tingled, waiting. I couldn't take it anymore. I opened my eyes.

The shapes above me took a moment to resolve into a person, but when they did, it didn't make sense. This wasn't Old Man Jenkins. It was her—the woman from the cabin by the beach. She was supposed to be dead! Instead, she clutched something small and oddly shaped, holding it over me like she was about to strike.

I jerked to the side, catching her legs up in mine and twisting. She yelped and fell. Whatever she'd held arced through the air away from us.

I stood, and my vision blacked out with pain. Clutching my head, I stepped back, not wanting to turn away from the woman. "What did you do to me?"

"You know." The woman army-crawled through the brush until her hands clasped around what she'd dropped. She scrambled to her feet. "I didn't want to do it, but you know. You saw me."

"What do you mean? I thought you were dead."

"Liar!" She brandished the object in front of her, and as its shape glistened in the moonlight, I recognized it as the hand rake from her garden.

I held my hands up like the rake was a gun. "I don't know what you're talking about. Let me go."

"Don't play dumb. You saw me with his body in the woods. I caught you watching from his campsite."

His campsite? I remembered staring into the forest after hearing that strange sound, but I never saw what was making it. Was it her? With a body? Hair raised on my arms. "It was dark. I couldn't see anything."

"Then why were you glaring at me when you drove past in your car?"

"Glaring at you?" Then I realized—the silhouette. "I didn't know that was you. I swear." Everything I'd suspected of Old Man Jenkins—it had all been her. He'd been the one to die, not her, and it looked like I would be next.

"At this point, I've told you enough that it doesn't matter what you saw. I can't take any chances. The second they even suspect murder, I'm screwed. He's my ex-husband, and he only died a few yards away from my cabin. Stupid man never knew when to leave me well enough alone. Anyway, it looks too suspicious. A few extra victims should throw them off my scent."

A few? "Mark—"

She lunged, cutting off my question. I dodged to the side, just managing to grab her rake arm as she passed. I tried twisting it behind her, but she resisted, spinning back toward me. I kicked out at her and felt my foot connect with something in the darkness. She cried out and went down. I ran.

Movement magnified my headache, and every heartbeat blotted out my thoughts. I wanted to puke. Still, I kept moving, unsure how far behind me she was or where I was going. I didn't even have a phone to call for help. Running was all I had. If I could keep it up, eventually I'd hit campground again.

Something snapped in the forest right in front of me—not a twig this time but a full-fledged branch—and I stopped, my momentum almost carrying me off my feet. Grabbing a tree for balance, I saw it—a shadow in the already dark forest. Wet snuffles cut through the night air. A bear. There really were bears out here, after all!

I took a deep, quiet breath. It only came up a little past my waist—a black bear. I scanned my aching brain, trying to remember what to do in these situations. Tell it to leave?

"Go," I said in the most intimidating voice I could muster.

The shadow grew to my full height as the bear reared up to look at me. I swallowed. It took a half-step closer, and I raised my arms over my head, waving.

"Get out of here," I said, my voice even louder.

With a soft grunt, it dropped back down onto all fours and skirted around me, ambling off the way I'd come. Perhaps that would keep the woman off my trail. I listened to it go, itching to leave but afraid of activating its prey drive. Finally, when it seemed far enough away, I started out again, more slowly this time.

I walked another few minutes before lights shone through the trees. Picking up my pace again, I broke out of the forest. The bathroom loomed in the distance, and I stopped, sick at what might be inside. But I had to know. I forced myself to take step after step, and my view of the parking lot grew clearer. A pair of cop cars and a ranger's truck idled close to my Subaru. A figure leaned heavily on one of the cop cars, speaking with the officers. Someone moved, and suddenly I could see him.

Mark! He was alive! Tears spilled from my eyes, and it was all I could do to keep my knees from buckling as I called out his name. Gathering my last burst of energy, I ran into his arms and didn't let go, even as I told the cops what happened in the woods. Finally, we got a moment to ourselves, and I buried my face in his neck.

"I'm sorry," I said. Our arguments seemed so stupid now. "You never have to go camping again."

He pulled away to smile at me. "But I want to."

"What?"

"We're helping catch a murderer. This is way more exciting than staying home playing video games."

"But you got hurt, and you were so scared."

"Of bears, yeah, but now I realize that humans are worse, and they're everywhere." He rubbed his head. "Maybe next time, we can go deeper into the woods."

"You mean it?"

"Yeah." He winked. "It'll be fun. Just you, me, and the bears."

# 9

# The Whistler in the Attic

*Lorena A. Sins*

*For my father, Carl David Sins, who told me this story,*
*and for my grandmother, Ida Marie Stabb Sins, who lived it.*

## JULY

Ida was canning beans when she first heard the whistler in the attic. She was alone in the kitchen, and in the house, except for Grandma. Her three younger daughters, Helen, Marian, and Arlene, were out in the large vegetable garden next to the old farmhouse, picking more beans. Ida could really have used the help of one of the older girls with the cleaning and canning, but, as so often happened, Helen and Marian had fought over who had to go out in the hot, mosquito-filled garden and who got to stay inside and help wash, string, and cut the beans and sterilize the jars. Ida, pausing in her work to push a strand of sweat-soaked hair off her forehead as the whistling registered in her ears, thought it was six of one, half a dozen of the other as to whether picking beans in the garden or canning in the kitchen was more unpleasant on a hot day in mid-July. The garden had mosquitoes, but the kitchen, which trapped the heat and the steam of the double-boiler despite the open doors and windows, was wretchedly humid. Helen and Marian, she thought with disapproval, would fight over anything.

She eased another set of mason jars packed with beans into the water in the big pressure cooker on the stove, then tilted her head, listening to the tuneless whistling sliding along the breeze that had suddenly slipped into the kitchen through the wide window over the sink and out through the screen door at the front of the house. At first she thought it was Grandma Otillia, her husband's mother, who lay bedridden in the back bedroom. She was left alone for most of the day, with Ida and her girls so busy in the summer, but Grandma, senile, never noticed. She would sing to herself sometimes, in her old, cracked voice, but this sound was not Grandma; it was definitely whistling. Ida walked across the kitchen to the doorway that led to the hall and the formal front door. The family always went in and out by the kitchen door; the front door and the parlor to the right of it as one went in were only used for the most formal occasions: a baptism, a wedding, a funeral. Today, though, it was open to let the breeze run through the house from upstairs, where the windows were all open. Winters were hard on the little farm, only a stone's throw from the mountains that rose to the west, the Adirondacks, as harsh and beautiful as the winter moon. At least the blizzard winds that tore at the old farmhouse meant that in the summer the wind never stopped blowing, either.

Sure enough, there was someone upstairs, whistling. Who? She knew where her all her family was, and they weren't in the house. Her oldest, Florence, had got a job in Rochester for the summer, not far from Nazareth College, the Catholic women's school she would be graduating from in another year. Joe and Dave, Ida's sons, and their uncle, Jake, who ran the two Sins family farms with Ida and her children, were back at Kessler's, haying on the huge fields where a good share of the hay the two farms would need for the winter grew. The three girls were out in the garden picking beans. Ida, exasperated with the quarreling of the two older girls, had ordered them out an hour ago, and they hadn't been back in since. Ida's husband, Joe, was dead.

Yet there it was: a thin, tuneless whistling from which no melody ever emerged, the kind of whistling a man might do absently, out of habit, as he went about his work. Ida frowned, then walked to the foot of the stairs that led down to the front door. The stairway was open, with a banister that kept careless children from falling off the stairs onto the hard wooden floor of the hall. The sound floated over the banister, thin and hollow. She had no idea who it could be. She'd been in the kitchen since before milking that morning, fixing breakfast for her family and Uncle Jake, then washing up after breakfast, then making three pies for dinner and supper, then cutting and canning the beans. No one but the family had been in the house that day, and she had seen them all leave. None of them had come back in and gone upstairs; no one had any reason to, with hay to be made and beans growing thicker, tougher, and less tasty every hour they stayed on the bushes in the hot July weather. The last time anyone but family had been in the house, in fact, had been when the Schoff boys, her husband and Jake's nephews, had helped Ida's boys and Jake replace the old shingle roof with a new tin one on the main part of the house. But that had been a week and a half ago, when the sky had threatened with thunderheads, and no one dared cut more hay lest it get rained on and become less nutritious and palatable for the Holstein cows that would be eating it come winter. Unable to work in the hayfields, Jake had decided that he and the boys, helped by their cousins, would work on replacing the old, rotting shingles. After the weather finally broke and rained itself out, everyone had rushed out to cut hay. The roof work hadn't been completely finished, but Jake figured it was better to let the attic get wet than the hay.

"Who's up there?" she called tentatively, but no voice answered her. Only the whistling replied to her query, rising and falling, as it seemed, on the currents of the breeze. *Well, then, I'll just go and see for myself,* she thought, but no sooner had she set her foot on the first stair step did the dizziness start. She felt her heart stutter in her chest, and the dizziness washed away on a wave of faintness. Ida managed to stagger back into the kitchen and collapse on a wooden kitchen chair without falling over. She had already been sweating from the heat in the kitchen, but the drops forming on her forehead now felt clammy and chill. She pulled her handkerchief from the pocket of her calico house dress and wiped them off.

She was still sitting on the chair, trying to catch her breath and waiting for the sickly twitching of her heart to steady itself, when the three girls came back in, the two older ones each carrying two baskets of beans and little Arlene valiantly lugging one with both hands.

"Are you all right, Ma?" Marian asked anxiously, setting her baskets on the table and hurrying to her mother's side. "You look white as snow."

"I'll be fine," Ida said, forcing herself to smile so as not to worry her girls. "It's another one of my spells, that's all."

"Aren't the pills Doc Hershey gave you doing any good at all?" Helen asked, going to the sink and working the pump to fill a glass with water for her mother. Ida accepted it gratefully and drank. The cold well water felt like a blessing in her mouth.

"No, not really. Doc said that the best thing for it would be if I could lie down for an hour when I get like this." Ida chuckled, a little bitterly. "He didn't volunteer to come can vegetables and tend to Grandma so I can rest, though."

When she was a little girl, Ida had contracted scarlet fever. Doc told her that the spells of dizziness and faintness and shortness of breath were the result of that fever long ago. It had damaged her heart, which had not been helped by the eight babies she had carried after she got married. Her first baby, Mary, had been born without a brain and died within an hour of her birth, and she had lost a boy when she had been crushed between two cows while milking one morning. But she felt lucky that six of her children survived, and that she herself had lived long enough to bear them.

Ida looked up at the three young, anxious faces clustered around her. Be strong, for them. "Well, it's passed now," she said, standing up and smoothing her apron over the front of her dress. "You won't need to pick any more beans today. We'll just get this lot done before Unk and the boys come back for dinner before it's time to do the milking."

"I'll go back and check on Grandma," she told them. "Arlene, you come with me. You can bring water and towels and hold them for me in case Grandma needs to be cleaned."

Halfway through the hall on their way to the back bedroom, though, Arlene stopped suddenly. "Ma, who's upstairs? I hear someone whistling." Sure enough, the whistling, thready but clear, was still coming from somewhere upstairs.

Ida opened her mouth to tell Arlene to go upstairs and check, but a sudden wave of apprehension made her close it again. Her spells always made her feel weak and overly anxious. There was probably nothing uncanny upstairs, but still . . .

"I heard it, too, before you girls came in from the garden. I don't know who it is. After we see to Grandma, I'll go up and look."

When she had finished cleaning Grandma and turning her so that bedsores wouldn't form on her wasted back and buttocks, she went up the stairs, trailed by Arlene. They looked in all the rooms, but there was no one there but them.

Back down in the kitchen, Helen looked up briefly from cleaning beans. "Was that you whistling, Arlene? I didn't know you'd finally learned how."

"I didn't, El. I still can't, see?" Arlene puckered her lips and blew hard, with her cheeks puffed out with the effort, but only the breathy sound of air rushing came out.

"I don't know what's making that whistling," Ida replied. "We went up and checked, just now. There's no one up there."

"Joe and Dave went out with Unk," Helen said, frowning.

"Well, it's probably just a bird, perching on the chimney. It'll fly away soon enough." Ida went to the stove, opened the little iron door, and put in another piece of stove wood.

"It doesn't sound like any bird I've ever heard," Marian chimed in thoughtlessly. "It sounds just like Pa used to when he would whistle in the barn."

"Nonsense," Ida said again, much more sharply. "It's a bird, that's all, and I don't want to hear any more about it. Now finish up there. The men will be back from Kessler's soon, and they'll want their dinner."

The girls bent to their tasks again, subdued, and Ida went to the stove to pull the batch of jars from the boiler and tighten the lids before they cooled. Upstairs the whistling went on, riding up and down the breeze, fading away, then wailing shrilly, wandering lost and alone through the empty rooms of the house.

## AUGUST

Ida stood sweating in her black dress, hat, and shoes, looking at a tombstone. Mass at the Church of St. Michael the Archangel had just finished, and rather than staying outside the church doors to visit with the neighbors, Ida had gone to visit her husband instead. Even though it was a fine haying day, and Father Driscoll was lenient and understanding about farm folk missing Mass when there was hay to be brought in, the church had been full. It was the anniversary Mass for Joseph Achilles Sins, who had died suddenly just a year earlier that week. Joe had been popular and well liked, and the neighbors still missed him. Ida had endured once more the condolences and handshakes due a recent widow, but as soon as was polite, she had slipped away to the cemetery behind the gray stone church.

The stone that marked the resting places of Joe and his father was large and imposing, made of polished gray granite. Joe, always extravagant, had bought the granite marker when his father died, and it seemed fair set to last as long as the granite mountains that stood to the west.

Ida had automatically bowed her head and recited the Lord's Prayer and the Hail Mary before the stone, for the repose of the souls of her Joe and his father, another Joe. Then she raised her head to read the words graven deep in the granite. On the side facing the church were the names of her father-in-law and his wife, Otillia, who lay in the sunny back bedroom in the farmhouse three miles away. Joseph Henry's birth and death dates were there, but only Otillia's birth date. A kindness if You would let her come to You, Lord, Ida prayed, thinking of the old woman lying in bed, wandering in her mind. The few times she was lucid enough to walk in the present for a few steps, she wept for her lost husband and son.

Walking around to the back side of the monument, Ida stared with hard eyes at Joe's name and dates. Beneath his name was hers, Ida Marie Sins, wife of. As with Otillia, only her birth date was there. Looking at their two names, Ida's eyes prickled.

She should have known when she married him that it would end this way, with her standing on the earth and him lying under it. The dates on the stone said it all: he had been born twenty years before her. Ida hadn't thought to ever marry; at twenty-four when Joe started courting her, she was already an "old maid" schoolteacher in the little one-room schoolhouse in Lewis, the little hamlet near her parents' farm. His family's farm and hers were cross-lots from each other; a quick two miles' walk through woods, swamps, and meadows would bring him to her father's front door. So their families knew each other, of course, but what interest would a grown man have in a little girl a generation his junior? They first got to know each other when both attended a dance at the grange hall in Lewis. Joe was lively, with a quick sense of humor, well liked by everyone who knew him and the center of the group that laughed most often at the grange hall dance. He was prosperous and generous, and handsome, but still unmarried, somehow, at forty-four. Ida, on the other hand, was awkward and shy, happier with her books or in front of her class of little scholars than at a dance. The only reason she had gone to the dance was because her Stabb cousins had dragged her there, convinced that she needed to meet some nice young men, even though she had assured them that she didn't want to meet a nice young man. Joe had spotted her, with her back pressed against the wall and hands clasped tightly before her from nerves. He had unclasped them and seized them, pulling her onto the dance floor, and even though she danced awkwardly, only ever having done it with her girl cousins to no music in the cow barn, where her mother couldn't see and scold, he danced only with her.

He had driven her and her cousins home in his buggy that night, and after that, it wasn't long before he'd asked her to marry. He would walk cross-lots from his farm to her parents' farm, bringing gifts of cheese from the cheese factory his father had built and which he and his brother Jake ran together, giving the farmers in the area a convenient and profitable place to sell their milk. He would bring flowers, too: forget-me-nots, yellow cowslips, and purple irises from the swamps that lay between his farm and hers. She could pick her own swamp flowers, of course, but the gesture touched her.

When he proposed to her, she did not love him, and she was put off by the difference in their ages. Her practical side had won out, though. No other suitors for her hand had ever appeared, and it seemed unlikely that they would if she turned Joe down. Before Joe came courting, she had resigned herself to never having a husband or children, but after, she found, to her surprise, that she really did want to have children. In addition, she had to think of the future. Her brother Frank would inherit her father's farm, and she didn't want to be indebted to a sister-in-law for the roof over her head. Joe and his brother jointly owned and ran two prosperous farms and the cheese factory that was built between them. Jake, who was even older than Joe, seemed unlikely to ever marry. Any children that Ida and Joe might have would inherit both farms.

So despite not loving him, Ida had married him. She liked him well enough. It was only after their first great tragedy together, the death of their first-born child, that she had grown to love him. After Joe's sister, Tillie Schoff, who had served as midwife to Ida's labor, quickly took the tiny child away from the birth-bed and baptized her Mary Anna with clean, if unblessed water in the name of the Father, Son, and Holy Ghost, she had hurried out of the small bedroom off the kitchen where Joe waited anxiously, to tell him of the baby's death, even before she told Ida. Joe had come into the little room where Ida lay, exhausted, and before turning to his wife, had taken the small, towel-wrapped bundle in his arms, uncovered the tiny face and the poor, deformed head, and wept for his child who had only taken a few breaths before she went back to God who made her. Then Joe had gently set the baby down in the cradle that he had made for her and turned to Ida. With him kneeling beside the bed and her lying on it, they had held each other and mourned for their daughter. After, while Ida slept, Joe had taken the spade out to the hill behind the house, where Ida loved to go, when she had time, to watch the sun set over the mountains to the west, and dug a small grave. He laid Mary to rest near the flat rock where he knew Ida sat to watch the sun set, so that she could be near her baby and pray for her innocent soul during her moments of peace at the end of the day.

Joe was her strong support during the hard times, and her best comrade during the good ones. He stood between her and his irascible brother Jake, who made his resentment of his brother's wife clear with every harsh word and cutting glance. His defense of Ida would draw Jake's ill temper onto Joe, of course, and Ida appreciated his kindness in shielding her from Jake's bitterness.

A year after Mary, Ida had given birth to Florence Marie, and Joe was ecstatic. He spent his evenings, when the work was done, holding her. On the day the baby was baptized at St. Michael's Church, he presented Ida with a gold knot-pin that he had bought in Peru, the nearest town large enough to have a merchant who could take orders for the jeweler in Plattsburg. He still brought her wildflowers whenever the work of the farm and cheese factory allowed him time, and once he bought a tiny lilac bush and planted it next to the house for her, where it grew and thrived and put out heaven-scented purple blooms every spring. After Florence came Joseph Anthony, their first son, then another son and three more daughters. Like the wife in Psalm 128, Ida was a fruitful vine, and her children flourished like olive shoots. With each healthy birth, and Joe's delight with each new child, Ida grew to love him more and more.

And then he had died and left her. She thought again of that day, only a little more than a year ago, when Clarence Schoff, Joe's cousin, came driving up to the farmhouse in his buggy to tell her. In the middle of the school board meeting, of which Joe was, of course, a member, out at the new school in Lewis, Joe had collapsed and died. Doc said his heart had just given out. Hers had felt like giving out, too, but she wouldn't let it. She had children to take care of. She hadn't let herself cry, either, biting the inside of her cheek till her mouth filled with blood, over and over again, so the pain would drown out the grief. She had been afraid, then, that if she once started to cry, she would never stop.

As she stood, staring at Joe's grave, she thought again about the whistler in the attic. She hadn't wanted to think of it, but she couldn't stop herself. She was a religious woman, a devout Catholic, but she was also imaginative. One of her pleasures was reading poetry and novels in her scant free time when the chores were done at the end of the day, and she loved literature that hinted at things beyond the mundane world, supernatural things. She had thrilled to Mary Shelley's *Frankenstein* after going to see a film version of the tale at the theater in Peru. Her favorite poems from *The Pocket Book of Verse* were ones that were ghost stories: the ballad "Two Sisters of Binnoire," Thomas Hardy's "Ah, Are You Digging on My Grave?," Poe's poem "Annabelle Lee," and "The Greenwood Side" by Francis James Child. She knew that it was wrong to believe in ghosts, and that the dead went to Heaven, Hell, or Purgatory, depending on the state of their souls when they died. But poems that involved ghosts sent a delicious frisson up her spine. Now she couldn't keep from thinking, what if? What if the whistler in the attic really was Joe, trying to comfort her in death as he had in life?

She shook her head, angry at her own foolish fantasies. Of course it wasn't Joe. What it was, she didn't know, but Joe's soul was in Purgatory or in Heaven, not whistling to her from upstairs. She turned and walked back down the gravel drive toward the church, biting the inside of her cheek to chase away the thought, the hope, if she was honest with herself, that Joe had not forgotten her.

After the buggy ride back home from church, Ida hurried up the front steps and into the kitchen to check on the beef roast that she had started before milking that morning. She had sent Young Joe on a special trip to town to get the roast from the town meat locker, where the family's slaughtered beef and pork were kept on ice in the summer. For the cost of renting space in the locker, Ida's family could have fresh meat any time of year. Ida wanted to make sure that the roast was cooked just right. Satisfied with the state of the beef, Ida left Helen and Marian to start the potatoes and beans and went to the back bedroom to check on Grandma and make sure she was presentable. Father Driscoll was coming to Sunday dinner and to give Communion to Grandma and Marian, whose turn it had been to miss Mass to tend to Grandma. It wouldn't do for the old woman to be less than immaculate when Father arrived.

*Otillia was having a good day*, Ida thought. She was sitting up, and she greeted her daughter-in-law by name as she entered the small, sunny room. Ida bent over and hugged her. "Hello, Grandma! We're back from Mass. Father is coming for dinner. He's bringing the Host with him, so you can take Communion, and he'll hear your confession, if you feel up to it." She smoothed the old woman's sparse gray hair, which Ida had combed and put up in a small bun after she had put the roast in the oven that morning. It was still in good order. Then Ida straightened, frowning. The air in the room felt still and close. The windows had been closed all night, since Grandma didn't like the cool night air, and they were still closed. Ida went over to the room's two windows and opened them, propping them up with adjustable screens that kept the mosquitoes and flies out while letting the fresh air in.

She paused, looking out the west-facing window at the mountains and marveling, as she always did, at the soft-looking slopes clad with maple, ash, and cherry low down and dark spruce higher up. Highest of all were the bald summits, gray against the green of the trees. When she was a little girl, she always imagined God setting His feet on those peaks, like a boy crossing a creek on stepping stones. The only things strong enough to hold up God were those mountains, she had thought then.

She was pulled from her daydream by Grandma's querulous voice, "Ida! Did you hear me? I said you've got to tell Joe to stop whistling!"

Ida walked over to the wooden kitchen chair by the bed and sat, coming back to herself after her brief sojourn of the spirit to the mountains. "Joe? Just now? Joe was at Mass with us today, and now he's out unharnessing Blaze and helping Dave and the girls shuck corn for dinner. He hasn't been in the house since we got back from church."

"Not Young Joe! My son Joe! The whole time you were at Mass, he was upstairs, whistling. It's not fitting, him upstairs whistling on a Sunday, and everyone else at Mass! You tell him to stop! Tell him I said to!"

*Not a good day, after all,* Ida thought. She doesn't remember that Joe is dead. Well, she would let her live in a happier world than Ida's own for a little while. "All right, Grandma. I'll tell him."

"Go do it now, Ida," the old woman replied. "I don't know what he's thinking. Whistling on a Sunday, and the priest coming for dinner!"

"All right, Grandma," Ida said again. "I will." She stood up. "I'll go check how the girls are doing with getting dinner ready. As soon as Father gets here, I'll bring him back so you can take Communion before you eat. I'll be back soon." She kissed the old woman's cheek absently, then headed out through the open door.

"Don't forget to tell Joe!" Otillia called as she left. "Tell him I said to stop whistling!"

Ida turned and looked at her. "I'll go do it now, dear," she said. "I'll let him know it bothers you. You rest, now, before Father gets here." She walked through the parlor and out into the hall toward the kitchen, but as she came to the foot of the stairs, she stopped. Suddenly, she began climbing them, before she could think the better of it, step after step, as fast as her tired heart would let her. At the top of the stairs, she walked around the stairwell, until she reached the attic stairs. Breathing hard now, she climbed those stairs slowly, pushing aside the heavy door that blocked the opening up into the attic. She walked across the attic floor, around the stove pipe that led from the parlor stove, through the attic, and out through the roof. At last she reached the attic's only window, directly above the window in Grandma's room, the one that faced west. She stood at the window, listening to the whistler, as she gazed unseeing toward the mountains. Then she whispered, "Joe? Joe, your mother says to stop whistling." No voice answered, but gradually the whistling grew softer and fainter, until it stopped altogether.

## SEPTEMBER

Ida carefully placed teaspoons of molasses cookie dough onto her iron cookie sheet as the intermittent sounds of hammering and of men's voices came into the kitchen from above. The haying was finished. The weather had been good in August, with only a few showers, none of which had lasted more than half a day. Now it was early September, and the men were working on finishing the last bit of the roof, hurrying to get it done before it was time to dig the potatoes.

Ida dropped the last of the dough on the sheet and slid it into the oven. It didn't take cookies long to bake, so she took the opportunity to sit down and rest. She would have a reason to be sitting, she thought resentfully, if Jake were to come into the kitchen. There wasn't time to start on another task before she would need to check the cookies. Ill health was no excuse, as far as Jake was concerned. He would be sure to nag her if he found her "taking it easy" in the middle of the day.

Ida still hadn't recovered her strength from the illness she had endured for most of August. She had caught a summer cold when she went into town with Dave and the girls to see a movie on one of the rare rainy days that summer. She had felt low, with muscle aches, fever, a bad cough, and a short temper for two weeks. When she didn't feel better, and with the cough actually getting worse, she had gone to see Doc Hershey. He diagnosed her with bronchitis and ordered her to bed before it turned into pneumonia. She wasn't able to go on bed rest completely, of course. There was too much to be done, and the girls couldn't do all the housework and take care of Grandma on their own. But she had rested more than usual, and after she had seen the doctor, she had spent five solid days in bed except for tasks that were absolutely necessary for her to do or oversee. Now, in the first week in September, she felt like she might finally be getting well again.

While she had been resting in bed, she had had time to think about the whistler in the attic. When her cough had been at its worst, she had felt cloudy headed, like there was a thick cheesecloth curtain between her brain and the world. She had lain in her bedroom, the one that had been hers and Joe's, and listened to the whistler. Everyone else had been at work in the hayfields, with the girls turning the hay in the windrows to help it dry faster, the boys forking the dried hay onto the hay wagons, and Jake driving the team. At milking time, one of the girls and one of the boys would bring in the cows and milk while Jake and the other boy got in one last load of hay before nightfall. The older girl who was not milking, helped by Arlene, would get supper ready and see to Grandma. With everyone but her and Grandma gone from the house for most of the day, Ida felt like the girl in Tennyson's poem, "Mariana": dreary and aweary and nervously aware of the little sounds and small presences in the empty farmhouse. In her surreal state of mind, she felt it the most ordinary thing in the world that a ghost should haunt her with whistling.

Though it was fickle, sometimes not sounding at all for two or three days at a time, the whistling, when it did come, kept her company and gave her comfort. Otillia's occasional spells of singing and talking to people who weren't there were far more eerie than the sounds that came to her from two floors above her bedroom. Otillia, after all, was preparing for the momentous leap from physical life to the Afterlife. The old woman seemed stuck halfway, not quite in the Afterlife, but barely in Life, either. Joe, as she now thought of the whistler, had made the leap boldly and suddenly, charging into Death as boldly and suddenly as he had done most things in life. Now, she felt sure, he was coming back to encourage and comfort her when the ordinary work of day-to-day life seemed almost more than her strength and courage could bear.

With all the hammering, talking, and heavy work boots tromping up on the roof, Ida couldn't hear the whistler, but she felt sure he was there. She might not be able to hug him, talk to him, or even see him, but the warm, loved feeling she had, knowing that Joe was there and still cared about her and the children, stayed with her whether she heard him or not. She kept joy in her heart, a tiny treasure, and it sustained her throughout the long days. Someone knew how hard she worked, and appreciated it, not like the children, who knew only their own cares and struggles, or Jake, for whom her best efforts were never good enough. Joe was with her in his whistling, and his whistling told her that he still loved her.

Ida pulled herself to her feet on the edge of the kitchen table to go and check on the cookies. The boys would be wanting a snack after working on the roof, and she needed to make sure that the treats were not burned. She had just taken the last batch of cookies out of the oven when Dave came charging through the porch door and in to the kitchen, letting the screen door bang and bounce behind him. "David!" Ida admonished. "How many times have I told you not to let the screen door slam like that! You'll break the frame, and the flies are bad enough in here already!"

"Sorry, Ma!" Dave said breezily. "But you'll never guess! We found out what's whistling in the attic!"

Ida's heart gave a lurch that was almost painful. "You ... you found ..." she stuttered. Not "who"; Dave had said "what." She tottered away from the stove to rest her hands heavily on the table top.

Dave was unaware of the shock his announcement had given his mother. "Come up to the attic, Ma! You've got to see this!"

Ida slowly followed her son up the stairs to the second floor, then on to the attic. How many times had she climbed those stairs, looking for what wasn't there? As she climbed, she heard the whistling start up, thin and clear. When she got up to the attic, Dave was already at the open window, hanging halfway out and talking excitedly to his cousin Herm Schoff, who was up on the roof. "Well, what do you want to show me?" Ida gasped. The climb up the stairs had winded her.

Dave moved aside so that Ida could lean out the window. "Look! Right there! Show her, Herm!"

Black-haired and gray-eyed Herm leaned perilously far over the eaves of the roof and grinned at her, upside down. "Hello, Aunt Ida! Look at the knothole in this rafter! That's where your whistling is coming from. When the wind blows just right, it goes through the hole and whistles, just like a man whistling!" Herm put his hand over the knothole, and the whistling stopped abruptly. He moved his hand away, and the whistling started up again. Just like a man whistling.

"We're lucky we were up here when the wind was blowing in just the right direction, or we'd never have found it," Dave said. "The knot must have got knocked loose when we were up here working on the roof in July."

Ida took a deep breath. "Well, well. A knothole and the wind. I'm glad that you figured it out."

"What do you want us to do about it, Aunt Ida?" Herm asked. "Should we leave it?"

"No," Ida said, almost sharply. "Don't leave it. Nail something over it. That whistling gets on my nerves, and it makes Grandma fretful. There's a tin can lid on the kitchen counter, from the can of peaches we had for breakfast this morning. Use that to cover it up."

Waiting for her son to return from the kitchen with the lid, Ida stood at the window and watched the mountains. Her face showed no more emotion than the stone of the mountains, but in her throat was a tight lump that she could not swallow. She felt lost and bereft, abandoned all over again. Joe wasn't there; maybe God wasn't there. All she had was herself, after all, and she wasn't sure that would be enough. Gazing at the mountains, she willed them into herself, making granite of muscle and sinew. *Be like stone*, she told herself. Like a gravestone. Like the mountains.

Stonily she watched as Dave and Herm worked together to silence the whistler, with Herm holding the can lid in place from the roof and Dave leaning out of the attic window and stretching to drive two nails, above and below, to hold it securely in place on the rafter. When they had finished, Ida forced a smile. "Thank you, boys. I'll rest easier now that I know what made that noise. And that I won't have to listen to it any-more." She straightened her shoulders and took a deep breath. "Well. Are you two hungry? See if Unk will let you come down and have some cook-ies. I just finished baking them. They should still be warm from the oven."

That evening, after the table was cleared, the supper dishes washed, the floor swept, and her family gathered around the radio in the parlor, Ida walked out behind the house to the flat rock where she liked to sit and watch the sun go down. This time she didn't pray, not for the soul of baby Mary, nor for Joe, nor even to God for the strength to endure all that He had put on her. She just watched the mountains, and the sun setting behind them, thinking of nothing. She sat like that for a long time, her mind blank and empty. A thought came then, out of nothing, like the wind. The mountains are God's stepping-stones. They are the only things strong enough to hold up God. Them, and you, Ida.

She sat for a little longer, watching the mountains that were the first things she remembered seeing as a child and that would be standing long after she lay in the stony earth. Such comfort as there was to be had in the world came from them. They, and she, were God's stepping-stones, taking the weight of His unfathomable Will. The mountains endured. She would, too. She bowed her head to her friends and teachers, with the fading sun glowing red across their stony brows, then she stood up, smoothed her skirts, and walked back to her family.

# 10

# DEFCON 1

## *Woody Sins*

THE 556TH STRATEGIC MISSILE SQUADRON WAS OPERATIONAL FROM October 1, 1961 to June 25, 1965. Twelve Atlas type F silos, ten of which were in the Adirondacks, were hewn into solid rock, 154 feet deep, and 74 feet wide. These were the only ICBM installations east of the Mississippi River, and were built to bring the western part of the Soviet Union into range of the nuclear-tipped missiles.

Staff Sergeant Jed Lambert's upper lip was sweating, as he sat deep inside the man-made cavern hollowed out of solid gneiss. He watched the readouts with apprehension as the mighty silver missile slowly emerged from its coffin into the clear Adirondack air. This was no propellant-loading exercise. The white tip on the gleaming monster was no dummy load.

This was real.

Lambert had signed up for the U.S. Air Force (USAF) because his father's farm in Kansas had failed to entice him, and he couldn't afford college. He was intrigued by the occasional sight of the huge new Atlas missiles that sprouted out of the prairie from time to time, so he requested, and got, an assignment to Missile command. After basic training, he was assigned to the missile training school and earned his security clearance. He had hoped to be assigned to the air force base in Salina, near his home, after he completed his training. Instead, he was assigned to the 556th Strategic Missile Squadron in Plattsburg, New York, which was about as far removed from Kansas as possible, both physically and geographically.

Vladimir Demyanovitch was more familiar with the terrain. As a KGB agent, he was trained in the arts of the outdoorsman for his special missions. His current mission was of vital importance to the Soviet Union, and to the Party. This mission was also personal to him. These missiles hidden deep under the Upstate New York terrain were the only ones the United States had that could reach his family in Ukraine. Under no circumstances could he fail. If he did, he knew his duty, and he had the cyanide capsule sewn into his shirt to assist him in this duty should he fail.

Staff Sergeant Lambert had gotten used to the tranquility of the Adirondack Mountains surrounding his post at 556-6, near AuSable Forks—that is, when he wasn't being run ragged in keeping the missile systems in readiness. Action has really picked up since the fall, when the Soviets placed IRBMs in Cuba, bringing the United States and the Soviet Union to the brink of war. Propellant-loading, or PLX, drills were frequent, and the pressure was on. Also, a rumor that someone was apprehended in the pine woods near the silo was making its rounds. This person hadn't given a good account of himself, and was allegedly detained by the site guards, and then mysteriously died en route to the base in Plattsburg. No one would give the real story, though, and life at the silo continued in its frantic pace.

Vladimir climbed back through the hole he made in the fence around the perimeter of the 556-6 site with all of the stealth he could. It was dawn, after a cool late summer night. His disguise as a hiker had served him well, thus far. He had accomplished his mission, and needed to exit the area, fast. Suddenly, a klaxon rang out, and the massive doors that protected the missile began to slowly open. The noise startled him, and he tripped on a fallen tree, twisting his ankle in the process. He shouted out in pain, then immediately regretted it. Almost instantly, a patrolling guard was upon him. His ankle was now throbbing. Flight into the forest was not possible. He had been captured.

Armageddon was upon them. The launch console indicated that the Launch Control Center had gotten the coded message that all had feared. The Atlas SM-65F was now almost to the top, and Captain Ben Bolt, the Missile Combat crew commander, and his deputy stood with their keys ready: keys that would initiate the Commit sequence and the launch.

As the jeep bounced along the road to the base, Vlad worked the seam of his jacket. He had been briefly questioned in one of the large Quonset huts at the silo site, but apparently the interrogator was not satisfied with the answers. He was also in a hurry to evacuate the area, since the site seemed to be on high alert. Something larger than a spy was afoot. All nonessential personnel, along with the prisoner, were leaving the immediate area in a great hurry. The convoy was moving as fast as the road conditions would allow. Suddenly, the jeep was almost run off the road by an air force staff car, going recklessly fast in the other direction. The jeep driver cursed, and continued on his way.

After what seemed like hours, the gleaming rocket finally rose through the massive blast doors and reached the cap. Its gleaming aluminum body and white tip stood in stark, almost obscene contrast to the pine-covered peaks of the surrounding mountains, yet it had its own sinister beauty. Its warhead, a 3.75-megaton thermonuclear bomb, was poised to annihilate millions of people half a world away. Staff Sergeant Lambert also knew that, as soon as they launched, the Soviet radar would start tracking the missile, and a retaliatory strike would soon follow. The AuSable Forks silo was a prime target. The LLC and silo was designed to survive all but a direct hit from a nuclear blast, but even if the launch crew did survive, they would not exit the LCC to the pristine wilderness that now surrounded them, but to a blasted lunar landscape under the brown-gray pall of nuclear winter. How had it come to this?

Finally, the seam of his jacket had come undone. Vlad discreetly slipped the capsule into his mouth and soon slipped into darkness.

The Atlas sat poised with its monstrous payload. The liquid oxygen had been loaded, and the tip of the missile was shrouded in the condensed water vapor caused by the LOX venting. All that was left was to receive confirmation of launch. A quick turn of the two keys, and World War III would begin.

Suddenly there was a pounding on the blast door leading from the LCC. Captain Bolt started, and went to the door. The blast door was thicker than a safe vault, so whoever was pounding was doing so with great urgency to make it heard through the door. He opened the small door, next to the larger one, and saw the ID badge that had been placed behind it. It was the ID of Colonel Garant, the base commander. He checked the TV monitor. It was the old man, all right. The colonel was yelling at the top of his lungs. "ABORT!!!" With a very audible sigh of relief, the crew began to de-fuel and lower the beast into its confines, close the enormous doors, and return to standby.

The colonel immediately ordered a complete diagnostic of the control systems. It seems that the order to launch was a false alarm, narrowly averted when a USAF aircraft flying overhead reported the silo doors open, and the site had begun the launch sequence. Efforts to radio the site went unanswered, so the colonel personally drove through the rough Adirondack roads to stop the launch. The site was soon swarming with technicians and top brass. The warhead of the missile was removed, and the missile itself was soon on a transport back to Plattsburg.

Staff Sergeant Lambert tore into the launch control instrumentation immediately. Cabinets were opened, and the electronics within were tested and retested. Sabotage was high on everyone's mind. The person who was apprehended had not been identified, although it was clear that he was not a U.S. citizen. Had he somehow gained access to the LCC and initiated the bogus launch? There was no indication that he had done so before he was caught. If it wasn't him, then what was it?

The UHF launch control radio equipment was checked. It all seemed in order, except only a very weak signal was detected from the transmitter. It could receive nothing. Lambert was sent to the top of the antenna to investigate. There he found the answer. The wires that connected the small UHF antenna to the radio were cut through. The wire cutters that had done the job were found in the dirt beside a small hole in the chain link fence. The culprit had done his work with great skill. All of the chaos caused by the sabotage would keep the missile launch complex off line for months. Ukraine was safe, for the moment.

That particular mystery was solved, but it didn't explain how the order to launch was received, if the radio was dead. More system teardowns followed.

After many nervous hours with all the top brass looking on, the problem was finally located. One of the ever-present deer mice that make their home in the Adirondack clearings had somehow gotten inside the cooling vents for the electronics, and gnawed through some critical wiring, and electrocuted itself in the process. This caused a short, which gave a false launch signal. "Poor little runt. Almost caused the death of the planet!" said Lambert as he removed the mouse carcass by the tail.

After that, permission was granted to add another crew member to the LCC personnel, a tabby cat named Boomer.

# 11

# Snowy Mountain Retreat

### *Daniel Swift*

Sitting around the campfire, the scouts of Troop 28 listened intently to the ghost stories being told. The crackling of the fire and the howls of the brisk air set the mood for such an evening.

The soft moonlight glistened off the waters of Indian Lake as each boy, holding tightly to their marshmallow stick over the fire, took their turn to tell a story. The smell of burning marshmallows and chocolate wafted through the smoke of the fire and into the noses of them all. It was as if they were smoking s'mores in a meat smoker.

As the evening drew on, at the climax of one of the stories, a loud crash from the cooking pots startled them all nearly to pieces. An older boy, Greg, had waited for a scary moment in the story and knocked over the pots to scare everyone out of their seats.

"You're a jerk, Greg!" said Jerry through a heavily frightened breath.

Laughing, the scoutmaster said, "Okay, boys. I've got one more story for you before we turn in for the night. The boys moaned a groan that was their way of saying they did not want to go to bed yet.

"Okay, boys, settle down," he said sternly. He paused and then continued, "You all know that cabin up there by Snowy Mountain?"

"You mean the old lodge that my parents said they used to visit?" replied Jerry.

"The very same. Well, some years back a couple rented out that cabin for a weekend just before a big snowstorm. It is a true story, so why don't I tell it from the beginning," the scoutmaster stated as he shifted on the log he was sitting on. Then he began to tell the story as if he was there. Changing his voice to be in his spookiest storytelling voice, he continued.

🌲🌲🌲

Kacey and Samantha were a happy couple that were lost in everyday life. So, they decided that it was time for a weekend getaway. A retreat in the mountains.

"Kacey, I cannot wait until we get back to the cabin. It has been too long since we've been there," Samantha said, as she poured herself a glass of red wine.

Sitting in her dining room, across from the love of her life, she sat there gazing into his eyes as they ate. Their table, set for two, was nestled near the window with a great view of the children playing in the park across the street. Their home was modern and clean with the pungent smell of fresh paint wafting throughout.

In his quiet reservation, Kacey nodded. Then clearing his throat, he said, "You're right, babe. It has been far too long. Between work and . . ." He hesitated for a moment. "Well, time sure does fly by. We need this weekend in the mountains. Just the two of us."

Kacey had served in the Marines after high school. He was proud of his time serving his country and fell in love with the wilderness while enlisted. Being a city boy, his outdoor life never really consisted of actually roughing it in the wilderness, but rather camping in luxury in some campground for RVs.

🌲🌲🌲

"Sounds like Harry!" one of the younger kids interrupted with a chuckle.

"Oh, shut up!" replied Harry.

The scoutmaster gave them a stern look that told them to cut it out and then continued to tell his story.

🌲🌲🌲

After getting out of the Marines, Kacey landed a civilian job at the old air force base in Rome, New York. With all his training and survival skills, Kacey was perfect for a job training those skills to the Department of

Environmental Conservation (DEC), Fish and Wildlife Management, and local Search and Rescue teams. Aside from that, he made time to give back to the Boy Scouts and was the instructor most sought after for teaching Wilderness Survival, among other merit badges.

Now, Samantha grew up in Rome and loved the Adirondacks. Her father used to take her to climb a different mountain every summer, and eventually she earned her way into the 46ers.

After college, Sam became a schoolteacher and spent her free time going out on the lakes as much as possible. Mostly, she would kayak on Delta Lake due to its proximity, but she would frequent the Adirondack lakes and streams as much as she could.

One day, Sam had decided to attend a wilderness survival course and mountain-climbing weekend retreat that was led by Kacey. It did not even take the whole weekend for them to fall for each other and they were married a year later.

"Well babe, we should probably get some sleep. Gotta head out early tomorrow," Kacey said as he turned off the television.

"Yeah. Finally, back to the cabin," she mumbled through her audible yawn.

Kacey helped Sam up from the couch, held her tight, kissing her on the head. "I know, love. That place means a lot to me, too. No place is better than the quiet solitude of Snowy Mountain Retreat." Then they went off to bed.

In the morning, Kacey awoke early with the sunrise, as always, and made eggs and bacon. Between the smell of sizzling bacon and the fresh brewed coffee that filled their home, it was hard pressed to not mistake it for the smell of a small diner in some quaint Adirondack town.

On such a chilly morning, sunlight warmed the dining room as they enjoyed their breakfast. Kacey was looking at the weather reports on his phone. "Seems like that storm is supposed to stay north of Indian Lake. But we will bring the extra supplies just in case, babe."

"Okay. I packed warm. But we better not be doing anything but keeping each other warm this weekend anyway," she replied in a sultry voice.

"That is why we love the Snowy Mountain Retreat so much, babe. No cell service. No neighbors nearby. Nothing. . . . Just you, me, a crackling fire, and the mountain to keep us company."

"Mmhmm. Sounds like paradise to me, babe. I am tired of all the noise and distractions."

After finishing their coffee, Sam cleared the table and put all the dishes into the dishwasher while Kacey packed up the truck. Kacey had an old '90s Chevy pickup that he restored from top to bottom. Besides Sam, that truck was probably Kacey's prized possession, and although it was winter and there was salt on the roads, Kacey undercoated and rubberized the truck so much . . . he never hesitated to drive it in the winter.

"Anything else you got that needs to be put in the truck? Last call!" Kacey exclaimed in his dry humor from the front door.

"Just these bags here, love. Oh, and the snacks for the ride."

"Oh, of course. Must have the snacks." he said, with a chuckle.

"That's fine. I'll eat all the m&m's and trail mix myself then."

"Now let's not get greedy, babe."

Setting off down Route 49 through Utica, swinging north on 12 and then northeast on 8, they breathed sighs of decompression and inhaled the fresh essences that the Adirondacks offered to those who visited. Something that always reinvigorated their souls every time they trekked out of the city and into the woods.

"What's it been? Three years since we have been up to the cabin?" Samantha asked.

"Yeah. I think since the summer after we got married."

"Jeez, I cannot wait to take in the gorgeous view of Indian Lake from that bay window again."

The Snowy Mountain Retreat is set back from Indian Lake about four miles into the woods. The cabin is nestled in the deep forest, with Snowy Mountain as the backdrop from the window or the porch. And there was nothing but valley views and the stunning Indian Lake on the other side.

There is not much there other than the cabin itself and the wilderness that surrounds it. That is probably the reason it was booked out most of the year. City slickers visited the mountains for some much-needed connection to the earth and a break from the world of technology.

Turning off Route 30, Kacey stopped and flipped on the four-wheel drive. Getting up the long road to the cabin was no small feat in the summer, but here in the winter, it was even harder. The seasonal road was only kept up by the owners of the cabin.

But for those who were looking for that escape, the crushed rock road beneath the snow was worth the trek. It was like the yellow brick road to the Emerald City and the cabin was the wizard, ready to give you the courage to let your mind rest and your heart breathe again.

"Looks like they must have plowed this morning for us," Kacey said through his chilly breaths as he got back into the truck.

"Yeah, just take it easy up the road. Don't think for one minute I am pushing this truck out of any ditches," Sam exclaimed.

"Yeah, yeah. I got this, babe. No need for you to mess up that pretty manicure of yours."

Driving up the narrow roadway, through the snow-covered trees, sunlight peered through the clouds and warmed the scenic views of the southern Adirondack woods. The stunning beauty of it all was exactly what they needed. It melted away the worries of the world and brought about a calming sensation. Tranquility through the evergreens.

"Can you feel it, babe? Can you feel that feeling of being home?" Sam asked as they pulled up to the end of the road, parked, and then stepped out of the truck.

As they stretched in front of the log cabin hidden deep in the woods, the smell of fresh snowfall and wintery pine was all around. The soft sounds of the trees swaying in the cold winds was all that they could hear for miles.

Snowy Mountain Retreat was a rather large cabin for its remote location. As you entered from the lofted front porch, you could see it was filled with all kinds of Adirondack furniture, moose print curtains, and bear skin rugs. Warm and cozy Native American woven blankets lay on each couch, and there was a fireplace that seemed to be plucked straight out of the Hallmark movies . . . hearth and all.

On the other side of the cabin, with the mountain framed through the kitchen window like a painting, there was a pellet stove in the corner. On the back deck, two Adirondack-style chairs sat with a wooden table between them. It was a perfect place to warm yourself with a cup of coffee and watch the sunset over the mountain.

Off the kitchen were the bedrooms and bathroom. Décor matching the rest of the cabin filled the lodge. A dreamcatcher hung beside each bed, and over the giant log headboards were paintings of loons on Indian Lake.

Setting their bags on the bed, Kacey told Sam to unpack the food in the kitchen. Neatly, Kacey hung the clothing in the closet and placed them in the dresser drawers. He hid the suitcases behind the clothes in the closet and placed their emergency bag by the front door.

Samantha brewed some tea and made some ham sandwiches for them. "Hey, Kacey, want to eat lunch on the deck?" she asked from the kitchen.

"Yeah, that sounds good, babe. I'll build us a fire quickly and meet you out there."

Kacey grabbed some wood from beside the fireplace and built a crackling fire to warm the chill out of the place. He also set the thermostat for the pellet stove to 68 degrees and slid the sliding door open to join Sam on the deck.

Sipping the warm tea, clenching the cup tight in her hands for the warmth, Samantha gazed out into the vast wintery mountainside. "It is really something . . . the sense of peace. My soul feels at ease here."

As he sat down, letting out a slight sigh of relief, Kacey replied, "I know exactly what you mean, love."

The hours slipped away, and the two of them soaked up the silence between the breaking winds. As the sun set over Snowy Mountain, they enjoyed a nice meal and some rose wine. The fireplace crackled in the background making the light dance about the room. Light and shadow synchronized in harmony in a ballet set to the warmth and sounds of a roaring fire.

The time spent unplugged in the cabin with no communication sources, no good cell service, was just the break they longed for. Too long, they had been draining themselves into their work. Their friendships. Their families.

"I think I'm going to go to bed," Sam said through a loud yawn and a stretch.

"Yeah, I guess we should go to bed," Kacey said as he got up. He stoked the fire and placed the fire cage in front of the fireplace.

"You got it all set?"

"Yeah, babe. I will be in shortly."

"Okay, I'll see you in bed," Samantha said as she walked toward the bedroom.

Sam climbed into the bed and fell fast asleep. The sound of silence and the warmth of the Adirondacks made it easy for her to drift off.

Hours slipped by, and Samantha awoke to a chill creeping throughout the cabin. "Kacey . . . mm Kacey . . . it is cold in here." She said through her exhausted morning alertness.

After hearing no reply, she rolled over to wake Kacey, but he was not there. In her silent study of the room, she could tell that he had never made it to bed. "Kacey! Are you still in the living room?" she yelled to no reply.

She slithered out of bed and out of the bedroom, bundling beneath her robe to keep warm. When she reached the end of the doorway, she could see that the front door was open, and snow had worked its way in beyond the threshold.

Confused, she peered out the front door to see that overnight the storm must have rolled south and hit them after all. For yesterday there was just a few inches of snow outside but now there was at least two feet. The trees glistened in the sparkle of the soft sunlight and the heavy icicles hung from every surface. The wintery wonderland was cold and was chilling her to the bone.

"Kacey? Kacey!? Are you out here?" she yelled out from the doorway.

After a few attempts, she closed the door and went to the fireplace. The embers of the fire were still smoldering beneath the ash. She added a log and stoked the ashes, breathing life into the fireplace once again.

*He must be out gathering some wood or something*, she thought to herself as she examined the cabin for Kacey. He couldn't have gone far.

As the chill in the cabin disappeared and the warmth returned to her fingers and toes, Sam began to really worry. Kacey wouldn't have gone anywhere. He wouldn't have left without leaving at least a note.

She opened the curtain covering the bay window and saw that the truck was still there but barely visible buried beneath snow. There were no fresh tracks or visible disturbances either, and the firewood was still where the owner had stacked it.

She looked down at the foot of the door, and the survival pack was still sitting there. "Where the hell is Kacey?" she asked aloud.

Quickly she took account of anything that was out of place. Any disturbance. Any clue to where her husband had been. She could see the blanket he was using last night as they snuggled had been folded and placed on the back of the couch. Over by the door were his jacket and boots. He couldn't have gone far.

"Kacey! If this is some sick joke you're playing on me, well, it is not funny!" she yelled in a scared anger. "I swear to God, Kacey!"

Hastily pacing from room to room, corner to corner, Samantha looked for Kacey, but he was nowhere to be found. It just did not make sense to her. *Where is he?* she thought.

As the sun faded back behind the next wave of wintery snowstorm and the desperation of the unknown crept deeper into her mind, it began to race. Is he okay? Where is he? How far could he have gone? Where are the keys to the truck? Is there any cell service?

Really understanding that she needed to get some assistance in finding Kacey, she said aloud to only her own ears: "I need to get help, but there is too much snow out there now and no cell service to call anyone."

"If you ever find yourself in a situation where you cannot see a solution ... remember to stay calm. You need to collect yourself mentally before you can find a solution," she recalled Kacey saying at his survival lecture that she had taken all those years ago.

Slowing her breathing and calming her thoughts, she began to find her composure. The lessons she had absorbed, both from her father and her husband over the years, were still there. Even if she didn't realize it, she was listening to their survival rantings, and in this moment, they began to take shape.

Grabbing the survival pack and tossing it onto the table, she took count of the supplies inside. "One 100-foot roll of paracord rope, a compass and Adirondack map, one flashlight, first aid kit, glowsticks, duct tape, one black-and-one orange ..." she murmured aloud. "One MRE

(Meal Ready to Eat), water purification tablets, a rain poncho, flint and steel, a multitool, and a knife," she continued.

"He didn't take anything out of the pack," she said as she looked off into space for a moment in deep thought.

*Okay. If he went anywhere, he probably went west up the mountain. Probably to the Fire Tower to get better cell reception or to signal someone*, she thought to herself. "But why would he need to go there?" she mumbled aloud and then took a pause. "Why?"

Packing up all the supplies back into the pack, she wrangled her wild imagination from the bucking bronco it had become and tamed it. Settled and with a clear heading for which she planned to search, Samantha put on her warm winter gear and shut the door behind her. Leave the safety and comfort behind her in hope of finding Kacey.

The icy chill in the air nearly took her breath away as she walked down the front steps. The smell of fresh snow was like smelling fresh linen but with a dry, chapped aftereffect. She began to breathe shallowly, so that the cold icy air did not continue to freeze inside her lungs.

By now, the day had crested and the afternoon was in full swing. Trudging forward, through the thick snowfall, Sam plowed her way to the west. Into the uncertainty of the winter wilderness . . . without knowing if she would even find her lost husband or perish trying.

Each footstep was a gamble. For one step, she would skate atop the snow, and the next, she would sink up to her knee. Every time it faltered, snow was jammed into her pant legs and boots, freezing her to the bone and, in turn, turning her clothing into essentially ice packs.

Breathing heavy, streams of icy smoke rushing from her mouth like that of a dragon, she gathered herself with each passing breath. No signs of Kacey anywhere. She was working through the journey in her mind. Am I sure that Kacey would have gone this way?

Through her shivers, from the wind that whipped through the trees she recalled, "Sam, if when the sun is setting, and you need to gauge the amount of time before darkness falls, you need to do this." She then removed her glove and raised her hand up to the sky.

With her index and her pinky, she placed the index upon the spot where the sun could be seen through the clouds and rested the pinky along the horizon. "This unit of measurement is roughly one hour of time. If from where the sun sits there is space below the pinky, then do the same with your other hand to gauge the next hour of time."

Still holding her hand to the sky, she measured about two hours of light left before nightfall. *I need to turn back.* She knew that soon the darkness would take over and she could tell that she would not survive the night if she did not go back.

*I need to eat this quickly*, she said to herself while pulling out the MRE. Sam ate just enough to subdue the grizzly bears that were drawing in her stomach.

Her body weary and exhausted but her mind still pacing from "where is Kacey" to "what am I doing," Sam knew she could not stay still too long or she would not be able to muster the strength for the return trek.

Sam could hardly feel her toes. Between the sweat she generated and the snow that melted in her boots, her frozen waterlogged extremities were nearly immobile. The feeling of hypothermia was really taking shape.

Terrified, she recalled another survival tip, "When hypothermia takes hold, your body shifts the blood out of your extremities and into your major organs for warmth."

"I have to get up and go now," she mumbled almost incoherently through her chattering teeth. "Kacey wouldn't want me to die out here."

"So wait . . . why does this story have a lot of the stuff you have been teaching us in it?" interrupted Gavin.

"Happy coincidence, I suppose," the scoutmaster replied with a smirk and then continued.

Samantha gathered herself and, keeping the sun at her back, headed east toward the cabin. Abandoning her quest to find Kacey out here was something she knew was right. For if she ventured forth, she would most certainly meet her demise.

For what seemed like an eternity, she walked slowly back toward the cabin. The wind whistled and swirled past her while nipping at her nose and chapping her lips.

The smell of snow no longer was something that gave her freedom but, rather, was a prison to her senses. She longed to be home in Rome with Kacey. To be sitting beside the window overlooking the park. To be gazing longingly into Kacey's eyes once again.

"Kacey . . . Kacey . . . where are you?" she moaned as she crested the last hill before the sight of the cabin was in range. *Where is he? Where is he?* she continued in her head.

As her toes began burning from the cold, she was back at the cabin. But something was different. Something was not the same.

The cabin looked unkempt. The rustic beauty was now cold and worn. The wood was weathered and cracked beneath her feet as she stumbled up the steps to the door. Waves of decaying smells traveled throughout the air and turned her stomach.

Puzzled, she stopped at the door and looked back out at the driveway. The wood pile was knocked over and looked as if it had been like that for years. Kacey's truck was still there but the paint was sun faded and rusty. "What the hell is going on?" she said aloud.

Turning around, she grabbed the door handle and slowly opened the door. The loud creaking of the door startled her. She slowly peered into the cabin.

No longer was the cabin warm and inviting but, rather, dark and dreary. Curtains were torn from the windows and the furniture was turned about the room. Lamps were on the floor, and the fireplace hearth was broken.

"Kacey!" she hesitantly said aloud, stepping through the doorway.

Samantha tried the light switch, but nothing happened. Nothing but darkness lingered. Shuffling through her bag, she took out the flashlight and turned it on, blinding herself for a moment.

As she pointed the single stream of light toward the kitchen, she could see it was in shambles. Cabinets were torn down, and the fridge was open. Smears of dark red, almost dark cherry red, were about the room. And that smell of decay was more prominent the closer she got.

*What the hell is going on? What happened here?* she questioned in her mind.

Slowly she crept closer and closer toward the refrigerator. The countertop was covered in the same dry red smears, and the window that faced the mountain was broken; glass shards were all over the sink.

Grasping the fridge door, she swung around and peered inside. The soupy mess of dead rats and mice that had decayed and petrified to the shelves was the cause for the smell. "Oh my God!" she yelled as she slammed the door shut and covered her mouth and nose.

From the bedroom, she heard a creaking that sounded like someone walking. "Kacey! Is that you?" she questioned with reservation.

Slowly she moved toward the bedroom, grabbing a kitchen knife that was still on the counter. "Kacey . . . is that you?"

With the tip of the knife, she pushed the door open to the room. To her astonishment, it was just as she remembered. Although it was now covered in a heavy blanket of dust.

She shined the flashlight into the closet, to find the suitcase and her clothing were still hanging neatly on the hangers. Although it was as if they had been there for years untouched.

*What happened here?* she thought again.

Suddenly the wind howled, and the cabin shifted. The icy chills blew throughout, and the tiny hairs on the nape of her neck stood up. Her breath poured from her tightly clenched teeth like smoke as she crept back into the living room.

"Hello? Is there anyone there?" she asked in an almost whisper.

Dashing the flashlight from side to side . . . stopping momentarily on things just long enough to see what they were, her heart rate quickened and she began to sweat. Without even noticing, she began to cry. Not sure as to why but the fear that crawled inside her mind was turning her into a petrified mess.

As she slumped upon the floor, tears welled in her eyes; she could not understand what was going on. The cabin was in shambles, and Kacey was nowhere to be found. The dried red substance that was all over the place now has become more noticeably old blood, and Samantha was lost in the depths of perpetual horrified wonder.

*Where is Kacey? What happened? Did something happen? Did I kill him?*
*I couldn't have killed him.* All these questions danced about her mind as her flashlight slowly faded into the darkness.

"Oh, no. Not now. Please. Please. Please!" she stammered as she fumbled with the batteries to no avail. She inevitably sat there alone. Alone and tormented by the blinding darkness and the unanswered questions that plagued her mind.

Suddenly the fireplace started to glow, and a flame emerged. The light danced about the cabin, and in the corner of the kitchen was the shape of a man.

The cold swirled around her, and the air grew thin and hard to breathe. Her gaze fixated on the man through the flickering of the fire. *Was that Kacey? Why does he look so weird?*

"Kacey? Is that you?" she asked as she rose to her feet.

The fire flickered again and became brighter, filling more of the room with a soft amber glow. Samantha could see that it was indeed her lost husband in the kitchen. But something was wrong. Something was really wrong.

She crept closer and closer until she could see it clear as day. Kacey had blood all over him, and the knife that was on the counter earlier was now protruding from his chest.

She froze in a moment of despair. And then, to her surprise she was instantly standing in front of Kacey, and she was holding the knife that was still in his chest. The water in his eyes glistened in the glow of the dancing flames behind them.

Kacey struggled to remain standing, whispering through his last breath, "Why? Why?"

The fire flickered once more, and Sam was now standing over Kacey with the bloody knife still in her hand. Shaking, she tossed it onto the counter and stood there sobbing.

Suddenly something caught her attention. A small sound in the distance. She listened intently, focusing on it as it grew closer and louder. It was an almost ticking sound but steady in time.

The louder the sound got, the more it seemed that the darkness that entrapped her was disappearing. A blinding brightness had soon taken over the room, and she struggled to see through her struggling squinted eyes.

🌲🌲🌲

"Sam. You are safe," said the doctor. "I am sorry we had to go through this again. You did great."

Sam sat up and was in a trembling trance. The blinding brightness of the room was hurting her eyes, and the smell of fresh paint tingled her nose.

Behind the desk sat a large man who was taking notes. The doctor had to be about six foot five and weighed about 250 pounds. He almost looked like he could have been an athlete or a Navy Seal.

Behind him on the walls were plaques and diplomas. Bookcases full of old books lined a wall and opposite the bookcases was a window that overlooked a park. Samantha could hear children playing in the distance.

The doctor spoke. "Samantha. You are in Adirondack Psychiatric Hospital for the Criminally Insane. You were found guilty of murdering your husband five years ago. Do you remember that?"

🌲🌲🌲

One of the boys interrupted. "Wait a minute, Mr. Thorburn. Is this story about you?" asked Jerry.

"Why do you ask that?" he replied.

"Well, you had said that their home smelled like paint and overlooked a park . . . and how the hospital is the same," Jerry answered.

"Yes, it is. I was given this case many years ago. And to this day, the authorities still cannot figure out what exactly happened that night. For years, I was trying to get Sam to recount the events and fill in the gaps in the story using hypnotherapy. To have her answer the questions the detectives still had. But she kept taking the surroundings of the hospital and making them part of her story. Each time I tried, it seemed like more questions arose and less were answered. We even took her back to the cabin once so she could see it all again, but she never fully confessed to the murder of Kacey."

As the boys sat there listening to Mr. Thorburn, the winds flowing through the pines faded into a whisper. The glow from the smothering embers of the fire grew dim, and the light from the moon grew more apparent.

"Ah man, that story was not that scary, Mr. Thorburn," proclaimed Bryan, another one of the boys, as he stood up to go to bed.

"Well, Bryan, I did not tell you the scary part."

"Oh, well what is it?" he replied sarcastically.

"She escaped our custody about a year ago, and we haven't been able to find her. Some say she went north to Canada. But not me. I think she came back to Indian Lake. I think she came back to the cabin where Kacey had died. The local folks even say that sometimes they can see smoke coming from that direction." He paused for a moment and then looked across the lake. "And look there!"

In the distance, centered in the moonlight over the silhouette to the treetops, billowed a single stream of smoke. "Look, boys, the cabin fireplace is burning bright as I tell the story of the Snowy Mountain Retreat."

The look of terror filled all their eyes, and Mr. Thorburn creepily stated, "Have fun sleeping tonight, boys. Hope she doesn't make her way over here to find her next victim. Good night!"

"You know that cabin is on the other end of the lake, right?" whispered the assistant scoutmaster to Mr. Thorburn.

"Oh, of course. . . . But they don't," he replied in evil laughter.

12

# Patchwork Prospectors

*Gigi Vernon*

BIRDIE MCALLISTER SURVEYED HER REALM—THE ADIRONDACK HAR-vest Craft Fair at the town hall. As the showrunner (in the common parlance of the day), she aimed to make this fair one to remember. She made her way through the aisles with a clipboard, ascertaining there were no infractions, no manufactured or imported goods, nothing blocking corridors. Greetings were called to old friends and to her, and old rivals studiously ignored each other. A few compliments came her way for the rainbow-hued crocheted dress she wore—couldn't be missed, which was half the point.

The hall was fragrant with baked goods, Christmas decorations, and scented candles and bright with goods for sale—handmade quilts, jewelry, antiques, jams and jellies, Kanien'kehá:ka (used to be called Mohawk in her day) traditional beadwork and pipes, Adirondack chairs and cane baskets, traditional wood carvings, and more. Ladies and gents of the region put the final touches on their booths, helped by their grown daughters or young granddaughters and an occasional son or grandson. All was well. It was going to be a wonderful fair. Her inspection finished, she returned to the entrance and threw open the doors to the public. Up and down Main Street, parking lots were already filling. The day was clear and crisp, the maples ablaze with color.

The roar of a motorcycle distracted her and immediately set her off. There was a noise ordinance in this town—didn't you know? The motorcycle—hog she supposed—was an enormous chrome beast ridden by a figure in glossy black that resembled a rain slicker and a helmet with a mirror visor. It rode abreast and illegally close to some kind of long, low classic convertible painted a pale green with a New York license plate. Both were going more than the speed limit of twenty miles per hour on this stretch of Main Street. Tourists! Where was the sheriff and his deputy when you needed them? Probably staked out on the interstate; that's where they usually were at this time of day on a Saturday.

They parked down at the end, the motorcycle on one side of the street, the convertible on the other. A young man in a black suit, narrow tie, and white shirt climbed out of the car dressed like he'd just attended a funeral or a business meeting. Couldn't be more out of place. Definitely a tourist. The motorcyclist removed the helmet and shook out long blonde hair. A young woman. She glared at the man in the suit. He glared back without speaking. Were they spouses in the midst of a divorce? Opposites attract, sure, but hard to imagine an odder couple.

On high-heeled boots, the young woman strode toward an antique store. On the other side of the street, the young man entered a gift shop.

A few minutes later, she emerged, empty handed. So did he. Watching each other, she dashed into the next shop as did he. And so it continued, antique shop by gift shop, both of them hurrying like their lives depended on it.

What was going on? Rooted to the spot in fascination, Birdie watched. Were they in a race?

They hustled up to Birdie, side by side, eyeing and elbowing each other like kids trying to get ahead of each other in the school cafeteria line.

Birdie stepped in front of them, blocking their entrance. He wore cologne, and she wore thick eyeliner, but now that they were close, there was a faint family resemblance— and it wasn't just their taste in flashy vehicles and their fondness for wearing black and the same unpleasantly arrogant scowl. Birdie never forgot a face, but she couldn't quite dredge up names. These two shared the same bone structure, same restless leanness, same nose, and same shade of eyes. Siblings rather than spouses.

"Tickets, please," Birdie demanded.

"Tickets?" he said, spitting the word, like he was mortally offended.

"How much?" the young woman asked.

"Singles are five or two for eight."

"Single," they said in unison and scowled at each other.

He dug out a money clip from his trouser pocket and peeled off a twenty from a wad. "Keep the change."

"Well, thank you for your donation," Birdie said, fighting the urge to refuse it and not feeling the slightest bit grateful. "You're not from around here. You two from New York City?"

"Not really." The young woman dug in her slick black jacket and brought out a couple of credit cards. "Do you take plastic?"

"Afraid not, dear. Cash only."

The young woman dug through her pockets and produced a fistful of wadded dollars and coins and counted them out into Birdie's palm.

"Thanks. Names?" Birdie asked.

"You need our names for tickets?" he asked, puzzled.

"Yes." Names weren't actually required. Birdie was just being Birdie and Birdie was nosey.

"What if we don't want to give them?" the young woman in leather asked, folding her arms over her chest.

"Then I'll refund your money."

He pressed his lips together.

She glared at Birdie.

He muttered, "Stanley."

So Birdie did know him but she poked anyway. "Last name?"

"Smith."

"And you, dear?" Birdie asked.

"Petra Smith."

"So you're married or siblings?" Birdie asked, pretending she didn't know and not relinquishing the tickets.

Stanley nearly shouted, "Siblings."

"Twins, actually," Petra said.

"Smith. There's a William Smith who founded Smithstown over in Fulton County. You any relation?"

"Smith is a common surname," Stanley said.

Maybe. "Where are you from?"

"Enough with the inquisition," Petra said. "Give us our tickets."

Fair enough. Birdie handed them their tickets.

Petra leaned close and whispered into Birdie's ear, "I'm looking for a quilt."

Craft types came in all shapes, sizes, and colors, sure, but these two? You could have bowled her over. "Quilts, you say?" Birdie said.

Petra winced and cut her gaze toward Stanley.

What was so secret about quilts? "We've got an enormous selection of fine quilts," Birdie said. "There's a map of the hall and vendors posted across from the baked goods booth. What are you looking for? Anything special? Martha Roe does a wonderful Wild Goose Chase quilt. And Samantha does Pinwheel, Log Cabin, Churn and Dash. There's—"

But the twins were not listening. They shoved each other, each trying to get through the door first, and preventing either of them from entering, like cartoon characters. Rude, just rude these youngsters were, like a pair of barn cats. She'd like to pick them up by the scruffs of their necks and. . . . "Hey!" Birdie said. "Where are your manners?"

Ignoring her, Petra pushed through into the hall. Stanley was on her heels.

"This is a family event. We don't want any trouble," Birdie called after them.

They made a beeline for the quilt section, one of the largest sections. Stanley started at one end, Petra at the other.

Stanley stopped at Martha's booth. Obviously puzzled by the sleek young man who looked like an undertaker, Martha tried to be helpful, asking Stanley questions, holding up this item and that, but he rudely ignored her and continued to fling quilts aside, some of which slid to the floor.

Meanwhile, across the aisle at Samantha's booth, Petra was being just as disrespectful, rooting through quilts, leaving behind wreckage. Samantha, who'd always been as shy as a new bride, though she had to be in her forties, became flustered, red faced, and tongue tied. She caught Birdie's eye, and Birdie saw the telltale lower lip tremble.

Birdie approached in time to hear Samantha offer, "I-I take custom orders. . . . If there's something you have in mind . . . I'm on Etsy."

Petra didn't respond and just kept riffling through the wares on display like a terrier frantically digging for a bone.

"Everything all right, here?" Birdie asked.

"Yes," Petra said, rolling her eyes as she stalked off.

Samantha blinked and blew her nose.

"Don't let them get to you," Birdie said.

"I know. I know. It's just.... Well, my quilts didn't win last year. I didn't even place. I've always placed before."

"Doesn't mean anything," Birdie said. "Judging is subjective. You're one of the best quilters in the entire Adirondacks, and don't you forget it."

Birdie wasn't having these two newcomers, who probably wouldn't know a quilting hoop from a hula hoop, wreak havoc on the fragile egos of the artisans showing at the craft fair. They'd need to take their impatient snobbery elsewhere. "Why don't you get a cup of coffee and a slice of pumpkin bread from the baked goods booth? I'll be back to check on you later."

Birdie accosted the twins. "You two. We need to have a word."

They ignored her.

"Harry," Birdie called.

Harry, the fair's volunteer security guard, lumbered over, sucking on a large neon-pink Slurpee and wearing a black-and-white-striped referee shirt that did double duty as a kind of highly visible uniform. Harry was a good kid; he had gone to high school with several of Birdie's grandsons. "Is there a problem?" he asked, his voice mild and gentle.

"What are you going to do? You can't arrest us," Petra said with a sneer and folded her arms over her chest.

"No, you are perfectly correct," Harry said. "I don't have the authority to apprehend malefactors. But I do have the ability to escort you from the premises and request that you never grace us with your presence again, and that would be humiliating and unpleasant for us both. I don't recommend it, personally."

"Okay. Okay." Stanley made a halting gesture. "We don't want any trouble."

"Let's speak in my office," Birdie said.

"If we must," Petra said, rolling her eyes. "Where is your office?"

Birdie didn't have an office. By office, she meant the sidewalk outside of the hall. She took them outside.

"What do you want?" Petra scowled.

"I don't even know your name," Stanley said.

"Thanks for asking. It's Birdie McAllister. I'm in charge of the harvest craft fair. I used to be the principal at the middle school. Now, I run the craft fairs as well as the holiday festival of lights and the summer 5k and 10k run-walks for cerebral palsy. I serve on the town board, and I'm the town librarian and historian. Pleased to meet you." She stuck out her hand.

Stanley took her hand like it would bite and dropped it without actually shaking it.

Petra's grip was firmer but left a lot to be desired.

Where had these kids been raised? "You have to understand. The artisans at the fair put a lot of effort into their crafts and setting up their displays, and you two just bowl through them like toddlers with sticky hands."

"Sorry," Stanley said, brusquely, not seeming the slightest bit contrite.

"So what's all this about? This race the two of you have going on?" Birdie asked.

"There's no race," Petra said.

"We're . . . looking for a gift . . ." Stanley said, obviously improvising. "A birthday gift for our . . ."

"Favorite aunt," Petra said.

They finished each other's sentences in that twin way.

"Plenty of fantastic handmade gifts made with loving care here. Take your pick," Birdie said.

"She's, um, very particular," Stanley said.

"Nope. I don't believe you," Birdie said.

"Our aunt—Priscilla—is very picky," Petra said. "It has to be, um, a certain kind of quilt."

"And what kind would that be?"

"Antique."

"Family heirloom."

Fishy as all get out. "And you're competing with each other to find the right one?" Birdie asked.

"Um. Yes. To see who can impress her the most," Stanley said.

"Nope. Come clean. What are you really up to?"

"No, really, that's it. Honest," Stanley said.

"Cross our hearts," Petra added.

"Hogwash. Would this entail money by chance? An inheritance?" Birdie asked.

Petra widened her eyes, feigning innocence. Stanley looked away.

So it was about money. Go figure. "Antique, you say. Our fine town historical museum has a fine collection of antique quilts."

"Really?" Stanley regarded her with sudden interest, leaning toward her in his eagerness. "Anything acquired recently?"

"The museum is always receiving donations. We happened to receive a very generous donation from the Smith family recently, including some antique quilts."

"That's it! It's got to be it," Petra exclaimed, then clapped her hand over her mouth.

What was it?

"Museum?" Stanley looked at Petra for the first time.

"We didn't think of looking in museums," Petra said, using *we* for the first time.

Stanley turned back to Birdie and began, "What would it take—"

"A museum is not a shop," Birdie interrupted. "We don't sell items from our collections. You can't purchase something as a birthday gift for your Aunt Priscilla—was it?"

"No, of course not. We wouldn't think of it. But maybe we could we just view the quilts? All we need is a look."

A look? So they thought a quilt held some important information? "Museum's closed until Monday," Birdie said.

"Monday!" they exclaimed in horror in unison in that twin way.

"We can't wait until Monday," Stanley said.

"You'll have to. Stay the weekend. It's a lovely area. A lot to see and do here. I'd recommend the Running Creek B&B, right around the corner. Charming rooms, and they're known for their big, delicious breakfasts."

Petra finally actually looked at her brother, really looked at him, her eyebrows raised.

"What if we paid for a private tour?" Stanley asked Birdie. "We realize it's an inconvenience, and we're willing to recompense you quite handsomely for it." He took out his fat money clip and peeled off several large-denomination bills.

Birdie accepted them and tucked them in her pocket. "The Girls & Boys Club thanks you for your donation."

"We just want to see it," Petra pleaded. "Just a peek. We'll be quick. We promise."

"The only way I'd even consider allowing you to visit the museum after hours is if you tell me the whole story first," Birdie said. She hoped it was a good story. She liked a good story.

The twins looked at each other.

"And you'd have to wait until the craft fair is over," Birdie continued. "Doors close at five, then there will be cleanup. Six thirty–seven before I'm free."

"I'll compensate you for your time," Stanley said. "It wouldn't take more than a few minutes. . . . If you could just see your way to leaving earlier . . ." The money clip came out again.

Birdie shook her head. "Out of the question. I've got responsibilities here I can't neglect. You'll just have to wait. Find something to do with yourselves until then. A hike would do you both good. Or a picnic lakeside."

🌲🌲🌲

They didn't take her advice. They sat at the baked goods stand and watched her.

At 6:47 p.m., Birdie said goodnight to Samantha and Martha, the last two crafters to leave, locked the hall doors, and pronounced herself finished.

"Where are you parked?" Stanley asked.

"No need to drive. The town historical museum and library is only a couple of blocks away. We can walk."

They put her between them. So they still weren't talking. Or did they think she would try to make an escape?

Their breath hung on the leaf-scented, chilly October night air. She pointed out the sights of the town as they walked—the fire station, the oldest building in town, and the commemorative park. They seemed distracted and inattentive.

The museum and library shared an old Victorian building, the interior in fair condition but needing renovation, the exterior needing work, always needing work—a fresh paint job and patches on the roof at the minimum.

Birdie unhooked the keys at her belt and unlocked the door. Turning on lights as she went, she led them through the front exhibition hall. "Here's a reproduction of early maps, Kanien'kehá:ka arrowheads and axe blades, wampum, a model of a village, an exhibit on settler life, Dutch and French fur trappers. We'd like to expand into an addition, where we could install permanent exhibitions on natural history, geology, and the history of regional Indigenous cultures. We've applied for grants, but so far we've been unsuccessful."

They didn't even pretend to be interested until she pointed out a small display on the Adirondack gold rush of 1898. At this, they both stopped and peered wide eyed at the cases.

Ah ha. It was gold they were interested in. They'd somehow got it into their heads that a quilt held clues to gold deposits.

She took them back to her office, or rather cubby hole, just large enough for a small desk, two chairs, and filing cabinets. "I don't know about you two, but it's been a long day, and I could use a cup of tea. Care to join me?"

Petra uttered a long-suffering sigh. "No."

Stanley cleared his throat. "Um, we're in a bit of a hurry. We have to get back."

"Too bad. You may be in hurry, but I'm not. If you want my help, you'll let me get my tea." She turned the electric kettle on to boil.

The three of them stared at the kettle.

"Smith, you say?" Birdie asked, pretending like she didn't know. "You been out to the old house?"

"First thing we did," Petra said.

"We miss it terribly. We need money to fix it up," Stanley said.

Liars. The house had already been sold and fixed up into a boutique spa and hotel that was about to open, and they weren't even aware of it—that's how much they cared about it. It was sad, terribly sad.

"I knew your gran Eleanor, you know," Birdie said.

"You don't say?" Petra said, feigning interest.

"I knew you, too, when you were just toddlers. I guess you don't remember me. That was a long time ago." The twins had been a handful then, and they were a handful now. "Your gran doted on you." Eleanor would be so disappointed in them. "She used to tell you stories, I seem to remember, while she was working on her quilts. You loved her stories when you were little."

"Still do—did," Stanley said.

"But then you grew up, and I don't remember you visiting. Eleanor used to hope that you would visit."

"It was impossible," Petra said.

Sure. "And when she was in the hospital, I don't remember seeing you there," Birdie continued.

"No, I was in Hong Kong at the time," Stanley said. "I tried everything to get back, but I just couldn't make it in time. It will always be one of the greatest regrets of my life."

"Me, too. I was in London." Petra crossed her legs sheathed in slick black.

"My condolences on her passing. She was a truly amazing person," Birdie said.

"Thank you," Stanley said.

Petra bowed her head like she was grief stricken.

Fakers, both of them, and Eleanor had loved them so dearly. She'd been ill for a long time, requiring a lengthy hospital stay followed by hospice. They really hadn't been able to get back in all that time? Birdie didn't believe them. And here they were prospecting. The electric kettle beeped that it was finished, and she made her tea. "Those tales of untold riches to be had in gold deposits in the Adirondack peaks are just that—stories, you know. People want to get rich quick, so they believe what they want to believe."

"I don't know what you mean," Stanley said, stiffening.

"That's what this is about, isn't it? You believe a quilt will lead you to gold deposits."

"No, this is completely different. Absolutely guaranteed to be true," Stanley said.

"Really?" Birdie asked, skeptical.

Petra smirked with confidence.

Infuriating. So that's the way it was going to be. They weren't going to be dislodged from their obsession no matter what.

"But we need Nana's quilt," Stanley said. "It's the key to everything. Is it here or not?"

"Hold your horses. Eleanor did bequeath some items from the Smith estate. I can't say off the top of my head whether your quilt is among them. What did this quilt look like?"

"I, for one, would be happy to award the museum a generous finder's fee," Stanley said.

"Stanley!" Petra protested.

"And just how much would that be?" Birdie asked, blowing on her tea.

"Five percent."

Five percent of nothing was nothing, but if there was any chance. . . . "The museum and library could certainly put funds to good use. There's capital improvements to the infrastructure. Community programs and outreach and the like. Not to mention the new addition. Make it ten."

"Ten?" Petra said. "Stanley, no."

"All right. Ten it is," Stanley said. "Just please, can you show us the quilts now?"

"Ten whether it pans out or not?"

"Agreed," Stanley said.

"Stanley!" Petra wailed again.

"Not so fast. We need to draw up a legally binding agreement." Birdie was no lawyer, and she knew that any agreement they made here tonight wouldn't hold up in court, but it couldn't hurt to try, just to see what their reaction would be. She pulled out official museum stationery from a drawer and began to write up something in her best legalese—party of the first part, and so forth. One way to find out if she was dealing with lawyers. She slid it across to them. "How's this?"

They skimmed it impatiently, not taking it very seriously, it seemed to her. "Fine." They signed and slid it back to her. That settled that. Neither of them was a lawyer.

"And a check for the 10 percent?"

"Before we even see it?" Petra asked.

"Yes. That's the deal."

Stanley wrote out a check and laid it on her desk.

She tried not to show her shock and excitement at so many zeros. They thought this so-called gold was worth that much. If they had that kind of money, why did they even need the gold? Sheer greed. "What makes you think a quilt has the answers?" Birdie asked.

"Because Nana said so in a letter," Petra said. "Here."

Did they know how ridiculous they sounded? And obsessed?

Both of them produced documents at the same moment and offered them to her.

"See for yourself," Stanley said.

She took both. They were faded, dog-eared photocopies of the same handwritten letter that she recognized as Eleanor's expansive cursive. But it was all very ambiguous, if you asked her. Not really even a letter. More like instructions. Written years ago. Phrases leaped out at her—treasures of her heart and prove your worth in a quest. Weird language, especially from Eleanor. And it said nothing about gold. Seemed like it really was talking about mending relationships.

"Can we trust you?" Stanley asked.

"Of course." Birdie drank the last of her tea.

"Nana told us that gold had been buried by her ancestor, William Smith, who originally settled the land."

"Buried gold? What do you mean?" Despite her best skeptical intentions, she began to be intrigued. "Why? How? When?"

"During the French and Indian War, William Smith was afraid that they might be raided, so he buried a cache of Dutch guilders before they fled for Albany," Stanley said.

"Dutch guilders would fetch a lot on the open market these days," Petra said.

"Are you sure this just wasn't one of your gran's fanciful stories?"

"It's true. We've verified it."

Birdie still wasn't convinced. "So you're looking for a quilt that contains a map or a code?" It was true that Eleanor had a taste for abstract depictions of places and maps in her quilts, which made them quite unique and artistic. When Birdie had asked her about it, Eleanor had told her it was a family tradition. That didn't mean that it would lead to gold.

"The quilt mysteriously disappeared before anyone realized its significance," Stanley said. "We've been searching for it ever since."

"Nothing mysterious about it. Your gran donated all her quilts to the museum. All above board and legal, and I've got the paperwork to prove it, if you'd care to see it."

Stanley waved it away.

Definitely not lawyers. If Birdie had to guess, Stanley was a banker and Petra was in marketing. "Why aren't you working together to solve this mystery? Instead of competing with each other?" she asked. "Your gran would be ashamed of you squabbling like this."

"I'm happy to team up. But Petra won't," Stanley said, hanging his head.

"Me? You!" Petra said, her voice rising, gesturing wildly. "You're the one who contested the will."

"Well, you're the one who ran off. And have been running ever since."

"Have not."

"Have too."

Birdie held up her hand for silence. "Enough." They shut up. Apparently, she hadn't lost her principal's touch. "Seems to me like your quarrel is a misunderstanding, and it's time to clear it up."

They folded their arms over their chests and scowled at her.

"You'll need to work together, or I won't show the quilts to you." Birdie stood, rattling her keys.

They bolted expectantly to their feet and hurriedly agreed. "Okay. Okay."

"Shake and give each other a hug," Birdie ordered them.

They did so reluctantly, awkwardly.

"Wait here while I retrieve the quilts from the storeroom and bring them out to you." Birdie didn't want anyone to see the museum storeroom. It was a disaster. They kept meaning to get it better organized. But every volunteer they assigned started out enthusiastic and ended up defeated.

The acid-free corrugated cardboard boxes (which cost a pretty penny) were organized by acquisition date on the shelves. She pulled a box out, unwrapped a quilt from its acid-free tissue paper (expensive), and studied it. Gorgeous and a real work of art. Now that Birdie knew what to look for, she could see it, plain as day—a map of the house and surrounding land and a patch of gold brocade in one corner near the stream. As a matter of fact, Birdie knew the spot.

Such a shame, really. If Eleanor wanted the twins to have the quilt and its secrets, why hadn't she left it to them? Instead, she'd left it to Birdie for the museum. Eleanor had planned for this eventuality. Birdie carefully folded the quilt back up, slipped it back in the paper and box, and took down another box holding more of Eleanor's quilts. She carried it out to the twins.

They were standing at the threshold waiting for her.

"Visitors are not permitted in the storage areas," Birdie said sharply.

"We thought you might have gotten lost and needed help."

A likely story. She locked the door behind her. "In here." She led them to a shabby conference room and turned on the lights. "There are quilt hangers on the wall." Get the two of them working together.

Once the first quilt was hung, they stepped back. It was a lovely piece of needlework. Looked like a sunburst. Intricate. Scraps of fabric in just about every hue. And at least a hundred years old. Still smelled faintly of mothballs and wood smoke. "Fine piece of original work that your gran lovingly repaired," Birdie said. "We plan to show it next year in a new folk art exhibition."

The twins ignored her, standing close and examining it myopically for clues.

"Here." Birdie handed out magnifying glasses.

"What are we looking for?" Petra whispered to her brother.

"Clues," Stanley whispered back.

At least they were talking now.

Stanley took out his phone.

Birdie coughed.

"Is it okay if I snap some pics?" Stanley asked.

"I suppose so," Birdie said, pretending reluctance. "Just don't post them on the web." Not that there was much chance of that with these secretive two.

"Of course not. I don't think it's this one," Stanley whispered to Petra. "Let's try another."

Birdie looked at her watch. It'd been a long day. She had just about all she could take of these two. She was ready go home, feed the cats, and put her feet up.

The twins studied each quilt and photographed them with a notable absence of bickering. They'd turned a corner in their relationship, so it seemed. Eleanor would be pleased. Birdie almost relented, but then she thought of the years of their neglect of Eleanor and her own plans for the museum addition.

The twins worked through the box, growing more frustrated. What if they guessed none of these was the right quilt and demanded to know if she had more in storage?

They hung up the last quilt.

Petra gasped and pointed to an intricate patch.

"Is it . . .?" Stanley asked with bated breath.

"I don't know. Maybe," Petra whispered. "Look at the needlework in gold right here."

They put their heads together.

Stanley glanced over his shoulder at Birdie in case she was eavesdropping (she wasn't, but she could hear them just fine). "That's the big oak."

"The one we used to climb on as kids?" Petra asked.

"That's the one. That's it. Good work, Petra."

Birdie breathed a silent sigh of relief. People believed what they wanted to believe.

"Let's get out of here," Petra whispered to her brother.

"You read my mind. It'll be too cold on your motorcycle. Let me give you a ride," Stanley said. "I'll put the roof up on my car, and we'll be toasty inside. Okay?"

"Like old times. Thanks."

Stanley turned to Birdie. "I think we've got what we need. We'll be going now. Thanks for everything."

"My pleasure," Birdie said as she ushered them out. Tomorrow morning, she'd go out to the spot at dawn with a shovel and be back in time to open for the last day of the harvest craft fair.

# 13

# Mr. and Mrs. Ghost

*Dennis Webster*

Awake. The footsteps across the hardwood flooring in the hallway woke him up. Ronald Rust walked the second floor of his Great Camp Evermore with a flashlight in his shaking hand. The female ghost had startled him awake with her loud moan. He had seen her full-body apparition the night before. A young lady with curly blonde hair and a blue dress. He stopped and shined the light on his wristwatch, and it was 2:37 a.m. This had been happening every night at the same time for months and with growing spiritual intensity.

"Who are you?" asked Ronald as he stopped and clutched his chest. He was one hundred years old and knew he had not much life left. He lived alone in his large camp on the shore of Mirror Lake. There was a chair in the hallway. He sat and shut off the flashlight leaving a slight slim moonbeam breaking through the window at the end of the hall and the rest of the camp interior in a squid ink view. He had the window open in the summer heat and could only hear the faint song of the crickets. He looked back and forth knowing she was gone. He whispered, "What do you want?" He had lived all his life in Camp Evermore and never had paranormal activity until the day he turned a century old. In the morning, he would take his boat across the lake and into the village to place an ad in the *Lake Placid News*. He had to find a person to end the madness and give the ghost and himself peace while he still had time left.

Ronald sat in his Adirondack chair with his bare feet nestled in the cold August water of Mirror Lake. He had an ice cold Utica Club beer in his hand. A boat approached and pulled up to his dock. He recognized Xavier Smith and his 1950s wooden Chris-Craft with the large U.S. flag flapping off the tail but not the couple who stepped out of the boat with the man carrying a small black case. Xavier waved then took off back toward the Lake Placid side of the lake. The couple walked toward Ronald, and he knew right away they were ghost hunters. He'd been inundated by them after his national ad placement, including a local paranormal team. None proved anything, and none had solved the mystery. The moaning lady ghost would disappear every time the opportunistic hacks crossed the threshold of his grand camp. He regretted placing a financial reward of $100,000 for proof of the haunting and discovery of who the lady was and what she wanted with Ronald.

"I'm sorry but I'm no longer offering up Camp Evermore for ghost hunts," said Ronald as he stood up and walked out of the water toward the couple dressed in all black that was a stark contrast to the summer tourist look of bright-colored puffy shorts and neon crocs. He paused and took a sip of his Utica Club.

"I thought you might say that, Mr. Rust," said the man who took off his black fedora to reveal a slick white head with no hair and no tan. The lady next to him was tanned with a black dress and revealed bright white teeth from her friendly smile. "I'm Dennis Ghost and this is my wife, Darsy Ghost. Before you say no, please allow me to give our credentials," he said as he handed Ronald a business card that was plain white heavy stock with only the words *Mr. and Mrs. Ghost* printed on it. There was no contact information, no e-mail, and no cell number.

"Let's get out of this sun and go talk on the front porch," said Ronald as he set down his beer can and picked up his cane. He meandered across the grass in his bare feet up the sloped hill toward Camp Evermore. Ronald felt at ease with the couple. He'd been chasing away others who came, but he knew the Ghosts were different. They all sat in the chairs; Dennis set down the black case he was carrying.

"I think you will find, Mr. Rust, that we are different than anybody who came here previously. We are both disciples of the grand dame of the paranormal, Bernadette Peck. We both were paranormal investigators for her and part of her team, the Ghost Seekers of Central New York. We apprenticed for decades before her passing. She had sixty years of paranormal investigations with the best results of any team of ghost hunters on the planet."

"You can call me Ron. I'm curious what makes you both so different. I've heard of Mrs. Peck. She had been on television a number of years ago."

Darsy leaned forward and placed her hand upon Ron's. "We are a spiritual-based ghost-hunting team. We use little to no technical equipment as our paranormal human senses guide us. We pray before and after an investigation, and we never charge for our service. We feel the good karma flows between the realms and delivers results."

Ronald smiled and said, "I want this mystery solved. I feel good about you two."

The trio walked throughout the entire outside lakefront property before stopping at a small cemetery out back that was on the slight hill adjacent to a large maple tree. A bakers' dozen of aged gravestones, stained with dates from the late nineteenth century to the 1960s, dotted the landscape. There was a small, black, iron fence circling the holy ground. Mr. and Mrs. Ghost stopped, looked at each other, and smiled.

"This cemetery," said Dennis. "This has a role to play in the mystery, Ron."

"Those are my relatives," said Ronald as he leaned on his cane. "My parents and grandparents are buried here as are my great aunts and uncles. When I die, I will have to be buried in the North Elba Cemetery as they stopped burials on private grounds. I wish I could be here for eternity. I was born in this house, and I'll die in it. I'm one hundred years old so I'm on the downslide," he said as he cracked a smile showing a few missing teeth, but the ones still in his mouth were pearl white.

The trio walked out of the shade of the maple tree and toward the large camp building. It was one of the larger camps on the lake.

"How old is Camp Evermore?" asked Darsy.

"Built 1870," replied Ron. "The Rust family has owned this land and built this great camp. Nobody but us has owned it."

They walked up the stairs to the front door, and Dennis stopped and rubbed his hands on the porch's hand-hewn posts that were worn but still had the beauty from the origin. "Do you have any children, Ron?"

"No, Dennis. I do not. The Rust lineage ends with me as this place will be owned by another family. I just hope they love it as much as we have loved it. Mirror Lake and Lake Placid are the most beautiful places in the Adirondacks and the world. And Camp Evermore is the most glorious great camp."

"It's marvelous," said Darsy as she walked in front of the group and through the front door. "I feel the presence of a woman spirit."

🌲🌲🌲

The sun had gone down on Mirror Lake, and the darkness was met by the serenading crickets. Mr. and Mrs. Ghost had decided to keep Ronald in the house and make him part of their paranormal investigation. He was the conduit and the one the ghost was comfortable communicating with. The only equipment they had was a small handheld digital recorder and a small flashlight. They waited for many hundreds of minutes until it was the witching hour. The spiritual safari would begin. They had just held hands with Darsy saying the St. Michael prayer of protection against bad ghosts then asked for the good spirits to come forth. They walked the house without saying much when they halted on the first floor hallway that led from the living room to the bedrooms and bathroom. It was long and wide enough that the three of them stood shoulder to shoulder with plenty of room leftover. The Camp Evermore spaces, hallways, and walls, more than 150 years old, were all expansive, roomy, and thick. They were lumberjack strong and craftsman built to destruction-proof standards. Ronald had to lean against the hallway wall as Dennis and Darsy started their otherworldly communication.

"Are you the lady haunting this house?" asked Dennis as he turned the flashlight off to engulf the group in utter darkness. "Come closer. Don't be afraid. We are friends."

The team was silent for a minute giving the ghost a chance to respond. Mr. and Mrs. Ghost had explained to Ronald how electronic voice phenomenon (EVP) sessions were conducted.

"Tell us your name," asked Darsy. She held the digital recorder out toward the empty hallway.

They stood still and quiet for a few minutes when Ronald spoke up and said, "She's here. I can't see her, but I can feel her."

"Yes," said Darsy. "I can see the woman with my third eye. She's blonde and wearing a blue dress. Her hair is done up in curls of a Roaring Twenties style."

Ronald stared at Darsy through the flashlight that Dennis was holding. He had an astonished look on his face as he had never told anybody what the female ghost had looked like. He felt weak in his knees as he said, "I'm sorry, but could you please get me a chair from the end of the hall? I need to sit down."

Dennis went to the end of the long hall with his flashlight leading the way so he wouldn't trip on anything. The window at the end of the hall was open, and the wind was pushing the scent of summer mist off the lake mixed with summer-baked pine needle. He grabbed the small wooden shaker chair and carried it to Ronald who sat down and put his cane across his lap. "You okay?" asked Dennis as he placed his hand on the old man's shoulder.

"Yes. Darsy floored me. She described the ghost that I had been seeing. She had been in hibernation for quite some time but she's back."

"She's here, Ron," said Darsy, standing with her eyes closed while the men watched her connect with a spirit of the dead. "I'm getting a name." Darsy stood there as all were silent for a minute that seemed an eternity; the sounds of the night went mute, including the wind off the water and the dew-soaked grass crickets. "Mary Grace," whispered Darsy.

"That can't be," said Ronald with his words trembling through his shaking lips. He got up from his chair and moved away as quickly as his hundred-year-old body could move, leaving Mr. and Mrs. Ghost still as they respected his flight from the paranormal.

🌲🌲🌲

It was morning, and Dennis sat at the large oak table within the expansive kitchen at Camp Evermore with his laptop on and his headphones plugged in as he was listening to the recorded ghost hunt from the previous night.

His cup of coffee steamed, but he paid no mind as he needed his full attention to listen for possible responses from Mary Grace. Ronald had been shaken the night before but settled down before giving Dennis and Darsy the grand bedroom to sleep in. It had large windows facing Mirror Lake. They had all woken up early, which was surprising considering they had all been up late. Ronald was in the living room talking to Darsy and had been reminiscing about his parents and his beloved Aunt Mary Grace Rust. He had not seen his aunt since he was a little boy. Ronald recalled how her big smile lit up a room. When he was an adult, he had learned that she had been denied marriage to a young lad truck driver from Tupper Lake who was in love with her and wanted to be together. Mary Grace had disappeared, and the family had never heard from her again. Most assumed she had run away to California with her trucker love. Ronald's parents had told him when he was a teenager that she ran away with her beloved. They never again spoke of Mary Grace. Until the day they died, Ronald's parents refused to speak of Mary Grace, and any pictures, clothing, or items left behind had been purged from Camp Evermore.

Dennis had listened to more than an hour of the recording and was getting close to the end when he heard it. It was time stamped on the recording at 2:37 a.m. He perked up and stopped the digital recording on his laptop and backed it up and played it again, but this time he pushed on the earphones to hermetically seal them to his ears and closed his eyes to devote his entire sensory to his ears. He played it again and knew it was a word spoken by a female voice, but it didn't make sense. He went and retrieved Darsy and Ronald as they were talking about the ghost of Mary Grace. Darsy had stated that she had communicated with Mary Grace and that she said it was dark and cold where she was and wanted to be among her family. "She told me she's lonely, Ron," said Darsy as she held the old man's hand. "Does any of this make sense?"

"I don't understand the breadcrumbs she's leaving," answered Ronald.

"I have a large crumb right here. Listen to this," said Dennis as he unplugged his earphones from the laptop and turned up the sound to 100 percent.

The trio sat in chairs, and Dennis hit the play button. You could hear Darsy ask, "Where are you?"; a female voice replies, "Wall."

"Does that mean anything to you, Ron?" asked Dennis. Ronald was quiet and was shaking his head with his jaw slightly dropped.

"That's my aunt's voice. I was a little boy, but I distinctly remember she had a deep, smokey voice like my mother. How is that possible?"

"It's what we call an intelligent haunting," said Dennis. "Mary Grace is aware she is dead and is communicating. She spoke this one word from the realm of the dead, but it's obvious she is trapped here and doesn't wish to be. But what does this last breadcrumb mean?"

Darsy stood up but still hung onto Ronald's hand. "I think I solved the mystery," said Darsy. "Let's go to where she spoke to us last night."

They walked to the hallway where they had seen, felt, and heard from Mary Grace. They brought in the chair so Ronald could sit. He held his cane and was watching with eyes wide open. Dennis stood back and let Mrs. Ghost perform her medium and psychic duty. Darsy walked to part of the hallway where the plaster was a little misshapen from the rest and placed her hands on the wall. She closed her eyes. She rubbed her hands up and down the wall then pulled them back fast, which startled Dennis and Ronald.

"Sorry about that," said Darsy as she rubbed her hands together. "My entire body lit up with paranormal energy. There's something hidden in this wall that Mary Grace wants us to find."

"Dennis," said Ronald. "Go out back and go in my small shed. In there, you'll find a pickax. Bring it in here and open a hole in this wall."

Dennis left and went outside. The summer sun was warming up the grass with the dew evaporating. He went into the shed and got the implement with the long wooden handle that had a hammered iron pick at the top that was rusty but could cause significant damage to whatever it struck. He came out of the shed and paused to look at Mirror Lake that was steaming as the morning mist was dissipating. He came back into Camp Evermore, and Darsy was still holding her hands on the wall with her eyes closed. "Are you sure you want me to do this, Ron?"

"There's a clue planted in that wall. Go ahead and strike away, young man."

Dennis smirked at the comment as he was in his fifties and wasn't young anymore, but to a century-old man he was a youngster. Darsy stepped back. Ron got out of his chair and walked with Darsy down the hall to a safe distance. Dennis struck the old wall, and plaster flew. He struck several more times until he had a dinner-plate-sized hole. He set down the pickax, grabbed the edge of the plaster wall, and yanked. A large piece came loose and slammed onto the hallway floor. Dennis stood in silence. For a moment he couldn't believe what he was seeing. "Oh, my God," said Dennis as he took a step back.

Darsy and Ronald walked forward with their steps crunching on the plaster chunks strewn across the hardwood hallway flooring. They stopped and looked into the large hole in the wall. They were in shock for a moment. It was a human skeleton trapped within the wall. It was obviously a woman as it was wearing a blue dress that had white lace on the collar. Ronald took a step, placed his hand on the cheek of the skull, and said, "Hello, Aunt Mary Grace."

It was a year later. Dennis and Darsy stood in front of Mary Grace's headstone that had been placed in the family cemetery at Camp Evermore. Darsy had a bouquet of wildflowers she had picked on the side of the road just outside Tupper Lake. The discovery of Mary Grace's body inside the wall of Camp Evermore drew national attention as it was something right out of an Edgar Allan Poe story; except this was not fiction—it was real. Mary Grace had been allowed to be buried in the family plot behind the camp as Ronald had her skeletal remains cremated. He planted his beloved aunt in the ground and passed away that night in his lifelong bed in his cherished Camp Evermore. Ronald was buried in North Elba, and they had stopped to give their prayers to the sweet old man who had died in peace. Mr. and Mrs. Ghost had solved the mystery of the blonde-haired lady ghost in blue, but a new mystery arose. Who put Mary Grace in the wall of the camp? Theories abound that her parents did it to keep her from running away with her truck-driving boyfriend. There were no heirs left and no journals or clues anywhere. Camp Evermore had new owners who were kind enough to grant Mr. and Mrs. Ghost access to Mary Grace's final resting place. Darsy placed the flowers in front of the small headstone. She stood up, and she and Dennis held hands and said a prayer to the souls of Ronald and Mary Grace as they knew they were in another place, a better place for all eternity. Dennis took his one free hand, stuck it in his front right pocket, and pulled out what he had carried for this moment. He sprinkled the breadcrumbs on the ground in front of the headstone with some landing on the flowers. "Rest in peace, Mary Grace Rust."

# 14

# A Most Impressive Illusion

## Larry Weill

THE DATE WAS SEPTEMBER 11, 2011. THE LIGHTS IN THE WELLS FIRE house were normally shut off by this time of night—unless the local firemen or Sheriff's Department were holding a social event in the building. Tonight was one of those nights; a retirement party for one of the long-standing officers, Undersheriff Dan Clements, who was calling it quits after several decades on the force. In the midst of the darkened town, the fire hall lights burned brightly even though the clock read almost 11:00 p.m. The gravity of the date, September 11, had done little to attenuate the joy of the celebration.

The crowd in the office had dwindled throughout the evening hours as more and more of the sheriff's force left the party to head back to their homes. The only two remaining officers were Clements and Deputy Mike Creed. Although the two men had worked together for a half dozen years and were the best of friends, they were remarkably different in almost every way. Clements was sixty-three years old and the most senior member of the department. He could have retired almost twenty years earlier, but he chose to stay on and assume the duties of undersheriff of the local station. He looked every bit the role of "grizzled veteran," with closely cropped silver hair and a ruddy complexion. However, anyone who knew him was also cognizant of the fact that he possessed a jovial disposition, and was always willing to lend a hand or word of encouragement to anyone in the community. He used his backcountry redneck persona to hide a keen sense of forensic logic that had solved many difficult crimes in his thirty-seven years on the force.

The other occupant of the room that night, Deputy Mike Creed, was young enough to be Clements's son. Although only thirty-four years of age, Creed had been with the Sheriff's Office for close to six years, and he was known for his dedication to duty. An avid workout enthusiast, he had a physique that was envied by many of his peers, with a thin waist and bulging biceps. He looked up to Clements with God-like respect and tried his best to glean every bit of knowledge he could from the senior officer.

The two men sat in the meeting hall, surrounded by the remains of a massive decorated cake and piles of used paper plates and cups. Even though they had worked together for years, they never ran out of topics to discuss, and the conversation flowed freely as the hours passed. For Clements, it would be the last night he'd ever spend on the force, and he intended to savor every minute before making his final departure.

"So tell me, how does it feel, combining your retirement party with such a somber date as the tenth anniversary of 9/11?" asked Creed, finishing the last bite of his cake.

"Funny you should ask that," said Clements, his eyes taking on a reflective expression. "I thought about that a lot these past few weeks, and it didn't really bother me all that much. In fact, I thought about the other 9/11 a lot more."

"The other 9/11?" asked Creed. "What other 9/11, and how could it be any more significant than the death of three thousand Americans in an attack on our own soil?"

Clements chuckled lightly and gazed up at the ceiling, as though trying to look beyond the innocence of his youthful companion.

"That's okay, Mike, I wouldn't have expected you to know about that one. Heck, I'm probably about the last one still serving who does."

"Then please share," replied the suddenly livened Creed, "unless you enjoy keeping all the good stuff to yourself."

Clements's expression suddenly turned gravely serious. The contrast of his face from a moment earlier was stunning.

"No, nothing I'm about to tell you can be described as 'good.' But to us, meaning the old-timers, 9/11 means something else in addition to the World Trade Center disaster. But you have to go back to 1978 to understand."

"Okay, take me back to 1978. By the way, I was a one-year-old back then."

"Thanks for reminding me of my age," laughed Clements. "Anyway, have you ever heard of Robert Garrow?"

"Of course I have. You don't have to be in law enforcement to know that name. Anyone living in this part of the state is familiar with that murdering piece of slime. If I'm not mistaken, he was convicted of raping and murdering about a dozen people across the southern part of the Adirondacks, wasn't he?"

"That's right," nodded Clements. "And based on a map that we found after his death, we think that number was actually almost a dozen higher. But we'll never know for sure."

"So what's that got to do with 9/11?"

"Well, it was on the night of September 11, 1978, that we finally took him down. He tried escaping through a gunfight one last time, and it didn't work. Pretty messy battle, I might add. One of our officers got wounded pretty badly."

"At least you got him," sighed Creed. "From what I heard, a lot of other good men tried to trap him but missed."

"Yeah, if you read all the official reports, we got him," agreed Clements. "I think we did, too."

"You mean you're not sure?" gasped Creed. "How is that possible? Either you killed him or you didn't."

"Well, first of all, I wasn't there," explained Clements. "It was a team of crack professionals from the Correctional System that hunted him down. Second, the rumors about it being a look-alike were never substantiated, and the killings did stop as soon as they got their man. But still, there were a lot of rumors, and some strange goings-on afterward."

"Like what?"

"Well, everyone knows that he killed a camper in the town of Wells in summer '73. Actually, he kidnapped four youths in that one spree, although a couple of them got away to sound the alarm. But very few people realize that there was another victim from Wells who disappeared about five years later. It was a girl by the name of Paula Terrell, as I recall. Pretty little thing who wouldn't hurt a fly."

"Did he ever confess to the crime?"

"No, and it was never prosecuted," said Clements. "They needed to keep a lid on it because it held too many ties to clues in other cases. She was reported missing, and finally assumed dead, but it never hit the press the way some of the other killings did. Finally, the whole matter was dropped after Garrow was killed."

"Okay, so if you make the logical assumption that Garrow killed this Paula Terrell woman, what's the remaining mystery, except where he might have hidden the body?"

Clements reached over and took a long sip from his Styrofoam coffee cup, then cleared his throat repeatedly as he shifted position in his chair. "Rumor has it," he said in a lowered voice, "rumor has it that she was never killed. Or else that she was killed, and her ghost still stalks the site where she was murdered."

"Oh, lovely," laughed Creed, his face illuminated with glee. "And who thought up this piece of backwoods folklore?"

"I don't think anyone thought it up," replied Clements. "I think it just evolved on its own. Terrell was last seen by a truck driver who gave her a lift to a point south of Wells on the night of July 30, 1978. She said she was going to meet someone, and he dropped her off near a bend in the road with no houses and no buildings. She was never heard from again."

"Did anyone ever check out the trucker who gave her the ride?"

"Well yes, and it was the trucker himself who came forward with the information," said Clements. "He was an older fellow who was making his return trip to Gloversville that night. He passed a lie detector test, and was very forthcoming with his story. He wanted to help find her as much as we did."

"So what else is going on here that you haven't told me?" asked Creed. He knew the older officer well enough to recognize when details were being intentionally withheld.

"Well, there have been times over the past few years when strange sightings have been observed along that stretch of road on Route 30 south of Wells. Strips of purple wool, like the sweater that Terrell was wearing, have mysteriously appeared in the road. And even more bizarre, there have been Christmas lights sighted on a house way up on Moose

Mountain. They've been seen on numerous nights like tonight, on 9/11, and then on into the middle of December."

"Okay, so what's so unusual about that? Lots of houses have Christmas lights. That's not a crime."

Clements fell silent for a moment, looking at his partner through his wire-framed bifocals before answering in a slow, measured voice. "Mike, there are no houses up on the west side of Moose Mountain. There are no roads, no houses, and no power lines. Nothing."

The younger deputy weighed this statement for a moment, considering the possibilities. "There's got to be something up there or you wouldn't see a house lit up like that. You're missing something for sure."

"Mike, I've seen it with my own eyes. And I've hunted that entire mountain, so I know that it's devoid of any buildings at all. The folklore has it that Paula Terrell built herself a cabin up there in the woods, and she won't come out until she is certain that Robert Garrow was actually the man who was shot and killed in September '78."

Deputy Creed glanced at his wristwatch, and then back at the seasoned lawman sitting across from him. A gentle smile appeared on his face as he mulled over the implications of the conversation.

"You say these lights come out on 9/11, the anniversary of Robert Garrow's death? Well, it's almost midnight already. How about we see if your ghostly apparition has awakened to appear tonight. It's a nice night, and we won't have far to drive."

"You're kidding, right?" laughed Clements. "You're not really interested in this, are you? I've only seen the lights once or twice myself, but I have wondered about them ever since."

Creed was already standing, pulling on his coat and gloves. "Sure, why not," he said in an off-hand voice. "Let's let someone else clean up this place tomorrow. Heck, no one cleans up after their own retirement party." And with that, they headed out the door for their patrol car.

Not much was said as they pulled out of the fire hall lot and onto Route 30, with Deputy Creed behind the wheel and Clements riding shotgun. It was only a few miles of driving, straight south on the highway heading toward Northville. Before long, Clements motioned to Creed to pull over into a short loop of pavement on the right side of the road. Creed elected not to turn on the flashing police lights.

Together they climbed out of the vehicle and stood on the shoulder of the road. The night was cool and crisp, and the waters of the Sacandaga River were clearly heard below the embankment to their right. Clements pointed in an easterly direction, up into the hills on the opposite side of the highway. The faint moonlight barely illuminated the façade of Moose Mountain, rising into the night sky like a black hulking dome of rock. It was pitch black, without a speck of light across its impenetrable mass. As close to the town as it was, the entire mountain looked entirely devoid of life.

"Doesn't look like much up there to me," said Creed, scanning the skyline. "If your friend Paula is up there, I'd say she needs to get herself a good flashlight, because it looks pretty darn dark to me."

"It's not time yet," murmured Clements.

"Huh?"

"I said it's not time yet. Those who have seen the lights claim that they come on at midnight, and it's not midnight yet."

"Oh, good Lord, this is getting stranger by the minute," Creed retorted. "And tell me, do you believe that myth, too?"

"The only times I ever saw them it was right around midnight," nodded Clements. "I know, I know, you must think I'm insane, but it's happened to me, too."

"What time is it now?" asked Creed.

"A little after 11:30 p.m.," replied Clements, "but I've got refreshments to keep us warm until then." The senior officer reached into the squad car and retrieved a thermos of coffee and a pair of Styrofoam cups. "I hope you don't mind it black, because we left the cream and sugar back in the fire hall."

The two men opened the doors of the car and sat down with their coffee to wait for the midnight hour. The conversation resumed once again, although there was a high degree of anticipation in the air over the upcoming spectacle, or lack thereof. In fact, neither officer knew what to expect, only to sit and watch and see whether this was something that could be observed and reported by a respected source. They didn't have long to wait.

At two minutes to midnight, they exited the car once again and looked up into the hills. The darkness was absolute, as before.

"See, I told you this whole story was just a bunch of made-up poppycock," said Creed, an incredulous look on his face. "I don't know about you, but I've never believed a word about ghosts, or spirits, or any other supernatural phenomena. I've always found a way to explain everything I've seen."

"Okay, it appears that you're right," sighed Clements. "And I guess I've always known that, too, but you have to admit, it's kind of fun to imagine it." With that he turned around and started strolling back toward the car. "Come on, Mike, it's getting cold and late. Drop me off at my house, and I'll catch up with you when I stop in next week to clean out my desk."

Silence.

Sheriff Clements was reaching for the door handle when he noticed that he was alone. His partner had not walked back to the road's shoulder with him. Instead, he had slowly walked forward until he was standing in the middle of the empty highway. His head was tilted up, looking up the mountain as if in a trance. Clements slowly lifted his head, allowing his own gaze to follow that of his partner's. What he saw made him catch his own breath. There, on a location about two-thirds the way up the mountain, sat a house that was brightly illuminated with seasonal lights of red, green, blue, and yellow. From what they could see, it was a moderate-sized colonial dwelling with a wide front face and six windows across the front wall. It had appeared out of nowhere; one minute the mountainside was black, and the next moment it was a picture of the holiday season.

"Well, my Doubting Thomas, what have you got to say now?"

Creed remained silent for another minute, simply gazing up into the trees at the blazing apparition. "I think that there is a house up there. Period, end of discussion."

"I tell you, there is nothing up there, Mike. I've been all over that mountain, and there isn't even the trace of a road, much less a building."

Deputy Creed was finally able to drag his eyes away from the lights and turn his attention back toward his partner. "Listen, I don't care what we think we see; those lights are real. Whether or not there is a house up there, those lights aren't from a UFO. They're real."

"Tell you what," said Clements, poking Creed in the ribs. "How about you and I try taking a short drive down the road and see if we can still see this house from another angle."

"Sounds like a good idea," replied Creed. "Maybe we'll be able to see more of the house from farther down Route 30."

The two officers made good time heading south along the highway. Once again they opted to leave the police flashers off, as the road was deserted at this time of night. After covering a distance of only a mile or mile and a half, they stopped again and piled out of the car. The lights were just as visible as before, although this time they could see the lights affixed to the right side of the house as well.

"Well, I guess we have our answer," said Creed, still sounding mystified about the eerie sight.

"Answer? What answer?" replied Clements. "I still don't believe that there is a house up there. But I'm not ready to concede that Paula Terrell's ghost is up there baking Christmas cookies either."

As Clements finished speaking, the lights on the house suddenly blinked out. All that remained on the eastern horizon was darkness. Clements looked again at his watch. The dial read 12:15 a.m.

"Looks like the show only lasts for fifteen minutes," he exclaimed, glancing back up the hillside.

"Not even enough time to bake those cookies I was talking about," replied his partner.

Creed dropped his freshly retired partner off at his house just outside of Northville, and then continued on toward his own residence farther south. Clements walked into his darkened home where he lived alone. It was a quiet existence, as both his wife and his horse had passed away within the past four years, and he never considered remarrying. Before retiring for the night, he walked to the back room, which he had converted into an office. He stepped to the far back right corner of the room and pulled open a file cabinet that was bursting with different colored files. From that drawer, he extracted two folders; one was extremely thick with a bunch of papers while the other was much thinner. He moved these to the kitchen table, where he sat down with a half glass of milk and a pair of Oreo cookies.

One of the things that had contributed to Dan Clements's stellar reputation in the field of law enforcement was his attention to the minutest detail. Even though he had turned in his badge the previous day, his natural instincts took over and responded to his inborn curiosity. Maybe he had missed something along the way, he figured, as he pored back over the yellowed pages. He didn't spend long conducting his review. Once the milk and cookies were gone, he folded the files back into a neat pile and got ready for bed. It had been thirty-three years since Garrow had been shot dead. One more day would make little difference.

It was several weeks before Clements would think about the intriguing lights in the woods. In the interim, he had received a number of uninvited reminders of the Christmas light phenomena, which some locals rated up there with the sighting of a Bigfoot. Local businesses were posting signs along the highways advertising the "ghost house" as a reason to stop into their shops. A prominent area water plane pilot was hired to fly routes over the mountainous area south of Wells to try to sight anything out of the ordinary, but nothing was ever seen. And yet the small but dedicated knot of observers who started gathering along the stretch of Route 30 every night were treated to frequent light shows, in which the house appeared from the darkness in all its multicolored glory before disappearing once again after its fifteen minutes of illumination.

It was well into October, and the taller peaks were turning white with snow when the doorbell rang at Dan Clements's home. It was late on a Saturday morning, and Dan had been cooking up a deep pot of his famed "blacktop chili." He gave it that name because he claimed that he had once spilled a bowl of it in his driveway and the heat from the concoction had removed the blacktop from the pavement beneath. Clements gave the pot a final stir and then shuffled through to the front door.

Upon opening the door, he was greeted by an elderly woman wearing a dark brown coat and carrying a cane. A loose flow of very white hair appeared from beneath her wool hat, contrasting sharply with the material of her overcoat.

"How do you do," said Clements, surprised at the appearance of such a senior citizen alone at his door. "What may I do for you?"

"Please pardon me for the intrusion, but are you Deputy Clements of the county Sheriff's Department?" As the woman spoke, she tilted her head and looked at Clements with an appealing eye, as though she wanted a favor.

"Well, yes, I was Undersheriff Clements right up until about a month ago, when I retired from the force. But I still stop by the station on a regular basis. Is there anything that I can do to help you, ma'am?"

"Yes there is, but it might take a while for me to tell you my story."

Clements invited the woman into the house and seated her in a comfortable chair in his living room. He offered her a cup of coffee, which she politely declined.

"Sheriff, I don't want to take up too much of your time, so I'll get right to the point. My name is Anna Terrell, and my daughter was Paula Terrell. I believe you are familiar with her name."

"Oh my God, yes!" replied Clements, almost jumping out of his seat. "I was involved in the investigation and search for your daughter back in 1978. You might not believe this, but I was just looking over her file as recently as last month."

"Well, thank you for your concern, Sheriff," said the aged parent, "but she's dead. She's been dead for more than thirty years. So why won't they leave me alone?" As she spoke, the emotional toll began to show, and her lower lip quivered in anger.

"Who won't leave you alone?" asked Clements. "Please tell me what is happening and who is responsible?"

"The reporters and newspaper people," replied Terrell, who was on the verge of tears. "They keep ringing my doorbell and following me around, all asking about the Christmas lights that my deceased daughter put up on her house in the woods. Can you imagine that? My daughter is dead, Sheriff. It's hard enough living with that fact, and that I'll never see her face again. But why do they have to remind me at least once a week, every week of the year . . . and I live in Buffalo! Yet they keep coming, and coming, asking for interviews and to see the room where she lived. I can't take it anymore!"

The retired officer sat quietly and listened to the old woman as she finished her story, adding an extra minute for her to regain her composure. Then, he spoke as quietly and soothingly as he knew how.

"Mrs. Terrell, I know how hard this is for you, and what you must have been through over the past many years without your daughter. But I can tell you one thing; this thing with the lights is, in my opinion, simply a local ghost story that was never meant to hurt anyone. No one could have imagined the hurt that it would bring to you and your loved ones."

The senior citizen simply nodded back at Clements through her tears while dabbing her eyes with an embroidered handkerchief.

"There is one thing that I can promise I will do for you," said Clements, taking her hand in his. "I promise that I will find those lights, come hell or high water, and put an end to this myth once and for all. Then maybe you'll get your peace back."

"Do you really think you can do that?" asked Anna, her eyes brightening visibly.

"You just leave that up to me," nodded Clements. "I may be old, but I can still find a needle in a haystack if I set my mind to it."

Anna gazed back at the retired officer and squeezed his hand tightly. "Thank you, Sheriff," she said, the passion for her long-lost daughter still evident in her voice. "And now, I have to ask you one last question."

"Anything you want," replied Clements. "I'll tell you anything I know."

"In your opinion, was that Robert Garrow who was shot and killed that night back in September 1978?"

"Without a doubt," answered Clements, nodding his head enthusiastically. "Garrow was shot dead in a blazing gunfight with a full team of professional sharpshooters. His body was positively identified before it was buried. You may ignore all the rumors and fairy tales you've heard about this evil killer. He will never again harm a soul either here or anyplace else."

"Thank you, Sheriff. That's what I came to hear."

After collecting Anna's phone number and street address, Dan Clements helped her back into her car and bid her farewell. It had been a most surprising visit, and he felt the blood coursing through his veins as he considered his next plan of action. Until now, he had thought of the lights on the hill as a simple diversion—an amusing footnote to a chapter in local history that had been long closed. But now he felt differently, as though the happiness and mental stability of an elderly woman hinged on him solving this mystery and bringing closure to the case.

Clements had already made up his mind that he would conduct this search by himself. It didn't involve a current-day crime, and there would be no prosecutions resulting from his private investigation. He considered calling his friend Deputy Mike Creed to help him on his off-duty hours. But he quickly shot down his own idea, figuring that Mike had better ways to spend his time than searching for Christmas bulbs. It would have to be a solo activity.

Once the retired Clements made up his mind to pursue something, he didn't sit on his hands. This hunt would be no different. He would attend an early Sunday morning church service, and then head up toward Wells and into the upper elevations of Moose Mountain in search of his quarry. He spent the next couple hours assembling his pack and woods gear, well aware that he might be out for a full day without finding so much as a single light bulb.

Sunday morning dawned as a beautiful Adirondack day, with blue skies and light winds that swept across the narrow expanse of Sacandaga Lake. Following his normal routine, he made his standard Sunday appearance at the Methodist church for services, and then headed back to his house to change into his woods clothes. From there, it was a quick half-hour drive north to the base of Moose Mountain. For sentimental reasons, he had scanned in a photo of Paula Terrell and taped a copy to the middle of his truck dashboard. He hadn't been all that connected with the victim during the 1978 investigation, which turned up no clues to her demise. But somehow he felt that placing her photo in plain view might bring him better luck in the search ahead. He wanted very badly to put an end to the rumor of the lights, and thus provide some relief to her elderly mother. Thirty-three years later, it still mattered.

Clements parked his truck at the same pull-off where he had stopped with Mike Creed the night of his retirement party. It wouldn't be the most direct route up the mountain, but it was less steep, and also offered a path that was less rocky and strewn with debris. At sixty-three years of age, he wasn't as spry as he was in his youth, and he wanted to avoid as much of the bouldering as possible.

True to his plan, Clements spent the first two hours of his expedition merely climbing. The summit of the peak was just a few meters below the two-thousand-foot mark, and he accurately figured that the lights they observed from the road were somewhere between two hundred and four hundred feet below the summit. Still, it would be a rough go, with a heavy cover of small trees and vegetation blocking his progress at every step. The final few hundred feet of ascent to the peak were even steeper and more treacherous, although Clements estimated that the target of his search was established below the top two hundred feet of rock.

By the time his watch chimed 12:00 p.m., Clements was already at significant altitude, looking down on the slender ribbons that represented the Sacandaga River and Route 30. The wind had increased with the elevation, drowning out the sounds of the automobiles and mobile homes winding along the highway. Only the sounds of the autumn breeze and the screeches of the soaring hawks above broke the silence as the silver-haired retiree moved forward and upward into the higher reaches of the mountain.

By the time Clements attained his targeted elevation of sixteen hundred feet, it was already 1:00 p.m. He had already decided that he would commence his retreat from the woods at 4:00 p.m., in order to reach his car before dark. He knew that he had to move quickly to achieve his goal of finding this house, or anything resembling a structure that was capable of holding strands of Christmas lights. As he began his search, the message hammered repeatedly inside his head that this was indeed a case of little significance; that it wasn't worth risking his life by sustaining a serious injury in the rocky ledges of a deserted mountain. Still, the image of Anna Terrell and her long-lost daughter reappeared in his head, and he knew that he needed to succeed in his quest.

By 1:30 p.m., Clements had completed an initial survey of the slope and was ready to start a series of four-hundred-meter search lines. Moving over fallen trees and around car-sized boulders, he zigzagged his way across the face of the mountain, keeping a keen eye peeled for anything man-made or unnatural in appearance. It was a tiring process, repeated again and again as he worked his way laterally and vertically up the incline. He stopped several times for brief sips of water and bites from his pack of granola bars. Still, each time he resumed the hunt it was the same sequence of look, climb, and traverse, each time without result.

It was almost 3:00 p.m. when Clements decided that he needed an extended break. A lifelong devotee of the woods, he was unable to accept the fact that he was no longer a youngster, able to bound from rock to rock with unlimited vigor for extended periods of time. He had just completed a lengthy traverse from south to north, moving across a series of jagged rocks that tested the limits of his balance and agility. He was tired, winded, and on the edge of admitting that he needed assistance in his quest.

Alternating between the granola and the water, Clements wedged his body between a sturdy beech tree and an upright boulder, with his right leg propped up against the rock for stability. The sky in the east was already dimming, the sun beginning its daily dip to the horizon in the west. So far, nothing resembling a structure of any sort had been visible in his search, and his spirits sagged accordingly. He was not a man used to accepting failure.

As Clements rested, stabilized between the tree and the boulder, his mind went blank as he gazed out at the panorama that extended into the west. He chewed his food slowly, his eyes taking in the tapestry of landscape that emerged from below. All conscious thought evaporated, as though sucked from his brain in an attempt to rejuvenate his tiring body. He had been at the task for almost six grueling hours, climbing and searching and seeking the unknown that would end the suffering for a woman and a family in distress. He tried to focus on regaining his strength, although the very thought of the next pass up the rock face seemed to drain the life from his body.

After a single last gulp of water, Clements screwed the cap back onto his canteen and tilted his head skyward, as if to ask the heavens for a single burst of energy to complete the last search line of the day. He needed the energy boost badly, and he knew of no other way than to ask his spiritual Father in heaven for the lift.

That's when he saw it.

As Clements lay back against the base of the thick beech tree, he noticed an odd phenomenon above his head. A red squirrel, chattering and hopping from branch to branch, began a most unusual voyage from one tree to another. What made this passage so unusual was that it appeared to dance across an expanse of open air. Nothing was supporting this long-tailed rodent as it hopped gracefully through the void of space.

The officer's analytical mind immediately snapped back to reality, observing the bizarre event taking place overhead. He'd had the opportunity to watch a great many "flying squirrels," which used their light bodies to glide short distances between branches. However, this particular animal actually paused several times, suspended in a stationary position for several seconds as it viewed the scene below.

*Hmm, now that's something you don't see every day,* Clements thought to himself. Pushing himself away from the tree, he turned around and allowed his eyes to follow the path of the squirrel in both directions. And there, outlined against the afternoon sky, was a thin wire pulled between two tree limbs about ten feet over his head. The wire was supporting a line of Christmas bulbs, which were strung across the same expanse of space.

The sides of Clements's mouth turned upward forming a smile, which widened by the second until he was grinning from ear to ear. He threw off his pack and pushed his way up the incline another twenty feet, with more of the electrical lines coming into view with every step.

The setup was eloquent in both its simplicity and its complexity. The person who had erected this visual mirage had used trees and branches to frame out a perfect house shape out of nothing. They had even used a series of staple nails to form a base from which they could create the image of a framed door, and a second floor complete with a long row of windows. In fact, with a vivid imagination, a person could stand back and look at the strands of wire and actually envision the front of a house, suspended in space. Two additional cords that trailed off the right side of the site gave the impression of a three-dimensional building for anyone viewing the lights from the south. It was a most impressive illusion.

The time was now 3:35 p.m. By his own schedule, he had twenty-five minutes left to investigate the site and see what else he could find. His primary interests were to learn what powered the lights, and also to try to find clues as to who had perpetrated the construction of the phantom home. The answer to his first question was easy to find. By following the left side of the lines down a large maple tree, he discovered a trunk line that ran through a hole in a large metal basin. The basin had been turned upside down to protect a wooden platform, which in turn held a series of heavy truck batteries. The entire setup was regulated by a timer, which was set to turn on at midnight and off again at 12:15 a.m. It was all beautifully wired and connected; the individual who assembled this device knew his stuff.

Clements smiled and shook his head as he disconnected the wires from the batteries, allowing them to drop to the platform. He then removed the timer and placed it inside his backpack. It would be his "Exhibit A" when he finally confronted the accused.

Next, he began crisscrossing the ground below the lights, his eyes scanning the soil and rock and moss for anything that might identify the prankster behind the plot. There wasn't much immediately in sight, but Clements's eyes were trained to focus on the obscure, and slowly the clues began to emerge. First, he observed a series of all-terrain vehicle tracks above the site, which surprised him due to the ruggedness of the mountainside. He stooped low and examined the tire tracks, mentally taking note of the unusual pattern and size of the tire tread.

Next, he continued his visual sweeps down the slope, in the direction of the electrical box. When he was about halfway down, his attention was seized by a metallic glint from the base of another tree located on his right. It was about fifteen feet uphill from the battery platform, and he quickly moved over to investigate.

In a loose pile, Clements came across a collection of empty Pabst Blue Ribbon beer cans that had been opened, emptied, and crushed. He picked up each can individually and examined them for signs of aging. They looked relatively new, as though they had been discarded within the past month.

As Clements picked up the last can, he observed something else that had been resting beneath the can and was now exposed. A single bullet cartridge sat nestled on the soil, its metallic gleam reflecting the light back to the officer. He picked it up and turned it over in his hand, immediately noticing the heaviness of the shell. Rotating the cartridge to see the round striking surface, he saw the characters ".416 RIGBY" stamped into the metal.

Clements stared at the annotation for a solid fifteen seconds, digesting its meaning and processing the implications. Then the smile returned to his face, his head nodding in recognition.

"Gotcha, Jimmy," he chuckled, his entire body shaking with his growing mirth.

After another drink from his canteen, Clements put the shell cartridge into a ziplock bag, which he placed inside a side pocket of his backpack. He placed the beer cans into yet another bag, which he planned to use as additional evidence. Finally, he removed a small camera from his pack and took photos of the battery platform as well as the strands of lights suspended from the trees. With everything repacked, he hoisted the pack onto his back and prepared to start the trip back to his car.

As he started his return trek, Clements glanced at his watch to check the time. It was 3:59 p.m.; he had accomplished his mission with a full minute to spare. *Gotta stick with the plan*, he thought to himself as he started the descent to the road below. It had been a most productive afternoon.

🌲🌲🌲

It was mid-morning on Tuesday when Dan Clements turned his truck into the quiet mud road that entered the woods about two miles north of Wells. It was not a well-advertised driveway, and was unfettered with anything but a small sign that read "JS Guide Service" in black and gold letters. Not even a mailbox or route number was evident to advertise the identity of the resident.

The truck navigated an *S* curve that was punctuated by a series of deep water-filled holes. It was not a lane meant for passenger cars. Clements finally pulled up in front of a rather dilapidated house that was almost devoid of paint. The front porch sagged considerably, and one of the gutters on the front roof was hanging precariously off its mountings.

Chained to the deck of a trailer was a ruggedly built all-terrain vehicle with heavy tread tires. Clements took note of the size and details of the tires as he passed by. Even without a close-up examination, he was confident that he had a match.

Clements didn't bother ringing the doorbell. Instead, he removed his pack from the truck and walked around the back of the derelict structure to the garage out back. Having visited this address in the past, he knew that the owner, local guide Jimmy Sills, could usually be found tinkering about in his garage, which served as the office and workshop for his guiding service.

Even though Sills's back was turned, he seemed to know that someone was entering the structure. "Mornin' Deputy," he exclaimed in a voice that was more of a shout than a greeting. "Didn't expect to see you comin' along this morning."

"Good morning, Jimmy," replied Clements, still speaking to Sills's backside. "How's life treating you?"

"Oh, fair to middling, I guess," replied the guide as he put down the fly rod he was repairing and turned to face his visitor. "Long time no see, though. Last I heard you'd retired from the Sheriff's Department. That true?"

"Yeah, a little over a month ago. I'm getting too old to be chasing the bad guys up and down these hills. I decided to let the younger kids take over the show. Plus, I don't care for all the new technology they've brought into the world of law enforcement. Heck, you've practically got to have a graduate degree in computer science to do anything these days."

"Ain't that the truth," laughed Jimmy, who leaned on the wooden counter with both hands. "I never bothered learnin' none of that stuff. As long as I can catch me a fish, and I can teach the folks who pay me to catch 'em, I'm happy. So what can I do for you this morning?"

As Jimmy was speaking, Clements allowed his eyes to wander casually across the clogged mess that filled the garage. He immediately noticed a piece of bright purple material that was pushed into the corner of a work table beneath a side window. Without preamble, he strolled over and picked up the cloth, which felt like a piece of knitted wool. He felt it in his hands and unraveled it, observing the ragged edges from the strips that had been cut away from the piece.

"Oh, that ain't for sale," said Jimmy as he shuffled over to retrieve the colorful fabric from the officer. "I'll just take that and put it away . . ."

Instead of handing it back to the guide, Clements turned the other way so that his company couldn't take it away from him.

"Nice material," remarked Clements, fingering the purple strands. "Too bad it's ripped like this. I wonder how that happened."

Clements enjoyed toying with his subjects, playing the role of the unsuspecting investigator even though he already knew the truth. He often gained additional knowledge by watching the suspect as he questioned them in this manner.

"Oh, that ain't ripped," said Jimmy, nervously attempting to snatch the material back from his visitor. "Ye see, I use that material to make fishing lures. The brown trout seem to like that color, so I tie a few strands onto some of the flies, just to get their attention. Works pretty darn good, too."

"Ah, I see," said Clements as he handed the swath back to the guide. "But that's okay, that's not why I'm here. I actually wanted to get your opinion on a piece of electrical work. I know you're pretty handy in that line of work."

"Well, I wouldn't exactly call me an electrician, but I'll see what I can do for ye."

Clements lifted his backpack to the counter and slowly loosened the drawstrings. "I was wondering if you could help me out with this," he said as he pulled a timer from inside the pack. "I've been using it to turn my Christmas lights on and off for the past couple years, but for some reason it doesn't seem to work anymore."

Jimmy put his elbows on the counter and allowed his chin to sink into his hands. His eyes were focused downward at the timer, taking in the markings and scuffmarks that clearly let him know what he was seeing. After a lull of almost a minute, he looked up at Clements, all the while still cupping his chin in his hands.

"Okay, ye found it, huh?"

"I found it, Jimmy."

"And if ye don't mind, how did ye track it back to me?"

"Well, it really wasn't all that difficult. I found the tracks to your ATV up on the site. Not a lot of people around here use the GBC Motorsport Grim Reaper tires, Jimmy. If you hadn't shown them to me yourself at the county fair this summer, I never would have suspected you in the first place."

"Dang it all," cried Jimmy as he slapped his forehead. "I never would have thought anyone would see them tracks. And by the way, I had me a heckuva time gettin' those batteries up there. Ain't no way I could have done it without the ATV."

"That's okay, because you left some other signs up there, too. Like the cans of Pabst, which you've drunk for as long as I've known you. And your handiwork in rigging up the batteries and wiring for the lights. That was mighty nice work, Jimmy. Not a lot of folks around here are as handy as you."

"Yeah, but I still don't see how that narrowed it down to just me, Dan. Lots of guys drink Pabst, and I could name a dozen folks who could have rigged up a power supply. If I had to, I could deny everything, including what I've already said, and you wouldn't have a thing you could do about it. Face it, you ain't got a case against me, so why don't you just ease yourself outta here and leave me to my work."

Clements relaxed his facial expression and flashed a disarming smile. "Whoa, easy does it, partner," he exclaimed. "Before you go getting yourself all worked up, I'm not here to investigate anything. Remember, I'm retired, and there's been no crime committed."

"That's right," said the guide, "there ain't. But then just what is it you want from me?"

"But before you do any more denying, I'd like to return something to you." Clements extended his open palm, which was cradling the empty Rigby shell cartridge. "Now how many people do you know around here who own an original .416 Rigby rifle?"

Jimmy's body sagged once again, confronted with the indisputable evidence.

"Not many, I guess," he replied, his aging eyes looking haggardly across the counter at his accuser.

"No, not many," said the retired officer.

"I tell ye the truth, Dan," said Jimmy, "I'm damn glad you never decided to be a conservation officer. You see too dang much. Heck, ain't none of us would've gotten away with anything."

"Well, thank you, Jimmy," laughed Clements. "I'll take that as a compliment. But tell me, what made you decide to set those lights up on the mountain in the first place? I've been wondering what the heck was going through your head to trudge all that stuff up the mountain and set it up like that. It must have taken an awful lot of work."

"Nah, t'wasn't much work at all. I let the ATV do all the carryin'. I just had to get it up there and then hook it up. My brother helped me; it was him and me who thought up the idea one night. Thought it would be kind of funny to have people wondering where the house come from."

"How did you start the rumor about Robert Garrow and the Paula Terrell case?"

"That wasn't me, Dan. I don't know how that got started. But once the word started gettin' passed around like that, I figured it'd be a good way to bring in some local tourists and maybe pick me up some extra guiding business."

"Well, whether you know it or not, your prank has caused some relatives of Paula Terrell, who was probably murdered around that area, to relive part of the pain. I'm sure you didn't want to do that, did you?"

The guide looked back at Clements with a sorrowful expression. "Heck no! I had no idea that anyone connected with Garrow or the folks done in by him was even alive still."

"Then I hope you'll leave the lights off from now on, okay? Maybe you'd even like to head back up there and remove it all from the mountain?"

"Of course, Dan. Consider it done. And now, I ain't in any trouble, am I?"

"No, Jimmy, you're not in any trouble," replied Clements. He slapped the old guide on the back and repacked his rucksack. "But I'd burn that piece of purple wool if I was you, and remember, no more tricks."

Jimmy followed Clements out of the garage toward his truck, all the while trying to make amends. "Now, you ain't gonna go and tell any of your sheriff friends about this, are ye?" he pleaded. "Like ye said, ain't no crime been committed."

"No, Jimmy, I won't say a word. It'll be our little secret." And with that Clements climbed back into his truck and drove off the property.

It was only a few minutes north on Route 30 to the turnaround where Clements had started his search for the phantom house. He pulled his truck onto the fringe of the pavement once again, observing the flowing waters of the Sacandaga River as the sunlight streamed through his front windshield. The bright rays of the sun illuminated the front seat, and he noticed a few strands of statically charged purple wool stuck to the front of his own sweater. He pulled the photo of Paula Terrell from the dashboard, and then used the tape on the picture to affix the purple fibers to the photograph, which he held tightly as he climbed from the truck.

Clements walked over to the guard rail and stepped over it, stiffly lifting one leg at a time to clear the obstacle. He then headed through the brush and down the embankment until he was standing on the very edge of the river. The water danced over the rocks and other obstructions in the riverbed, forming a beautiful pattern of whitewater, eddies, and pools.

Even though the colorful leaves had almost completely dropped from the trees, Clements could not imagine a prettier place to live. Carefully balancing himself, he bent over the stream and placed the picture of Paula into the racing waters, setting her free to go where nature would take her. For at least a minute he stood rooted in place, watching her float away over the multitude of rippling wavelets until, at last, she was lost from view. Then he turned back toward his truck to start the journey home.

# ACKNOWLEDGMENTS

The authors would like to thank North Country Books and editor Jake Bonar for giving our Adirondack mystery stories a warm and friendly home.

# About the Editor and Contributors

**Cheryl Ann Costa** is a published and produced playwright, mystery writer, novelist, short story author, and well-known UFO columnist and published UFO statistics researcher. She's a story contributor to all three volumes of the Adirondack Mysteries series.

**Marie Hannan-Mandel** is a professor of English and lives in Elmira Heights, New York. She has been published in four anthologies, including volume 3 of the Adirondack Mysteries series, and shortlisted for the Crime Writers' Association (UK) Debut Dagger award.

**G. Miki Hayden** has a deep body of work that includes many pieces of short fiction published in small magazines, national magazines, and anthologies (including volumes 2 and 3 of the Adirondack Mysteries series and three Mystery Writers of America anthologies). Hayden has published several novels, including one alternate history lauded by the *New York Times*. Hayden, who has taught at Writer's Digest Online University for twenty-plus years, also has two writing instructions in print and has had an Edgar short story win.

**Marianna Heusler** is an Edgar-nominated writer of thirteen published novels and hundreds of short stories. Her cozy mystery series was bought by Harlequin and included in their book club. She lives in New York City with her husband, her son, and her rescue dog, Triscuit.

**Margaret Mendel** lives, writes, and draws in New York City. She is an award-winning author with short stories and articles appearing online and in print publications. Mendel has published two mystery novels and a collection of short stories. She is also a self-taught artist and began focusing on drawing portraits at the onset of the COVID-19 pandemic. She is a contributing writer and photographer at a California-based online magazine. Her photographs and drawings have appeared in several New York City exhibitions.

**Jenny Milchman** has written five novels, all of which take place in the fictional Adirondack town of Wedeskyull. Her debut won the Mary Higgins Clark award, was nominated for a PEN/Faulkner, and was a finalist for the Macavity and Anthony awards. Her third novel won the Silver Falchion award; four of her books were selected as Indie Next Picks; and all five have earned starred reviews, praise from major media such as the *New York Times*, and "Best of" spots on lists from such magazines as *PopSugar*, *PureWow*, the *Strand*, and *Suspense*. Jenny is a two-time contributor to the Adirondack Mysteries series and lives downstate in the Catskills.

**W. K. Pomeroy** is a third-generation writer with more than seventy-five published short stories, poems, and articles, and is adding a fourth "Adirondack Alchemist" story to this newest volume of the *Adirondack Mysteries and Other Mountain Tales*. His underemployed Bosnian research scientist, Damir Hemnon, is one of his favorite characters to write. Mr. Pomeroy is currently marketing a fantasy novel and a science fiction novel to literary agents, and he is pitching a collection of "Not-for-Children" Christmas stories to publishers. He served six terms as president of the Utica Writers Club and continues to support creative writers as a member of this group.

**Cheyenne Shaffer** is a graduate of the Odyssey Writing Workshop and the Never-Ending Odyssey, and she currently lives in Ithaca, New York, with her partner and two feline overlords. When she's not writing, she works as an emergency veterinarian to fund her addictions to books, cats, and fancy coffee. Her short fiction can also be found in *Aseptic and Faintly Sadistic: An Anthology of Hysteria Fiction*.

**Lorena A. Sins** was raised on a dairy farm not far from the blue line of the Adirondacks. She has a PhD in English literature from the University of Georgia. She has taught English, composition, and literature at Dalton State College for the past nineteen years. Her story "The Whistler in the

Attic" is based upon a true story from her childhood growing up on the farm. She lives with her husband in Dalton, Georgia, where the adjacent mountains remind her of the Adirondacks.

**Woody Sins** grew up near the North Country crossroads of West Leyden, New York. Now living in New Hartford, New York, Sins is a digital engineer working on radar systems. He's a story contributor to volumes 2 and 3 of the Adirondack Mysteries series.

**Daniel Swift** has climbed all forty-six Hike Peaks, canoed more than two hundred miles between the lakes, and spent every summer of his youth at Camp Russell on White Lake in the town of Woodgate, New York. After he gained the rank of Eagle Scout in the Boy Scouts of America, he continued to explore the Adirondacks and has loved finding different ways to enjoy the majestic views they offer. With that knowledge and understanding of the Adirondacks, Daniel brings some unique realism to his short stories.

**Gigi Vernon** writes thriller crime fiction. Her short fiction has appeared in *Alfred Hitchcock Mystery Magazine* and *Mystery Writers of America Presents Ice Cold: Tales of Intrigue from the Cold War*. Her short story "Show Stopper" received a 2015 International Thriller Writers nomination for best short story.

**Dennis Webster** is a paranormal investigator with the Ghost Seekers of Central New York and a member of the Punishers Law Enforcement Motorcycle Club. When he's not riding his Harley or chasing spirits of the dead, he's at his writing desk conjuring up his next book. He's the editor, story compiler, and contributor to volumes 1, 2, and 3 of the Adirondack Mysteries series. He's the published author of books on ghosts, haunted locations, true crime, and asylums.

**Larry Weill** got his start in the Adirondacks as a wilderness park ranger in the late 1970s and early 1980s. He has worked in both finance as well as Xerox Corporation's supply chain for thirty years. Weill is a retired U.S.

Navy captain, and has attained the rank of rear admiral as commanding officer of the New York Naval Militia. He enjoys writing both fiction and his memoirs about the Adirondacks, and he has numerous books published in multiple genres of Adirondack literature. He resides in Walworth, New York, which is located just east of Rochester.